Dancing Tides

A Pelican Pointe Novel

VICKIE McKEEHAN

Dancing Tides
A Pelican Pointe Novel

This book is a work of fiction. The characters, incidents,
and dialogue are drawn from the author's imagination and
are not to be construed as real. Any resemblance to actual
events or persons, living or dead is entirely coincidental.

beachdevils
PRESS
ISBN-13: 978-0615723068
ISBN-10: 0615723063

Printed in the USA

Cover design by Vanessa Mendozzi
Pelican Pointe map designed by Jess Johnson

Visit the author at:
www.facebook.com/VickieMcKeehan
www.vickiemckeehan.com/

Don't miss these other exciting titles by bestselling author

Vickie McKeehan

The Pelican Pointe Series
PROMISE COVE
HIDDEN MOON BAY
DANCING TIDES
LIGHTHOUSE REEF
STARLIGHT DUNES
LAST CHANCE HARBOR
SEA GLASS COTTAGE
LAVENDER BEACH
SANDCASTLES UNDER THE CHRISTMAS
MOON
BENEATH WINTER SAND
KEEPING CAPE SUMMER (2018)

The Evil Secrets Trilogy
JUST EVIL Book One
DEEPER EVIL Book Two
ENDING EVIL Book Three
EVIL SECRETS TRILOGY BOXED SET

The Skye Cree Novels
THE BONES OF OTHERS
THE BONES WILL TELL
THE BOX OF BONES
HIS GARDEN OF BONES
TRUTH IN THE BONES
SEA OF BONES (2018)

The Indigo Brothers Trilogy
INDIGO FIRE
INDIGO HEAT
INDIGO JUSTICE
INDIGO BROTHERS TRILOGY BOXED SET

Coyote Wells Mysteries
MYSTIC FALLS
SHADOW CANYON
SPIRIT LAKE (2018)

For all those who struggle in their dark places,
but manage to find their way into the light and
eventually into their own dancing tides.

"Life is a little like a message in a bottle, to be carried by the winds and the tides."
Gene Tierney

Dancing Tides

A Pelican Pointe Novel

VICKIE McKEEHAN

beachdevils
PRESS

Welcome to Pelican Pointe

Prologue

Eighteen months earlier
Leesburg, Virginia

Decked out in his Sunday best, a tux no less, he stuck his index finger between his sweaty neck and the collar of the scratchy, white shirt he wore, and nervously gave the fabric a tug as he waited at the altar for his bride to make that walk down the aisle where she would become Mrs. Cord Bennett.

Even though the stifling heat of Indian summer had the crowded church feeling airless, Cord tried to loosen his tie about the same time his best man, Paul Angleton, bumped his shoulder, and batted his hand away to put an end to the fidgeting.

Cord shot a thumbs up in the direction of Paul indicating he was A-OK, even though he was anything but.

Not even close.

His gut felt like the drummer in the band had gotten an early start and set up a steady beat in his stomach. The rehearsal dinner party the night before had gone on too long. He'd indulged in too much wine and woke up this morning with the hangover from hell.

But if he puked now, Cassie would never forgive him. So he swallowed down his bile and tried to ignore the sickening smell of all the flowers lining the altar.

In fact, it might have been the powerful combination of all those fragrant blossoms coming together along with the sweet-smelling blend of perfume from the hundred or so guests, packed like sardines into a chapel meant to hold no more than seventy-five, that had his upchuck reflex on overload.

Whatever it was, it had him wishing they'd get this show on the road.

He supposed every groom was nervous before uttering those two little words that would cement a bond for life. Thinking like that, his queasiness got worse.

Not because he was having second thoughts. No, he'd given his heart to Cassie three years earlier and knew for a fact no other woman would do.

For him, Cassie Spearman was it. At that precise moment though another whiff of magnolias hit his nostrils and almost brought him to his knees. The pungent odor had him wishing they'd eloped to Virginia Beach in a quickie service without all the fuss. He knew a buddy there who had taken up preaching since coming back from Iraq. Knew for a fact he could've had them married without a frill or a piece of lace. But Cassie had wanted to tie the knot in front of her entire family wearing the dress, the one that had cost her parents a small fortune.

And that, too, was apparently what regular families did. Family.

Cord didn't have a clue what it meant to be a part of that kind of a unit. He'd grown up in San Diego in the system, a ward of the state.

At first, around eight or nine he'd thought that somebody might come along and adopt him. But by the time he'd celebrated his tenth birthday that notion had died on the vine and he'd accepted the reality of his situation. No one wanted him. And too many didn't even care, not even the foster families he'd repeatedly tested to the limits. They'd taken him on, albeit briefly, and passed on making him a permanent part of their unit.

By the time he'd hit thirteen, his teen rebellion had kicked in for good about the same time he'd realized no family felt like taking a chance on a kid who never seemed to measure up to their expectations. There had simply never been a good fit. So he had stayed stuck in the foster care system until he'd struck out on his own at sixteen. He hadn't even graduated high school, at least not until much later when he got his GED in the army. In between his military stint and joining the California Guard unit, he'd managed to sandwich in two years of community college.

But Iraq had put an end to anything beyond that. His unit had been called up and, once again, he'd served his country.

So, if Cassie wanted to say "I do" in front of a bunch of relatives she loved and who loved her back, then he could damn well stand here in his Sunday best and breathe in the smell of a bunch of flowers, even though they made him slightly ill.

It had to be the lilies, that array of buds representing the tried and true language of love and tradition only a bride could fully appreciate, that smelled so freaking strong. They stood tall and straight, lining the dais in so many different shades of pink and white he could hardly keep them all straight without conjuring up a bottle of Pepto Bismol.

But the lilies were Cassie's favorite. And because of that he had no doubt she knew every blessed variety of petal or bud. The woman kept track of every stem and shade of color that had been delivered to the church that day. He would bet money on it. Because she had spent hours and hours with at least a half dozen different florists in town picking out just the right shade of pink—for the flowers alone. The ones she had bugged him about, the ones he'd barely given a second glance or given a second thought—because let's face it—he hadn't cared a whit about what kind of flowers she carried or what genus decorated the church.

As long as she said "I do" when the right time presented itself, as long as he could manage the same without choking or stammering or forgetting that one important line, he didn't give a good crap about a bunch of flowers.

But Cassie Anne Spearman did.

He scanned the small chapel and its sea of faces, checking out the rows of pews where family sat alongside friends and coworkers waiting for Cassie to take center stage.

His lips curved into a wide grin. These people had shown up to spend their Saturday afternoon watching the two of them tie the knot after a long courtship, a courtship that had included three tours of duty in Iraq for him, as well as numerous separations. Cultivating a long-distance relationship with a soldier during a war was never a good bet. But he and Cassie had weathered the storms, cut through the pitfalls and come out the other side better for it.

Here today, they were about to exchange vows and prepare to spend the rest of their lives together.

They'd been through a lot. So it didn't really matter to him about her choice of flowers or the dress or any of the details that had seemed to drive his bride-to-be crazy over the past several months.

He'd spent that time watching Cassie's careful planning, saying "yes" when it was expected, nodding his head in agreement whether the topic had been about napkins or the choice of caterers, or how many place settings they would need for the dinner parties they would surely give.

He'd let her choose whatever bridal registry was the best, let her be the deciding factor as to whether they served chicken or fish at the reception.

No, up to this point, he had been all about getting to the church and to this day when he would cease his bachelor existence and become husband material for all time to "the one."

Cassie Spearman was the one. At barely five foot three, the little blonde had managed to capture his heart, his mind, his soul.

And for him, she had been the first one to do so. Before Cassie he'd made sure he kept his heart from ever suffering any kind of major rejection or defeat in that department.

Good thing she had agreed to become his wife. Otherwise what Iraq hadn't been able to do to him, a broken heart surely would have.

And at six foot four, Cord Bennett wasn't an easy man to take down. Nor was he a pushover. At least not until Cassie had come into his life.

Not half an hour earlier his best man had reminded him that no matter what Cassie looked like in her dress, he was to make absolutely certain that the expression on his face told her, in no uncertain terms, that he was blown away by her appearance, by her dress, by her presence.

But when he spotted Cassie at the end of the aisle, about to take that step toward him in her soft white gown with her hair swept up off her shoulders on the arm of her father, there had been no need for pretending.

He had simply been blown away by the sheer beauty Cassie innately showed to the world. Her face lit up, standing there in the gown she had so carefully chosen with the bead and pearl bodice, the way the skirt showed off her curves and full figure.

He fell in love with her all over again. The nerves fell away. All of his unease subsided.

Staring at his soon-to-be wife, his mouth gaped open; he would have bet money on it. He was that awestruck.

But then, it all changed in a flash of gunfire.

By the time Cord realized what was happening, the uninvited guest had already fired a series of fatal shots. His eyes zeroed in on the man holding the Luger. Cord started running down the aisle toward Cassie. But he couldn't get his legs to move fast enough.

Bullets flew. People screamed.

Boom, boom, boom—the man kept firing.

Cord saw the shooter turn, take a few steps toward him, and aim his weapon. That's when he felt the burn in his chest.

As he went down, Cord saw Cassie's dress turning from the silky, shimmering gown of white to a blood-red splatter born of rage and hate and jealousy.

The last thing he remembered was the sickening sweet smell of blossoms as the air around him changed to the putrid iron odor of blood.

He'd survived three tours of duty in Iraq. But a gunman had taken him down in a suburban church in the middle of a quiet, residential neighborhood.

And with it, had ended the life he'd dreamed of spending with Cassie Anne Spearman.

Chapter One

Present day
Pelican Pointe, California

The dive along the docks known as McCready's rocked and shook with the after work crowd. The place jammed with people determined to cap off the end of their forty-plus hour week in tried and true fashion—happy hour drummed along in full swing.

Friday afternoon bar patrons were a mix of khaki wearers, mostly members of the town council, sitting amid the jeans-clad local fishermen and dock workers. Each group had their favorite thing to gripe about. The lousy economy had them stumped. The ridiculous cost of fuel had them pissed. Still others bitched about the girlfriend or spouse they'd ignored back at home.

They explored a variety of solutions—mainly how to make it through the end of the month—grousing about the week's sorry catch, and agreed that life would get infinitely better if they ever had the good fortune to hit the lottery.

Because they all wanted nothing more at the moment than to leave their troubles behind for an hour or more, no one dared mention the irony of blowing their precious dollars on booze. Or that McCready's wasn't suffering from any type of economic slump.

At the long, scarred, mahogany bar, crabbiness linked them in camaraderie. No matter what the subject matter, fellowship meant taking advantage of the happy hour specials, which happened to be either two dollar bottled beer or three-dollar well drinks.

The music on the ancient jukebox was loud and country, the smoke thick and smelly, the food greasy and typical bar fare. But on a Friday night the local faithful wouldn't have dreamed of blowing their hard earned cash or getting stone-blind drunk anywhere else except the place that passed for an Irish pub in Pelican Pointe.

And today, there were rumors stirring up the masses about some big wig corporation wanting to buy out all the independent fishermen in the area. In the way of small towns the gossip impacted all of them in one way or another. Everyone might've felt the pressure of surviving in the poor economic times, but some saw it as another greedy corporation going after the little guy—and one of their own.

Some compared the plight of the fisherman to the beleaguered American farmer when they were close to financial ruin. The townspeople were on the side of the local fishermen whether it was the professional man who made his living on the water, or the guy who fished for pleasure, the locals wanted the big wig outsiders to keep out and stay out of Pelican Pointe.

Progress be damned.

But regardless of the stress and the mood inside McCready's, the back room where the pool tables stood had an overflow crowd. Those that weren't playing a game were watching, either applauding shots, or making derogatory comments. It didn't matter which because in the end the players and watchers alike chalked it up to forgetting their troubles for a few measly hours enough to be sociable.

Cord Bennett didn't give a shit about being social.

His height alone caused more than a few to take a second look because he cut an imposing figure. Few were stupid enough to take him on in a fight. Even those who were sloshed and looking for trouble usually decided on the spot to re-evaluate the situation and move on.

Because when Cord got hammered, they'd better walk away or suffer the consequences.

Then there were the tattoos. One arm bore his black and red army ranger band designating his unit, capped off with a skull and crossbones. The other arm sported a snarling, black dragon.

If you could get past the badass look, there was his long, sandy blond hair that hung to his shoulders. And the fact his warm, brown eyes flecked with gold could soften at the drop of a hat. He had a tender heart for animals. He couldn't work around them all the time and not. He was a sucker for kids, especially those who had grown up hard like he had. And because of that soft spot he often lacked the ability to get tough or dish out hardcore discipline of any kind.

Sober, he ran to easygoing, even laid-back. Even when he did get upset, he could send out vibes with a look, and then rely on his size to diffuse a difficult circumstance.

In other words, it took a lot to piss him off. At least in years past that was true.

But now, when Cord drank, a person might get the surly attitude along with a willingness to fight just to prove a point.

The night was early yet, not even seven o'clock. Cord wasn't quite drunk. But he was steadily doing his damnedest to get there.

Nights like this one were the toughest, where memories of other more festive Friday nights lingered like the heavy smoke in the air or the unmistakable smells of fish along the pier.

Heartbreaking recollections of a time spent with the love of his life no longer mattered. But they were there, always there, hovering at the surface, filling up that corner of his mind that no matter how much he drank he couldn't completely get to go away.

He would've liked nothing better than to simply hit a delete key, like on a computer, and erase or somehow wipe away the memories of happier days. That way he wouldn't have to remember what had been.

He had to remind himself that he was content

wallowing in his miserable excuse of an existence. And if he got lucky tonight, more of the drink might, just might, wipe out even that stubborn corner where Cassie lived as if she had never been there at all.

When the hulk of an Irishman named Flynn McCready, who not only tended bar but owned the place as well, stared at him long and hard, Cord knew that look.

"You're done here, Cord. You've reached your limit. You'll get no more drink tonight from me."

Cord stood up with a curse and decided on the spot it wasn't worth a fight. Nothing much was of late. You had to care about something in order to fight for it.

And he'd given up caring for anything a year and a half ago.

Hell, he wanted to be by himself anyway so he shrugged off McCready's missive.

He'd simply take his business down to Murphy's before the place closed and buy his own bottle. It certainly wouldn't be the first time.

When he ran into Deputy Sheriff Ethan Cody, the law in these parts, coming in the door as he was going out, Cord swore again at his lousy luck. He glared at the town cop, his Native American features, and wished he'd had the good sense to leave the bar sooner.

Because now he'd get the third degree from Ethan. "Cord, I hope you aren't heading to your truck."

"And what if I am?" Cord bellowed back, not in the mood for a hassle.

"Then I'd have to take your keys."

Cord's eyes narrowed. "Christ, Ethan. Stop treating me like I'm the town drunk."

"Then stop acting like it," Ethan snapped.

Cord's face fell.

Ethan sighed and pulled the man farther outside, out of earshot of the other patrons, out onto the sidewalk. "Look, I know you've had a rough couple of years. But you have to stop this self-destructive shit before you hurt yourself." Or someone else, he wanted to add. Maybe Nick Harris needed to get tougher with his friend. Hell, maybe as a member of law enforcement, he did as well.

"Hurt myself? What do you know about it anyway? It's Friday night for chrissakes. I'm entitled to a drink now and again just like the rest of the town. You think McCready's is standing room only tonight because I'm the only one in town having a drink. Shit. Six days a week I bust my ass out at that farm. When I'm not there I'm doing chores at the B & B. I don't slack off. I do my share of the work. You don't believe me, ask Nick. Hell, Silas and Sammy will vouch for me, too. I'm a damn good manager."

It had been Cord's boss, Nick Harris, who had called and sent him in to pull Cord out of McCready's.

"So long as you don't drive in this condition, or start a fight, you can do what you want. But I find you drunk or disorderly on the street or the beach or any other public place tonight, Cord, and I'm locking your ass up. You got that?"

"Yeah, I got it. I'm not that damned drunk." But he'd been heading there. If he couldn't drive how was he supposed to get home?

"Bullshit. You're impaired. And in no short order you'd be three sheets to the wind. Don't even think about driving. You need a way home, I'll get you there."

"Fine. Let me lock up my truck."

Ethan watched as Cord staggered off toward the lot at the side of the building and to McCready's designated parking area. He watched Cord open the door to a silver-birch metallic pickup parked there.

Ethan shook his head and waited.

It was a damned shame a soldier like Cord, who had been wounded in combat and even survived three tours of duty in Iraq, had to come back home only to get shot during a spree shooting inside a church. Six people had died that day, one of them Cord's bride-to-be, shot dead right there in front of him as he'd watched her slip away.

All of them died because the bride had a very jealous, very crazy, former boyfriend.

Cord had come very close to being one of those six. But right now, he was headed down a path that was quickly leading nowhere.

After a few minutes, Cord came stumbling back. "I've changed my mind, Ethan. It's a nice night, gonna be a decent-looking sunset, too. I think I'll take a walk on the beach to clear my head first."

Ethan took the time to size up the man who stood in front of him on unsteady feet. Cord Bennett had a disheveled look about him that spoke volumes. It might have been due to the fact he wore his shoulder-length hair loose in a fuck-you-style that screamed, "I'm no longer in the military and not governed by anyone's rules but my own."

He wasn't sure why, but it seemed to Ethan as if the man desperately wanted him to believe he'd switched gears and was now the epitome of cordial and cooperative.

"Okay. But hand over your keys." Ethan gestured with his hand for Cord to give them up.

"Damn it, how the hell am I supposed to get back to the farm?"

"You take that walk, clear your head some and then come by my house, I'll drive you home."

"Well for chrissakes. I don't need a babysitter."

"Cord, if you don't get your act together, either you're gonna end up getting hurt or someone else will." Ethan pointed a finger at his chest to make his point. "And it will not happen on my watch. You got that. Now you take that walk, enjoy the sunset and look me up when you're ready to head home. You know where I live."

Cord reluctantly relinquished his truck keys. He set off in a huff down the street toward the pier, wondering all the while why people couldn't just leave him the hell alone. It had been a major mistake on his part getting dragged to this measly little town in the first place. Even worse, he'd hung around now for four months. He should've taken off on his own, left for greener hills somewhere, anywhere, someplace no one knew him, or knew about his miserable past.

Here, it seemed to him, someone was forever trying to fix him. And he didn't like it, not one bit.

The bitch of it was he really didn't have any other place to go. Pelican Pointe was it, the bottom of the barrel, which meant Cord Bennett had hit rock bottom right here along with this crappy little town.

Once he got to the wharf, he followed the wooden steps down to the rocky beach. He spotted a dry boulder jutting out where the waves were at low tide and plopped his butt on the flat surface. He looked out into the setting sun as it dropped over the water—and decided maybe it was time to quit kidding himself.

Ethan was right. He either needed to change his ways or make some changes.

He intended to make a change all right, a big one, a permanent one. The pain would at least finally end.

He stuck his hand in his jeans pocket, removed the shiny black .22-caliber Smith and Wesson he'd taken from the glove box of his truck. Good thing Ethan hadn't felt the need to pat him down or arrest him for some idiotic reason like public intoxication. He'd already been down that road before, too.

But ending it meant there would be no more drunk and disorderly, no more hurting inside, no more terrible guilt, no more nothing.

There were so many other times over the past year and a half he'd been right here in this same spot. Not sitting on the beach, of course, but it didn't really matter at the moment whether he was back in his bedroom at the farm or not, only that he'd finally found the courage to make up his mind to do it, once and for all.

Okay, maybe it didn't take bravery. He'd been in combat and knew how it felt to face the enemy. This felt different. He couldn't get a handle on this. Maybe he'd finally drunk enough whiskey, enough booze to know he didn't care anymore about the fight.

He looked around to make sure he was alone. Sure

enough, this stretch of beach was deserted.

He glanced out at the horizon and the dropping sun. The brilliant purples and pinks of approaching dusk didn't capture his attention for long.

Instead, he held the .22 in his fist, cocked the hammer, pointed it directly under his chin. But then all of a sudden, he wondered what would happen if the damn .22 couldn't get the job done? With the way his luck had been running he didn't want to chance ending up a vegetable if the gun didn't do the kind of damage he hoped it would do. And what if it misfired? What if it jammed? It had jammed before back in January, New Year's Day to be exact.

A boat out in the harbor drifting toward him caught his eye. He stared long and hard at the water.

An idea took shape.

Gauging the tides, he watched them come and go, dance in and out, to and fro and estimated how far he would need to walk out into the water away from the pier to let the ocean swallow him up.

He decided it would take a good thirty yards, forty to be on the safe side to make sure he dropped off into deeper water. The more he thought about it, the more he realized it was a much better way and not nearly as messy. The sight of blood didn't bother him exactly. No doubt if he did it here on this rock, he'd be leaving a mess for someone else to find.

But if he simply walked into the water, people would more than likely assume he'd decided to take a swim, had too much to drink, and simply—drowned—accidentally.

And because he was a strong swimmer, it was a good plan, a very good plan he resolved. He could just drift out, go down into the water at his own pace, and have his pain float away.

"Feeling sorry for yourself isn't cutting it, Bennett. You're a better man than this." "Screw you," Cord said with a nod of his head.

Expecting to see Ethan Cody standing over him he was shocked to turn and find Scott Phillips sitting to his left on a nearby rock.

The man, or rather his ghost, and his former captain in the Guard, stood there big as life, dressed in khaki shorts and a bright yellow T-shirt with a navy oxford shirt, unbuttoned, and hanging loose over the Tee.

Scott looked relaxed and in his element.

"You don't get a say in this, Captain, not this time. You have no idea what it's like to live without the woman you love."

Scott laughed. "You're joking, right? Dead here, Bennett, or don't you remember what happened to me in Iraq? You think I don't know what you feel, how much you're hurting. You're alive, buddy. Be grateful you're alive. Why can't I get you to understand that?"

"Because, damn it, I don't want to be alive. Don't you get it? I want to be free of the memory of watching her die right in front of me. I should've done more that day. If she'd told me that Robby pestered her in the past—I might've been able to—do something. I should've died that day with Cassie. That son of a bitch had perfect aim six other times that afternoon. Why the hell did he have to miss with me?"

"He didn't miss, Cord. You took two shots to the chest before one of the guests grabbed the gun out of his hand and wrestled him to the floor. The EMTs thought they'd lost you a couple of times on the way to the ER."

Yeah, well, they shouldn't have bothered. Otherwise I wouldn't have spent the last eighteen miserable fucking months drinking myself into oblivion.

But Cord knew better than to share those thoughts now.

Instead, he glowered out into the ocean, watched the dancing tides again for the best possible place to sink. "Look, I appreciate your trying to save me and all, but...you've been a pain in the butt for months now. I'm tired, Captain. I'm tired of living without Cassie. I'm tired of having the dreams. The dreams won't let me go. I've replayed that scene so many times. There's nothing you or anyone else can do. I've made up my mind about this."

With that, Cord unzipped his jacket, tossed it on the rock then kicked off his work boots, removed his socks and stood up. He started to wade out into the cold, murky water, still wearing his jeans and Tee.

Farther and farther Cord swam out until finally Scott shook his head. "But it isn't your time, Cord. It simply is not your time to go. When will you understand that?"

On the deck of the fifty-foot research vessel, *Moonlight Mile*, a renovated fishing trawler, marine biologist Keegan Fanning stood looking out to sea. It was one of those gentle evenings she enjoyed so much just before sunset as the boat bobbed and rocked up and down on the water.

Because the darkening skies splashed with bursts of purple and gold streaks it was times like these she could enjoy the setting sun. She could forget her troubles for a little while, watch the first evening stars pop out, and relish the reason she was out here in the first place.

Tonight, as the winter part of March refused to let go and give way to spring, she was on the hunt to find a sea lion pup. Not four hours earlier, the owner of a passing yacht on its way to Santa Cruz had called in to say the baby mammal was in some kind of distress due to what looked like an open flesh wound.

By four o'clock that afternoon she had boarded the *Moonlight Mile*, the boat Fanning Marine Rescue used routinely for water saves, and hoped like hell she could find the pup before it succumbed to the elements. She had already made several up and down searches along the coastal waters, but so far, she'd come up empty.

A few hundred yards off Smuggler's Bay, the boat rose in the tides as her indigo eyes continued to scan the water near the shoreline through her binoculars. Because of the chill in the air she wore a gray wool mackinaw that had once belonged to her beloved grandfather, Porter Fanning, the original founder of the rescue center where she now worked practically twenty-four-seven.

A battered, black and silver Raiders baseball cap tugged down low hid part of a mass of straight red hair she'd tried to bundle at the nape of her neck to keep it out of her way. The attempt had been in vain of course, as the damp wind wreaked havoc on the bulk of it, which no doubt gave her an unkempt, windblown look.

At the moment, she really could have cared less about her rumpled appearance. After all, the baby sea lion wouldn't care what she looked like once she located him.

Her brow creased when she noted the heavy marine layer forming off the port bow. "Hmm, we have to hurry and find this little guy tonight or we'll likely get caught out in the weather," she muttered to her dog, Guinness, a feisty chocolate Lab that adored the water almost as much as she did. "We don't want to give up on him but...let's face it, in three hours we should have spotted him by now."

Guinness gave a bark as if he knew she was weighing the pros and cons of staying out longer and he needed to somehow be the voice of reason.

She might be able to stretch another hour yet before the fog bank rolled in. She had thoroughly searched the bay and still had seen no sign of a distressed anything, let alone an injured sea lion pup. She hated to think the little guy might not make it through the night if she left him out here with a flesh wound.

But she'd learned long ago from that same grandfather it was foolish to thumb her nose at bad weather or tempt fate when it concerned Mother Nature, especially when it happened over the water.

Porter Fanning had been an incredibly gentle soul when it came to dedicating his life to taking care of marine mammals or any other type of animal in distress. A veterinarian, who nurtured and rehabilitated all types of wildlife over the years, who cared for them so much that he'd taken his inheritance from a once-thriving trust fund and started his own non-profit animal rescue organization. That was Porter Fanning.

He had devoted five decades of his life, along with his wife Mary by his side every step of the way, to saving a variety of animals. From pelicans to dolphins to sea turtles, up and down the California coastline, the name Porter Fanning stood for rescue and a sanctuary for the sick or injured where they would have the chance to thrive before returning to the sea.

Along the way, he'd gained a reputation for fighting greedy land developers and corrupt politicians. For in all that time, he never once turned down the chance to save a starving, stranded, or injured animal.

That is, until a heart attack at the age of seventy-seven put an end to a life that, up to then, had pretty much gained the respect of wildlife lovers on four continents. Porter Fanning didn't just preach about the preservation and conservation, he backed up what he said with his own dollars.

And then eleven months and five days after Keegan had buried her beloved grandfather, a broken-hearted Mary Fanning had gone to bed two days before Thanksgiving and died peacefully in her sleep.

Mary Fanning had followed Porter into whatever other realm exists.

Keegan liked to think that wherever they were, they were together and happy with all the animals that had come and gone in their lives over the years.

Their deaths though had left Keegan with an empty hole in her heart. She hadn't just been devastated the past few months but a little lost as well. She'd always been able to rely on them for anything and everything.

And now, she had no one.

It fell to her to keep FMRC up and running. And she was determined to do that. Her grandfather might have started off wealthy but he certainly hadn't ended up that way, a fact that his attorney, Aaron Hartley, had made clear to Keegan two days after Porter's funeral. It seemed his passion for animals and making sure the wildlife center, as well as the *Moonlight Mile* always stayed up-to-date with the latest technology and gadgets, had come with a hefty price tag.

The rescue center had long since zapped Porter's family fortune.

For the past decade, the center had survived on grants, donations, and bequests, many coming from all over the world, from the people Porter Fanning had inspired.

With the bad economy of late the center had seen a downturn in donations and those bequests. Keegan didn't intend to let her grandparents down though. Since their deaths she knew it was getting tougher and tougher to keep the center running, especially since things like medicine and food continued to rise in price. The care of the wildlife they rescued and rehabilitated took priority but it didn't stop fuel costs from climbing, or medicine from skyrocketing, or bills that had to be paid on time.

And since the center had lost its veterinarian, Keegan had put out plenty of feelers for a new one. But so far, not one qualified vet wanted to relocate to a small town the size of Pelican Pointe.

Even though Keegan wasn't a vet, she could administer antibiotics in a pinch and so far she'd been able to rely on the town veterinarian, Bran Sullivan, for counsel and emergency services.

She thought back to those days last November right before Mary had died. Keegan had known her grandmother had been sliding into despair. It seemed to her that since Porter's death, Mary had lost the sparkle she'd once had. She'd lost interest in almost everything. Yes, there had been a dozen signs that Mary wasn't coping well with her husband's death. For the first several weeks she hadn't wanted to get out of bed, acted as though she didn't want to face the day, or watch any of her favorite programs on TV.

Mary had even shunned spending time at the center

with the animals. That alone should've told Keegan her grandmother had been fading into an abyss of depression and had no interest in a comeback.

But she'd thought giving her time to grieve was the answer.

Keegan realized now that had been a mistake. She should've demanded Mary go see a therapist. Even though she couldn't imagine loving anyone that deeply or staying in love for as long as Porter and Mary had been together, she should've done more to help her grandmother.

At the age of five Keegan's mother had brought her back to Pelican Pointe for a visit to finally meet her grandparents, parents Maryanne Fanning hadn't always gotten along with. But on the same day the two of them had arrived in town, Maryanne had slipped back into her pride and joy, a sleek black 1989 Pontiac Trans Am with the lame excuse she needed to go pick up a pack of cigarettes at the gas station.

A five-year-old had bought the lie. But looking back, Porter and Mary Fanning had known their daughter wasn't coming back.

Mainly because Maryanne hadn't exactly been mother material, and hadn't for a very long time.

Keegan never laid eyes on the woman again, and as far as she knew, neither had Mary or Porter. She'd dumped Keegan in Pelican Pointe and went on to do whatever Maryanne enjoyed doing, which history said was mostly partying with bad boys who could supply her with a steady stream of drugs.

Maryanne certainly hadn't cared about her daughter. Keegan barely remembered what the woman looked like in the flesh even though her grandmother had kept pictures of Maryanne sitting around the house, on the mantel, on the nightstand beside her bed.

Keegan hadn't wanted to tell her grandmother those photos of Maryanne didn't mean a whole lot to her. In fact, she'd already boxed them up and stored them away out of sight, out of mind. The only pictures she needed sitting around were the ones of Porter and Mary and ones that reminded her of the good times they'd had together.

Keegan had never even known her father, didn't know the color of his eyes or his hair, or how tall he'd been, or what he did for a living. She didn't even know if he still lived or had died at some point. Maryanne mostly forgot to mention those kinds of details.

There were some things Keegan had never bothered asking. Maryanne hadn't hung around long enough. And asking her grandparents seemed to bring back memories they seemed reluctant to revisit.

Because none of it had mattered—the people who had raised her were now gone.

For more than twenty years, Mary and Porter Fanning had given her stability, a home-onboard life, unconditional love and acceptance. They'd sent her to UC Santa Cruz for her degree in marine biology. From them, she'd inherited their love of nature, of wildlife, learned to respect the sea, and the marine life that lived there.

As of last November, Keegan had inherited the compound south of the pier on Ocean Street where the rescue center made its home. That included an old two-story brick building and the little house adjacent to the ten-acre property.

To Keegan, both places seemed lonely and empty without Mary and Porter Fanning bustling around, hovering in their own way, to take care of everyone.

Keegan had discovered the hard way over the past few months that the animals, much like the center, did not wait for grief to pass. And stressing about expenditures and stretching a dollar wouldn't change a thing.

She squinted out into the horizon and decided that even if it looked like she had another hour or so before the marine layer rolled in for real, she'd consider calling it a night—at least on the water. She could always head for shore and wait there to see if the pup headed inland. Wounded animals, by instinct, tended to know it was dangerous for them to stay in the water where predators could make an easy meal out of them.

Realizing her stomach rumbled with hunger pains, she began jonesing for a greasy grilled cheese and salty fries from the Diner. Since the peanut butter and strawberry jam sandwich she'd eaten around noon seemed like a distant memory now, getting food sounded like a solid plan. She could always dash in, grab a quick meal and then eat it on the pier while she kept an eye out for the pup with her binoculars.

Because pretty soon the light would be gone anyway and she'd have to resort to using the searchlights, which tended to make sea lions skittish.

Reluctantly Keegan went to the helm, pushed the button to start the ancient engine—or tried to. She heard the grinding noise that always made her grimace. They might've spared no expense on the latest equipment onboard, but Keegan knew the engine on the *Moonlight Mile* would likely need a major overhaul before summer.

She'd have to see if she could persuade Wally Pierce, her best bud and all-around mechanic guru, to take a look at it, as well as the engine in the twenty year old Ford truck she used for land rescues. Sadly, both had been misfiring.

As soon as the motor roared to life, she turned and headed inland. All the while Guinness stood at the railing, tail wagging at the prospect of getting to shore soon and back to his dog dish for supper.

Heading due east, she brought the *Moonlight Mile* into the harbor—and noticed the man first. He walked straight out into the water, the entire time he seemed to be talking to himself. Odd, she thought. From this distance the man looked similar to the one she'd seen in town a time or two, the one who worked for Nick and Jordan out at Taggert Organic Farms.

Rumor around town said he had a major drinking problem—along with a questionable past, whatever that meant.

Keegan shrugged absently. Whatever his past held, it

was no business of hers. Having grown up in Pelican Pointe, she knew all about small-town gossip. People liked to buzz and needed someone to talk about, the newer you were, the juicier the tidbits tended to run.

But that didn't explain why the stupid man had decided to go swimming in the bay this close to dusk with all his clothes on. Sane people usually didn't go in the water on a chilly night in early March without an excellent reason or a wetsuit.

Idiot man, she decided. He obviously was unaccustomed to being around Smuggler's Bay and its changing tides.

She made a wide swing around the area where he drifted into the waves.

Spending the next several minutes getting the boat moored, she slipped the rope through the shackle and secured the lines. By that time, she noticed the man had disappeared entirely. Suddenly realizing a good ten minutes had gone by without seeing him surface, she scanned the water. When she didn't spot him, she turned to study the shoreline in case he had given up and gone back to sit on the sand.

But the beach was empty.

Guinness began to bark wildly. From the corner of her eye, she spied a body floating in the water, face down. Instinctively she took out her cell phone and dialed 911.

"I've got a potential drowning victim in Smuggler's Bay. There's a man in distress. Get an ambulance here! Now!"

While she talked, she pulled off the mackinaw and replaced it with a life jacket, shrugging it on. "He looks unconscious. I could take the boat out but I might stand a better chance if I simply go in and try to pull him out."

"You shouldn't do that. Wait for the EMTs to get there," the voice on the other end of the line cautioned.

"I wait; chances are he'll be gone for sure."

And with that, Keegan tossed the phone aside, threw off her Raiders cap, toed off her shoes and without considering the consequences, dived into the frigid, wet cold of the Pacific Ocean.

At that moment, an injured sea lion wasn't the only creature in need of saving.

Chapter Two

When Guinness jumped in after her, she shouted, "You go back, go on now, Guinness. Go back to shore. Now!" Keegan demanded, and watched her dog change direction, reluctantly heading back to land.

Good thing too, because now where the shelf dropped off into deeper water, she struggled mightily with the rip current. She had lived around the water for most of her life. If she wasn't in it surfing or swimming or netting marine mammals, she was on it.

But now, the tide kept pulling her farther out to sea.

By the time she caught up with the man, he was still face down, not moving. And they were both a good seventy yards from shore. Not only that, it felt like the man weighed a ton. She managed to turn him over, tried to get a good grip on him around his neck. She began to swim parallel to the beach.

At this point, she knew fighting the current would be useless. If she was lucky she might be able to tread water until the paramedics showed up.

She bobbed up and down before realizing that if she waited much longer to head for shore, she might not be able to revive the guy once she got him to the beach.

Because of that she began to kick harder and move them southward, *with* the current not against it. She'd gone what felt like forty yards across before she recognized the tide and current had changed in her favor. As soon as that happened, only then did she begin to kick and swim harder toward the pier.

His dead weight prevented her from getting him all the way up on land though. It took her forever to drag the man through shallow water. Even then, she collapsed on top of a sandy bed of gravel and rocks to get her breath back. She glanced around for the EMTs.

They still hadn't shown up.

But Guinness had. He immediately started licking the man's face.

She pushed the dog back long enough to lean over the guy's chest, put her ear to his heart, listened, and then realized he wasn't breathing.

She smelled whiskey, strong, overpowering.

But she opened his mouth anyway, made sure his airway was clear. She tilted his head back, lifted his chin up, and pinched his nose closed. She blew air into his mouth and began CPR.

Focused on her effort, Keegan didn't even hear the ambulance screech to a halt up above them on the pier.

But after almost a hundred reps, the man still wasn't breathing. As she continued to count, Guinness kept up his own steady lick to the man's forehead or whatever he could reach.

Just when she'd about given up, the guy coughed and shot out a ton of sea water onto his own already soaked T-shirt. The minute he took his first full breath, Keegan rolled him to his side and began rubbing his back.

Keegan heard him mutter, "Cassie, my Cassie."

Guinness woofed near the guy's ear and then got up close and personal, making the man blink in surprise. Once the dog had his attention, Guinness gave him a couple more licks to the face for good measure.

Stretched out on the sand, the man put a big hand on the dog's snout as if he needed the contact. With his other hand he shoved his mass of long hair back off his face.

About that time the paramedics came running up.

Over the top of Guinness' head, his wary eyes darted to Keegan's and held. Gruffly, he whispered, "Goddamn it why, why couldn't you have just left me out there in the damned water."

He made a weak attempt to get up.

Taken aback by his words, Keegan pushed to her feet and grabbed Guinness' collar then watched Deacon Jones, one of the EMTs out of San Sebastian, take over by attempting to get the man's vitals, wrapping his arm in a cuff to take his blood pressure.

But the man jerked his arm away. "Leave me the hell alone," he groaned and immediately began trying to remove the wrap.

For the first time since pulling him out of the water, realization dawned on Keegan. The man had obviously done this on purpose. He hadn't gone swimming at all, the current hadn't caused him to falter but rather he had tried to end his life by drowning.

Something about that pissed her off.

With the drop in adrenaline, she began to shiver in the cold.

Brian Driscoll, Deacon's partner, draped a blanket around her shoulders. "Good job, Keegan, looks like he'll be fine, doesn't seem to appreciate that fact though."

She puffed out an angry breath. So Brian had gotten the gist of the man's mindset as well. It was then she spotted Ethan Cody running down the beach with his wife, Hayden, in tow. Ethan looked determined and furious and Hayden had trouble keeping up with his stride.

Eyeing Ethan, the man on the ground did his best to sit up again, knocking Deacon's hand away when he offered it in assistance.

"What the hell happened?" Ethan barked.

"What does it look like?" Cord choked out. "I had too much to drink. I went for a swim and ended up going out a little too far. That's it."

Keegan pursed her lips together trying to decide what to say. Should she rat the guy out? What if next time no one was around to save his ass? What if next time he took someone with him? She didn't need this, didn't need the aggravation. She had work still to do, a sea lion pup to find. If the man didn't want to live—what the hell did she care?

She watched as Deacon and Brian started packing up their equipment. Neither man said a word. But all of a sudden Keegan couldn't let this go. "Bullshit," Keegan muttered, staring straight into Cord's gold-flecked brown eyes. "I watched you from the boat. I watched as you walked out into the tide. At first that's what I thought you were doing, that you were just in the mood for a swim despite the fact you looked out of it. But you didn't even try to swim, not once. And why don't you go ahead and tell Ethan about that gun you're carrying in your pocket."

She'd felt that, too, when she'd gotten him onto the beach.

Cord put his hands out on the rocky gravel and struggled to get to his feet. But in the midst of standing, he stopped dead still. His eyes landed on the mouthy redhead.

As if he'd just noticed the goddess for the very first time, he blinked and sucked in a ragged breath. Jesus. Long, straight, wet tresses skimmed down to her shoulders and clung to the creamy skin along her neck. The damp locks curved softly around a classic narrow face topped with saucer-sized, striking cobalt eyes. A cute, patrician nose turned up slightly at the end.

Despite the fact she was pissed, she looked like his idea of what a mermaid might look like if such things existed. Attraction had his belly tightening.

Lust aside though, Cord cursed under his breath and threw a look of disdain at the drenched woman before finally turning to face Ethan—and lied through his teeth. "I brought the gun with me for protection. It's just a little ol' .22, Ethan. You know how rowdy McCready's can get on Friday nights. I wanted to be prepared."

Ethan's eyes narrowed to slits. Realizing he'd been suckered not thirty minutes earlier, Ethan had heard enough. He quickly turned Cord around and cuffed his hands behind his back. He patted him down, retrieved the .22 from his wet pants pocket.

"Prepared for what exactly? Well, prepare for this," Ethan stated emphatically. "I'm taking you into custody for a weapons violation and then recommending to the judge you get a psych evaluation as soon as possible." To make a point, he started reading Cord his Miranda rights.

"You aren't serious? Who will Nick get to milk the cows in the morning, do all my chores and stuff? Silas and Sammy had a wedding to go to this weekend, dragged their cousins Marty and Ben along with them to Visalia. Even though the Miller boy is doing the evening milking doesn't mean he'll stick around for long tonight. That leaves Nick shorthanded."

"Yeah? Well, you shoulda thought of that before you brought a gun with you to take a walk off the pier."

Disgusted, Ethan hauled Cord up the beach, trudging through sand the entire way. "Damn it, Cord, not only do I have to spend the rest of the evening away from Hayden on a Friday night, but I'll be mired down with filling out paperwork, your paperwork for the rest of the damned evening. You know how I hate administrative shit, especially when I could be snuggled up to my wife of three weeks making out on the couch."

He turned to Hayden. "Sorry. Looks like Cord put a dent in our movie plans."

Cord watched as newlywed Hayden Cody leaned over and whispered something in her husband's ear. The simple gesture tugged at his heartstrings. Now he felt guilty for being the one to mess up things between a pair of newlyweds.

Cord considered his predicament. "You're actually locking me up?"

Ethan nodded. "You bet I am." He turned to plant a kiss on his wife's cheek. "Don't start *Clash of the Titans* until I get back, okay?" With that, Ethan shoved Cord in the back and headed up the steps to the wharf above.

Hayden hung back to study Keegan and realized the woman must be freezing. "Come on. Let's get you out of those wet clothes. You okay?" "I'm fine. Serves me right though for getting involved in this whole mess when I should've just let the paramedics handle it and mind my own business. I've got an injured baby sea lion to find."

Hayden put her arm around Keegan. "Tonight? Well, knowing you, you'll find it. But you need dry clothes. Cord is in a bad place right now, Keegan. You did the right thing."

"I know, but the way he looked at me that man hates me."

"Oh, Keegan, Cord doesn't hate you nearly as much as he hates himself right now."

"What's his deal anyway, other than the whole 'drinking himself into oblivion' thing?"

She patted her thigh to get the dog's attention. When the dog trotted over, she bent down to scratch his head and ears. "What do you say we go back to the boat and get our stuff, Guinness? Let's go, boy. You did such a good job, didn't you? Then we'll go get you some supper. That man was so lucky we were here to help him."

Keegan turned to Hayden. "You think he's going to be all right." She tapped a finger to her own temple. "Up here."

Hayden shrugged. "I hope so. Go get your stuff and I'll tell you all I know about Cord Bennett."

After retrieving her shoes, cell phone and the mackinaw, the two women took off down Ocean Street toward the Fanning Marine Rescue Center.

It didn't take Hayden long to go into a detailed account of what she knew about Cord's past, including the spree shooting that had taken his fiancée's life.

Keegan let her finish and then said, "Cassie. That was the first word out of his mouth after he regained consciousness." She shook her head. "That kind of love is something I'm just not familiar with, it's what my grandparents had. And look at you every time Ethan gets within ten feet, you light up like a gaudy neon sign."

Hayden snickered. "I know. You just wait, Keegan, once you find Mr. Right, once you take that fall, you'll be right there with me."

Keegan snorted. "Yeah. Sure. Whatever. You know

you're delusional, right? This is Pelican Pointe. If Mr. Right is around here he must be hiding underneath one of those large rocks on the beach I have yet to look under."

"Hey, you never know. It's possible." "You know what I hate?"

"What?"

"When a perfectly good friend goes gaga and starts seeing love in the air for everyone around her. You've been married, what, almost a month now? And you're still glowing. God that is so—"

"Wonderful?" Hayden finished, bumping her friend's shoulder and letting out a huge sigh. "Sue me because I want everyone else to be as happy as I am."

"Hmm, not a bad idea. I wonder if old man Hartley would let me sue you for false advertising. Maybe I could get some extra cash for the center out of that deal."

"You've got a lot on your plate, trying to keep a lot of balls in the air, losing your grandparents within a year of each other has to hurt. I told you I'd find you another volunteer or two. Lilly made me a sign I put up in the bookstore advertising the need for people to help protect the wildlife in the area and reminding them that we have a state-of-the-art, rescue center right here in Pelican Pointe that needs their continued support."

"Get any replies?"

Hayden sighed. "Just two, Hannah Broderick's son, Jason, and his friend, Connor Davis." Keegan couldn't help but laugh. "That's what I need, two very eager ten-year-old boys. Well, granddad always said to start 'em young, get 'em involved early and they'll appreciate the wildlife more in the long run. Seriously though, I'd love to bring on another couple of volunteers. It seems there are never enough hands for all that we need doing."

"How many do you have now?"

"It's down to a skeletal three volunteers, plus Pete. Pete is always willing to go that extra mile."

"He loved your grandfather."

"He did indeed."

"What kind of animals do you have in residence now, Keegan? Do you still have that cute little seal?"

Keegan snorted knowing how that cute little seal had grown to nearly three hundred pounds and almost ate them out of house and home. "We released the seal two months ago. Now we have a resident sea otter still recovering from starvation. We call her Minnie because she's so small, kind of like Minnie Mouse. She's pregnant, probably due any day now."

"Really? That's fascinating. How many do you think you've rescued over the years?"

"Me? Not that many, but granddad, he probably saved a thousand or more."

"What you do is—extraordinary—and your place is awesome."

"You think so?" Keegan asked. "Sometimes it feels a little like insanity."

They walked along a ragged sidewalk marred with broken pavement and passed a number of abandoned storefronts until they reached the section of town even more derelict than the rest. Here a group of warehouses hadn't seen an occupant in three decades.

Guinness trotted beside them, sniffing and inspecting every blade of grass and weed that sprouted up between the gaps in the cement.

When they reached a two-story red brick building originally built as a hotel back in the '40s, Keegan stopped long enough to pull out a small remote control from her jacket pocket and pressed the button. An iron gate began to slowly slide on its wheels along a track until it fully opened wide enough that a vehicle could easily drive inside. They walked across a paved lot, what once had been a parking area for the old hotel.

But these days the former lodge was a mere memory. Porter Fanning had gutted the place in the '90s and remodeled the structure into a marine wildlife hospital that rivaled those in bigger cities. Now it offered a state-of-the-art nursery with heated concrete floors, an exam room that doubled as an operating area, a small token office, and much-used laundry facilities.

Once inside the fence, the repaved area led to a renovated, modern compound complete with five roomy, outdoor cages all with their own in-ground pools so the mammals could exercise, swim and have plenty of space to move around.

At the sound of Guinness' "honey, I'm home" bark, a young, college-aged female emerged from one of the enclosures and sent them a wave. "Hey, Keegan, did you bring me back that pup?"

Keegan squinted in the direction of Abby Anderson, a sunny blonde with a deep, abiding love for wildlife. Abby was one of the brightest interns out of the current crop of UC Santa Cruz marine biologist hopefuls Keegan had interviewed.

Keegan considered it her good fortune she had snagged the energetic, cheery volunteer since most would rather work at more popular places like San Diego's Sea World or further north at the Monterey Bay Aquarium.

"Nope. Couldn't find him in the water—yet—but I'm not giving up. He might've beached himself already, that's why I'm going back out as soon as I get a shower and put on dry clothes."

"Hmm," Hayden muttered. "I can see you out in the dark walking up and down the shore with a flashlight before you quit for the night."

Keegan shrugged. "It's better than leaving him out there stranded and injured." She turned to Abby, "How's the pelican doing?"

"Better." Abby eyed the blanket Keegan still used against the chilly night air and asked, "Did you take a spill in the water or something?"

"Are you kidding?" Hayden burst out. "She saved a man from drowning in Smuggler's Bay."

"Probably some stupid tourist who decided to take a swim and didn't know how dangerous the undertow is in that area."

"Something like that," Keegan mumbled. She turned to Hayden, remembering the woman's ordeal last fall when she had people trying to kill her, and asked, "Will you be okay walking back by yourself or do you want Abby to go with you?"

"I'll be fine. You go on and take a shower. I want to see the pregnant otter and the pelican first though. What's wrong with the pelican?"

"Some good Samaritan brought him in last Saturday after finding him in the park in San Sebastian with a broken wing, starving to death. And you watch your fingers, Hayden Cody. Don't go sticking them in through the fence. Some of these animals bite. And that pelican is in quarantine until we know he's healthy enough to join the others."

"Yeah, yeah…I know, I know," Hayden muttered when Abby took off for one of the pens in the back to show her the injured pelican sitting away from the others in a cage by himself.

Keegan watched them go before following a walkway across the length of the complex and headed for the 1940 two-story Craftsman, painted a sunny butter color that sat on the other side of the property, away from the chaos and noise of the center.

The home her grandparents had occupied for almost half a century sported four squared stone pillars halfway up that turned neatly into wood trim they kept painting white for contrast. A huge dormer window, front and center, took most of the sloped, second-story roof.

When she got to the bright red front door, a permanent reminder that Mary Porter had had a spirited, creative side, Keegan paused to stare down at her grandmother's tidy flower beds, laden with a mixture of budding white gerbera daisies and bright yellow coreopsis. Daisies had been Mary's favorite flower.

Since last November she had tried mightily to maintain the plants. But after four months of reading all sorts of books on gardening she'd picked up at Hidden Moon Bay

Books, she didn't seem to have the same kind of green thumb.

She shook her head at the blossoms, the droopy leaves. First chance she got she needed to head over to The Plant Habitat and get a serious heads up on how to grow daisies, otherwise they were all going to wither away and die—just like her grandparents.

She sighed. Okay, so maybe she knew a little something about depression. Losing her grandparents had been heartbreaking and difficult. But despair, no matter how deep, didn't mean suicide was ever the answer.

She had to get the image of the man's eyes out of her head. She didn't want to consider how anyone could be that dead inside enough to want to end it all.

Because being down didn't mean you had to give up. Ah well, what she needed now was a hot shower, a meal, and out of these damned wet clothes.

After all, Cord Bennett wasn't her problem.

Chapter Three

After four long months of having the house to herself Keegan still couldn't quite get used to coming home to the silence of it sitting empty.

As soon as she opened the front door and stepped into the long, rectangular living room, Guinness barreled past her, sliding, as he always did, on the wide-planked cherrywood floors.

Wet and cold, she eyed the tail-wagging dog. "You have to be as hungry as I am. Okay fine, you get food first then I get a hot shower."

She headed to the kitchen and the pantry where she stored the dog food. Scooping out a generous portion, she heaped it into his dish, and then made a dash for the stairs. All the way up she heard the sound of Guinness crunching his way through his chow.

Once she got to the bathroom, she turned on the water and began unlacing her shoes. She tossed them into the hallway and started peeling off her top then her jeans.

She stepped under the hot spray, and tried to calm down from the ordeal at the pier. It wasn't everyday she played lifeguard and saved someone's life, especially since that someone didn't want to be saved.

What would make a person do that, she wondered as she used her familiar apricot scrub to get the sea water and salt off her skin.

She did her best to hurry because damn it, she was starving—and she needed to find the sea lion. But a little thought nagged in the back of her mind and wouldn't let go. If she hadn't been out on the water looking for the injured pup, she never would have been around when Cord

Bennett went into the water.

He could be dead right now, drowned from his own stupidity. There was something pathetic about that.

By the time Keegan emerged from the bathroom, warmer and cleaner, it was almost eight-thirty.

She pulled on a pair of clean jeans and pulled a soft, beige sweater over her head. She braided her wet, straight hair back into a tight tail and picked up the damp towels around her feet, then went back into the bathroom to hang them on the towel bar to dry.

For some reason, without meaning to, she couldn't get past what Cord Bennett's gentle brown eyes had looked like. But those dark eyes hadn't just been glazed over with an alcoholic buzz. They had looked incredibly empty— and sad. She'd never seen eyes like that on a living thing so vacant. She realized now he might be the first person she'd ever been around who had actually tried to take his own life.

When she spotted the blinking light on her answering machine she knew exactly who had called. She hadn't lived in a small town for two decades not to know how fast news travelled. She pushed the button on the machine and listened in sequence as half the town wanted to know how she was doing.

Small towns didn't need to go national when they had their own network full of people who cared.

Keegan had known these people for most of her life. She knew they meant well. They'd been great after both funerals. But it didn't mean her safety net wasn't full of holes. People had their own lives, their own sets of problems. They didn't need to dwell on hers.

Her stomach reminded her she needed to eat.

Even though she was craving a cold beer and that cheese sandwich and fries, she snagged a Snickers bar instead off the counter, grabbed a flashlight out of the laundry room and called to the dog. "You ready for another adventure. Let's get the truck and the netting and go find us a sea lion."

Sitting in the back seat of Ethan's police cruiser, Cord wasn't worried. This wasn't his first ride to the drunk tank, and certainly not spending the night at the county's expense. Nor was he too concerned about the psych evaluation. He'd seen at least half a dozen psychiatrists after he'd been released from the hospital and knew all the buzz words by heart, all those key phrases that would tell the shrink he was as sane as they were. He knew exactly what to say to push all the right buttons. He'd done it before.

"You gonna let me have a phone call, Ethan?" Cord grumbled. "I gotta call Nick and Jordan, let them know they'll need to get someone to do my chores."

"I have something better than that in mind. We're making a stop at the Cove. You can tell Nick yourself, face-to-face, man-to-man. If we don't stop, Nick will just make a point to drive all the way to Santa Cruz to pay you a visit. This way, I'm giving him the opportunity without having to leave his family on a Friday night to get in your face. You need help, Cord. That's what I'm saying and that's what Nick's gonna say. This is your chance to get it."

Cord watched as Ethan made the turn down a long driveway, past an apple-green sign that read Promise Cove Bed and Breakfast and pulled up beside an old Victorian.

At that moment, Cord didn't know he could feel anymore chastised. But at this point he had no doubt that if you gave Ethan Cody twenty minutes with a nun he'd find a way to make the sister feel guilty as hell about something.

It didn't help any that he knew he deserved it. So the minute Nick opened the door and Ethan came around to the back and pulled him out of the car, Cord prepared to go into apology mode.

He saw Nick step outside onto the porch and close the front door behind him. "Sorry, Nick. I..."

But Nick didn't let him finish. "Save it. Because we talked about this a time or two already I'll tell you straight out. You need help, Cord. Apparently it's more than what Jordan and I can give you. It's obvious we aren't in a position to provide you with what you need. We've tried but you seem content in wallowing in your own misery. You told me you were going into McCready's for a couple of drinks not to get drunk. I told you when you came to work for us I'd put up with a lot but I wouldn't tolerate you drunk around Hutton or Jordan, that's bottom line."

Cord shifted his feet listening to Nick's assessment. He knew Nick would be disappointed in him but this was a new way to go. Guilt. "I wasn't drunk around Hutton or Jordan and you know it," Cord put in.

"Ethan pulled me out of McCready's, I admit to that. I went for a walk on the beach, decided to go for a swim and sober up, wandered a little too far out in the surf. People are making a big deal out of nothing."

Nick pointed his finger and stated, "Right there is the problem. You really think I buy that. Keegan Fanning pulled your ass out of the bay not more than half an hour ago. With the rip tide you both could've drowned. You think she wanted to take an impromptu swim in freezing water tonight? Of course you don't think of anyone but yourself and how miserable you are. You're damned lucky she was around."

Cord moved his shoulder around to show Nick his manacled wrists. "Ethan's locking me up!"

"Because you had a gun! You tried to end it all! You seem to forget, not that long ago, I walked in your shoes. But despite all my guilt I never once tried to kill myself. Do something about it, Cord. Agree to counseling or find another job."

"You don't mean that."

"Yeah, I do. It pains me but you get into grief counseling and a program like AA, maybe rehab or so help me we're done. You have to want to help yourself. Maybe Jordan and I can't make you go. But as your employer, I can, and will. As the owner of Taggert Farms, we have a liability if you have a drinking problem on the job and now it seems you're suicidal."

"Come on, Nick, I do not drink on the job and you know it. The Miller boy wanted to make a few extra bucks tonight to take his girl over to Santa Cruz next weekend. I gave him work, the evening milking and some other chores. He gave me a little free time tonight. I work my ass off during the week. A guy's got a right to an evening out where he can blow off a little steam once in awhile."

"And you headed straight to McCready's, got drunk and then decided to what? End it all? Jordan invited you to dinner tonight. Remember? You didn't have to go anywhere except right here. Instead of heading over here for dinner though, you chose to get drunk. Well, I get it now, Cord. Thanks for letting us know where Jordan and I fit into the grand scheme of things. You aren't getting better. No, you're heading toward rock bottom as fast as the wino in the gutter and I won't stand around watching it happen."

Cord sighed, ran his cuffed hands through his still-damp, shoulder length locks. For the first time he began to see the seriousness of it all. "Look, I had five whiskeys. Up to about three hours ago, I hadn't had a drink all week."

"And when you do you don't know when to stop." Nick let out a sigh of his own in frustration. "I care about you, Cord, so does Jordan. You and I, we've been through a lot together, something we shared while we trained, and once we got to Iraq that bond got stronger in war. But I need you to understand you can't treat people like crap wherever and whenever you want. We understand you've had a rough two years. But until you decide we aren't the enemy…" Nick's voiced trailed off as he started to pace up and down the wooden porch.

"I had a momentary lapse in judgment and made a

mistake. Everyone's acting as though…"

Nick lost it then. "Getting drunk isn't the only issue at play here. And you know it. Jordan and I understand you're grieving. And we've formally offered our support by giving you a job and a place to live to get you through this rough time, but you have to decide just how far downhill you want to go. You have to take that first step to change your life. We can't do it for you. We won't babysit you anymore, Cord. Think about it while you spend the night in county lockup. Get your act together or don't bother coming back to Promise Cove or the farm."

"Let's go." Ethan took Cord by the arm and pushed him back toward the cruiser. To Nick he said, "He'll get a hearing in the morning, probably see the judge on call for the weekend. I'll make sure they order him to talk to a psychiatrist as a part of his release. Until then what should I do with him?"

"That's up to Cord. Let me know what he decides."

As soon as the police car disappeared down the driveway, Jordan stepped out onto the porch beside her husband. Six months pregnant, due in June, Jordan rested her head on Nick's shoulder and ran a hand over her nice, round, baby bump. "Tough love is always difficult."

"So you think I was too hard on him?"

"I didn't say that. You've tried everything else. Who knows, maybe he'll come to his senses sitting in a cell. It won't be the first time though. Maybe we should've gotten tough a lot sooner. You sounded as if you were practicing for when we have teenagers."

Nick paled. "God, I hope not." He placed a hand over the one that rested on her belly, rubbed gently in a circular motion and said, "I'm not putting this little guy or Hutton in jeopardy by hoping Cord finally sees the light enough to change. He's a ticking time bomb. Trying to commit suicide woke me up. Hell, I didn't even know he had a gun. I knew he was messed up, but... What if Keegan hadn't been around to pull him out?"

"Don't think like that. Keegan was practically raised

out on Smuggler's Bay. What is the likelihood she'd be right there when Cord went in and needed help?"

"I don't even know how she got the guy to shore. She must be a helluva swimmer."

"I don't know that much about her really. She was still in college when Scott first brought me back here. Then when Scott left for Iraq, I wandered around town one day and found myself inside the center. Mary Fanning gave me a tour. But let's face it, both Keegan's grandparents had their hands full with so much to do. Even then, they were well into their seventies so I'm certain they were preparing to hand off the reins to her to run the place. The only other time I was inside the center, Hutton was about a year old. I took her to see a couple of baby seals they had at the time. Noisy things, but Hutton loved watching them play."

Nick grinned at that. "I forget that checking out a couple of seals passes for entertainment in Pelican Pointe."

Jordan laughed. "Don't knock it. When it's gray and chilly and you need something to pass the time just to keep from going crazy, you'll get creative. Do you think Cord's crazy, Nick?"

"I honestly don't know. They say PTSD can do a number on a person. I know it did on me. But that was before I met you." He gave her a quick kiss and went on, "What if he'd done something like that over at the farm, Jordan? What if you or I had gone into the barn or the house and found him…like that?"

Nick shook his head at the thought and couldn't finish. "I'll have to call Ben Latham and let him know. Maybe he can make a trip to Santa Cruz while Cord's locked up, talk some sense into him. God knows, I've tried—and failed."

She laid a hand on his heart. "It's okay, you're upset and you're afraid for your friend. But really, Nick, I doubt Cord will be locked up that long. I think Ethan's determined to get him some help. Ethan might want to be a famous author one day, but he takes his duties here as deputy very seriously. He cares for the town."

"True, but I've also got a responsibility to you, to my

family. I don't think Cord would hurt anyone but then I didn't think he'd get desperate enough to try and kill himself either."

He leaned over kissed her cheek. "Besides, thinking about our kids growing up, they'll be perfect and not give us a day of distress."

Jordan wheezed out a laugh. "You just keep thinking like that, daddy. Let's not spend time dwelling on the terrible twos or what we have to look forward to during their teen years down the road. With kids, you do your best and hope it's enough for the right outcome. The same has to be true for Cord Bennett. Do you think he'll get out tomorrow?"

"Probably. I think Ethan hopes spending the night in the drunk tank will wake Cord up. But whatever time he has there, Cord will have some decisions to make. The ball's in his court."

Two hours later Cord had been fingerprinted, booked and stripped. He found himself dressed in an orange jumpsuit and locked away in a solitary cell under suicide watch. Cameras hung above his bunk, watching every move he made, which included taking a piss.

He spent the first couple of hours in rage mode, angry with the world, which of course did him little good. But goddamn it, he was not wallowing in self-pity. For God's sakes he'd lost someone he loved in a violent shooting. Hell, he'd watched her not twenty feet away as she lay dying, watched as she had taken her last breath.

And what the goddamn hell had he done about it?

An image of his beautiful Cassie as she was in life smiled down at him. Lying there drunk and sick on his bunk, he wanted to believe, no, he needed to believe her appearance was real. Instead of the camera, he saw her angelic face.

"What have you done to yourself, Cord? You don't even look like the same man I fell in love with. What's with the hair? If you were back in Leesburg...Daddy would give you grief about wearing it that long and insist you get it cut."

Cord dismissed the criticism as he always had. "I miss you. I want you back. You were the only good thing that ever happened to me in my whole miserable life. You know that."

"Yes, I know that. But I'm gone now, Cord. You're still here among the living. Get on with your life. You need to stop wishing you were dead and find what you're missing. It won't be me. It will never be me. But that's okay. I'm happy here, Cord. And remember, you made me happy while I was there—with you. Life was too short for me but you, you still have a chance at what you want. Don't blow it, okay?"

Cassie started to fade away.

"Don't go. Don't leave me alone again."

"I'll always be with you, Cord." She placed her hand over her heart. "I'll be there in yours. Always. But you need to let me go now. You have a good life, Cord. Don't stop looking for possibilities. Your destiny was never to be with me in Virginia. Your destiny's here, Cord, not where you started out, not in San Diego, but in that little town. Put down roots, Cord. Okay? Don't blow it. You always have a tendency to blow it." "No, no, don't go. Cassie!"

Whether it was Cassie's ghost, the image of her as an angel or something else, it dissolved into nothing.

Surrounded by raw smells of sweat and urine with a little stale cigarette smoke thrown in for good measure, he wished he'd never left the farm. He thought of the tidy rows of the vegetables he tended, the cherry and apple orchards just beginning to blossom and realized he wanted more than anything to be outside.

He missed the earthy smells of hay and cows, the views of the Pacific Ocean from the cliffs. He longed to see the stars, to sit outside in the old porch swing that creaked no matter how many times he oiled it during the week.

He decided then and there if he ever got out of this place, he'd do whatever Cassie wanted him to do to straighten out his life. He never wanted to think of Cassie disappointed in him.

Closing his eyes, he drifted off to sleep and dreamed about a woman for the first time in two years who was not Cassie Spearman.

Tall, she stood at least five-eight with a mass of titian hair and a spattering of light freckles across the bridge of her nose. She looked a lot younger than his thirty-four.

She had saved him.

Her eyes were so huge and azure, like pools of gleaming sapphires. Penetrating, is the way he would've described them. They had bored holes in him. If he thought about it long enough, he might even describe them as glaring. They had shot daggers at him when she'd caught him in a lie. Those eyes of hers had shone coldly blue, then furious.

But her lips, she'd had the softest lips. He might not remember her mouth on his but he could imagine what it felt like.

She'd breathed life back into him.

Her name was Keegan. That's what Nick had called her. What kind of woman had a name like Keegan anyway? She'd acted as though she actually cared—cared about a stranger, a worthless piece of shit like him who wanted to end his useless existence.

God. He did need help.

He had to wonder if it was too late to make that change everyone kept talking about. He had to hope it wasn't.

Cord sat up on his cot and looked around. Jesus, he scrubbed a hand over his face and remembered now that Ethan Cody had locked him up, caged him, like one of the barn animals at the farm.

His eyes scanned upward to the camera overhead.

Okay, Bennett, you need to get real serious about convincing these people you are one hundred percent sane and very, very sorry for ever taking a short walk into the ocean.

Chapter Four

Three thousand miles away, locked inside Sandhurst State Mental Hospital, Robby Mack Stevens worked on his escape plan.

For the past year and a half he'd done everything he could to convince his own lawyer, as well as the mealy-mouthed judges he'd stood in front of using his hang-dog persona, along with a variety of head doctors, that he was a schizoid.

What fools they all were for believing that. Robby Mack was as sane as the rest of America.

Though they'd sealed him away in a mental ward and put him on meds he didn't need and that he often spit out, Robby kept up his ruse. He religiously attended his anger management classes three times a week, even though it pissed him off to do so. Old Robby Mack was no fool. He made sure he maintained his cool throughout the sessions. He even made sure he pretended remorse and contrition.

The suckers always wanted a decent member of society to show regret and remorse for what they'd done. Robby knew the drill—by heart—and was more than willing to play his part.

At least he wasn't forced to wear an orange jumpsuit at Wallens Ridge State Prison near Big Stone Gap where they were prone to putting murderers in solitary confinement and throwing away the key. Nope, the con he'd been running for the past eighteen months had prevented that from happening.

Here at Sandhurst, Robby Mack simply bid his time in this crap of a hole-in-the-wall until he found a way out. He'd been scouting the best possible way off the floor each and every time they made him take the walk down the hall to spend a little more time with the shrink.

It was only a matter of time until he found a way out. He did, after all, have someone willing to help him.

Blonde bimbo, Terri Lynn Cranston was a little on the fat side for his tastes, but she didn't need to know that, at least not yet, not until he was done with her. A born charmer, the six-foot-tall Robby liked to think he could talk his way into any woman's panties, on any given day of the week. Once there, as long as he could bend her to his will, women were of use to him. Terri Lynn was no exception. The woman was desperate for some attention. And ol' Robby Mack intended to be around to give her whatever she needed every time she needed it.

Whatever sob story worked, Robby would hone in on the poor woman's weakness, manipulate her to do whatever he wanted then keep her on a tight tether. Women needed guidance and a schedule. That's what they understood. Without it they were adrift in a world not suited for the weaker sex.

As the orderlies walked him to an elevator that would take him down to the first floor and to the therapist, Robby once again checked out the layout. Thanks to chunky Terri, she had given him a better idea of the hospital's design.

He intended to make the most of her generosity.

He figured it had to be his trusting, gray eyes. Women seemed to always comment on his eyes. But Robby knew. His eyes hid his dark, cold side, the predator side like a shark.

It wasn't his fault he had never been able to connect to the pain of other people, especially females.

He shook his head. A guy could only put up with so much before he had to take a stand. Women seemed to forget their place in his world. They were there to do a man's bidding—his bidding.

And in getting women to "bend to his thinking" department, Robby always won first prize. Even locked up, he could recognize a woman suffering from low self-esteem from two miles away. No one could ever accuse Robby Mack of not knowing how to play on a woman's insecurities like a drum.

Oh, yeah, he was excellent at telling a woman like Terri Lynn what she wanted to hear. Robby Mack was a sweet-talker who could and would get a woman to believe every word out of his lying set of lips.

Women were so gullible when it came to believing his compliments.

All you had to do was make it sound sincere and bam—you were in like Flynn.

In the meantime, Robby Mack would do what he did best.

He would work plump Terri Lynn Cranston into a frenzy believing he had been wrongly accused, wrongly charged so that she would continue to help him plan his escape from this nasty godforsaken place.

Because when he got out, he intended to make his freedom count.

He might've put an end to that bitch Cassie Spearman, for that he could be proud. But as soon as he could, he intended to go after more, much more. He'd only taken out six that day. If given the chance, he knew he could do better. He'd go after that bastard, the one who had gotten away. He wanted, no, he needed to finish what he had not been able to do eighteen months earlier.

Because Cord Bennett had survived, he intended to remedy that fact. And in that, Terri Lynn had already come through for him.

He knew exactly where the son of a bitch lived now. But first he had to find a way out of the loony bin.

Chapter Five

At five-fifty-five the next morning, a guard woke Cord up by sliding a plastic tray with runny scrambled eggs and stale toast through an opening in his cell door. The whiskey from the night before had his brain fuzzed and pounding like someone had decided to hammer some sense into his hard head.

He rolled over on the uncomfortable cot in time to see a very large cockroach scurry across his breakfast. The insect pushed the urge to barf over the edge. He barely made it to the metal toilet in time to throw up.

Of course there was nothing in his stomach but nasty-tasting, alcohol-induced bile.

More determined than ever to get out of this place, he bided his time with the pounding in head getting worse by the minute. He would've given five hundred dollars for one lousy aspirin.

Four hours later Ethan appeared at his cell door with a piece of paper in his hand. Cord waited impatiently as the door slid open and realized he was never so glad to see a friendly face than now.

"Come on, Cord. The judge is waiting."

"What does that mean?" he asked as he got in step beside Ethan as they walked down a long row of cell doors. "Listen, I'll agree to anything to get out of this place. Anything, Ethan. I'll go to AA. I'll go to grief counseling, just get me the hell out of here."

Ethan stared at him, did his best to determine if Cord was playing him again or whether this time, the man might be serious about getting his life straightened out. Deciding maybe spending the night here had been well worth it after all, Ethan nodded and told him, "Good, because I hear this judge is a real hard-ass when it comes to suicide attempts in a public place carrying a gun. If you're lucky, she might just kick your ass all the way back to Pelican Pointe."

Judge Helen Harrington was indeed a no-nonsense lady. But lucky for Cord Bennett, she was also willing to waive confinement pending the evaluation from a qualified psychiatrist.

Her lecture on the preciousness of life made sense even though he only caught about half of what she said. Either he was way too hung over, or too humiliated.

It might have been the still-pounding ache in his throbbing head that caused his lack of focus. But whatever the reason, he got the gist of her speech. He willingly agreed to see a board-certified psychiatrist, ten sessions to start which meant twice a week trips back and forth to Santa Cruz. At that particular moment though, he would have willingly agreed to anything just to get outside. So he nodded his head at the appropriate time.

Just when he thought she was done with her sermon though, Harrington hit him with attending mandatory AA meetings. She even assigned him a sponsor. Reading through his paperwork, wearing her glasses, the judge didn't even look up when she calmly asked, "You're from Pelican Pointe, right?"

She didn't wait for Cord's response but instead flipped a few more pages in his file, made a few more notations and then added, "Ethan Cody says here that Patrick Murphy heads up the Pelican Pointe chapter and that Pete Alden has agreed to be your sponsor. The AA chapter there meets at the community church Sunday afternoons at three o'clock."

The judge finally looked up, removed her reading glasses and stared straight into Cord's brown eyes. "That's tomorrow, Mr. Bennett. You miss that meeting and I'll issue a warrant for your arrest by six o'clock tomorrow evening. Are we clear here?"

"Yes, ma'am, clear as rain."

And with one resounding tap of her gavel, Cord Bennett walked out of the hearing a chastised, but free man.

"Do you think Nick will take me back?"

Behind the wheel of his police cruiser heading back to Pelican Pointe, Ethan pointed out, "He didn't fire you, Cord. He left the decision up to you. It seems you decided."

"Didn't have much of a choice, now did I? You hit rock bottom the only place to go is..." he gestured with his thumb in an upward motion. "I bet that old Flynn McCready had my truck towed by now."

"It's parked in front of my house."

"Thanks Ethan. And not just for that—for everything. Who is this guy that's supposed to be my sponsor, this Pete Alden?"

"Gosh, Pete's been around Pelican Pointe for probably fifty years or more. Used to be a shrimper before he sold out to Clance Hopkins, had three boats that went out every day, seven days a week, the *Ruby Tuesday* and the *Potted Shrimp*. He sold the *Moonlight Mile* off a decade or so back and Porter rehabbed it into a research vessel. Now Pete spends his time working at the rescue center."

"Okay, so this old dude is my sponsor. Got it. What rescue center?"

"Pete's a character. He and Porter Fanning used to be best friends. Porter started the Fanning Marine Rescue Center."

"Wait. Fanning? I take it the Keegan woman is related to this Porter guy."

"Granddaughter. She runs the place now." Ethan told him about Keegan's recent loss and how she had been out on the *Moonlight Mile* searching for an injured animal in need. "She knows that bay like the back of her hand. The

Moonlight Mile belongs to the center."

"So this Pete and the grandfather were tight. I guess it isn't a coincidence that the names of the shrimp boats and this renovated fishing trawler are all Rolling Stones' songs?"

Ethan laughed and rubbed his chin as if considering that. "No coincidence. I guess Porter and Pete were big time Stones' fans. They were certainly leftovers from the '60s. As I recall Pete captained the boats for forty years or more before the fishing drastically fell off around Smuggler's Bay."

"What can you tell me about the Keegan woman?"

Ethan cocked a brow. "Interested in the redhead, are you?"

"Who wouldn't be? Since she saved my life I need to find a way to thank her for it. She could've waited for the paramedics to get there. I heard them talking. She didn't. If she'd waited—I might not be sitting here now. You think I don't know that?"

Ethan took his eyes off the road long enough to give Cord a hard look. "I want to believe you had an epiphany in lockup last night but—"

"I don't know as I'd call it an epiphany maybe more like a realization that Cassie wouldn't exactly approve of what she sees in me these days. Besides, I have to accept the fact that Cassie's gone. I need to think about keeping my job and my place to live, do something with my life other than wish I had died that day."

"Glad to hear it." But the Chumash shaman in Ethan, always fighting an energy from within, picked up on an underlying vibe he wasn't sure was genuine. For now though, he determined it was nothing more than his law enforcement cynicism kicking in and decided to let it go. Over the next few days, he'd just have to wait and see, keep an eye on things and judge how serious Cord was.

"So?" Cord prodded.

"Keegan Fanning is about as rock solid as they come. She's a hard worker, and does her damnedest to keep

FMRC up and running every day. After Porter died, she had staffing issues. Interns transferred to other places, thought they could learn more elsewhere than from a girl. Plus, it takes an incredible amount of money to keep that place going. Porter was good at fundraising. She has huge shoes to fill in trying to replace not one grandparent, but two, who were fixtures at that place for decades. She lost both of them within a year of each other. She's juggling a lot of balls in the air right now and lately seems stressed out—to me anyway."

For the rest of the drive Cord pumped Ethan for both fact and fiction about the redheaded mermaid lookalike with deep blue eyes. He learned all he could about the woman who fascinated him with her boldness, with her sense of right and wrong, and with how she'd instinctively jumped in the water to save a stranger.

Ethan made him realize the woman's work habits rivaled his. And he didn't think that was possible.

She'd grown up without her natural parents, something he could relate to but at least she'd had grandparents. They'd taken her in and stepped up to the plate to raise her.

There had been no one to take that step for him, never had been—until Cassie. Cassie, he supposed, had filled that void. At one time he'd craved a family. He'd wanted grandparents, even a wayward uncle, maybe even a flighty aunt. But he'd long ago accepted the fact he'd been solo at an early age.

Family. That word had a tendency to rankle him.

The minute he got back to his truck, the first thing Cord did was head to the florist. He might not have had a woman in his life for a long time but he knew they liked getting flowers. Even though going inside a flower shop wasn't where he wanted to be at the moment, it was something he had to do. In his mind there was no better way to say "thanks for saving my sorry life" than sending her a bunch of roses.

But once he stepped inside Drea's Flowers a familiar

smell hit him and he knew this idea had been a big mistake. Unwillingly, he inhaled the scent of lilies. At least he thought it was the sickening, fragrance hitting his nostrils that had him ready to bolt back out into the street. On an empty stomach from not having eaten in almost twenty-four hours, he wanted to get his order placed and done with and get out of there.

When he spotted the perky brunette standing behind the counter arranging long-stemmed white roses in a dark blue vase, he swallowed hard and gutted it out.

He cleared his throat. "What can I do for you?"

"Do you know Keegan Fanning?"

Drea eyed the man with open curiosity. He had the most gorgeous deep brown eyes and his long blondish hair made him sexy as hell, even if his face looked as though he hadn't shaved in a couple of days. Scruffiness aside, she decided a customer was a customer. "Sure, I went to school with her from first grade on. Why?"

"I want to send her roses. If you know her well, maybe you could pick out something for me you're sure she'll like." He reached in his back pocket for his wallet and his credit card. "Those white ones you're working on will do fine, or something else just às nice, whatever she likes."

The brunette's eyebrows arched in unmistakable, curious fashion. She grabbed her order pad. "You want to send Keegan Fanning white roses? Keegan Fanning the woman who runs the rescue center, right?"

"One and the same. Why are you so surprised?"

"Well for one thing, as far as I know Keegan Fanning hasn't gotten flowers since senior prom. Those were violets, a wrist corsage as I recall, had to be almost ten years back. Keegan likes the color blue. This arrangement here is for Myrtle Pettibone. It's her birthday today, seventy years young. Her sister, Prissie Gates, wants to surprise her."

Cord didn't hear the last part. All he knew was that violets were not pink like lilies. Lilies were Pepto Bismol pink and not blue. His hands went clammy, sweat popped out on his forehead. "Okay. Something blue then. Violets are fine. Look, I'm in kind of a hurry, whatever you pick out I'm sure it will work." He needed to get out of there.

Drea tilted her head to study the man. "What's the occasion, first date?"

Cord shook his head. One thing even a newb like him could count on in a small town was that one way or another, everyone sooner or later wormed their way into knowing your business. There wasn't a doubt in his mind that by afternoon most of the nosy locals would be flapping their gums about the fact that he'd sent flowers to Keegan Fanning.

"I want to say thank you."

Drea was beginning to get a better picture of this man. With her hand, she air-waved back at his chest. "Wait, you're the guy she pulled out of the ocean last night."

"Exactly. Now—"

"I've got just the thing for her." With that, Drea disappeared into the back room.

Annoyed, Cord stood there like an idiot, looking around the small shop. He noted lots of sunny yellow blossoms, lots of red roses, lots of sweet-smelling carnations, but he didn't see a single blue petal of any kind. Violets were simple. Why couldn't he just pick out a bunch of them and be on his way.

But when she came back she held a cluster of brilliant, bluish, huge purple flowers in her fist. "These babies are blue parrot tulips. I got them in yesterday. My parents own The Plant Habitat." Eyeing his confusion, she added, "The nursery in town."

Cord nodded. "I'm familiar with The Plant Habitat. We mostly rely on growing our own seedlings in the greenhouse, but there are certain kinds of hard to grow vegetables we get from your mom and dad."

"I know. Asparagus is one of them. My dad's got this reputation as a guru when it comes to developing hardy vegetables. He has a side interest though in flowers, specifically tulips. For years now he's been on this kick experimenting, trying to grow his own kinds, trying to produce different colors other than the norm, you know, something other than red or yellow, something out of the ordinary. Anyway, these babies are the result." She sat them on the counter and stood back proudly waiting for his reaction.

As long as they weren't lilies, anything would work. But Cord noted they did make a striking bouquet of blue without being frilly. The petals almost matched Keegan's eyes. And they were long-stemmed like she was.

"I'll take 'em. Will you see that she gets them today?"

"Of course," Drea said amicably, reaching for his credit card. "She's four streets over. I'll have them there in thirty minutes or less." The man hadn't even asked about the price, making him, in her eyes, a one-of-a-kind customer. Before she swiped his credit card though, she asked, "You want them boxed or arranged in one of my clear stock vases."

Cord tightened his mouth, trying to decide. "Boxed, I think. That way she can display them in her own favorite container." He didn't have a clue if she had one or not, but it seemed to him he remembered women usually liked doing that sort of thing. They always had one special vase.

Pleased with his decision, Drea sent him a wide smile and said, "Trust me. She's going to love them. Here, don't forget to fill out the card. Make it zing, okay. Keegan deserves something special."

On that suggestion, he totally agreed. So he took the tiny card in his huge hand and scribbled down his message, making sure it came from the heart.

Keegan had started her day treating the sea lion pup she'd finally located on the beach last night barely alive, tangled in a mass of kelp. The little guy had suffered a six-inch bite wound that had pretty much left his rear flipper in shreds. From the teeth marks she could say with some certainty the bite probably came from a much larger predator like a shark.

Thanks to Bran Sullivan showing up at midnight to do emergency surgery on the baby and a healthy dose of antibiotics, this morning the pup looked a lot more alert.

"Well, don't you look all chipper," Keegan cooed at the sea lion she'd nicknamed Dodger because he'd obviously dodged becoming shark supper. She stroked his fur and added, "You look ten times better than when I first set eyes on you."

Keegan was in the process of doing a temperature and weight check when Abby bounced in between the row of large indoor cages. "How's our newest patient?"

"It's amazing what a little TLC does along with some decent food. Isn't that right, Dodger?"

"Dodger?" Abby snorted at the nickname. "I suppose that's fitting. How old do you think Dodger is?"

"Has to be around eight months since sea lions usually breed no later than July. But his weight's down and he looks much younger than that because he's very malnourished and dehydrated. And he still acts like he wants to nurse."

"I could bottle feed him," Abby volunteered. "And before you ask I already updated the website, posted all the new photos we took yesterday and did a load of towels."

"Okay." Keegan smiled. That's what she liked most about Abby. The girl was always willing to go the extra mile or attack some chore with what Keegan deemed her "Abby-Spirit."

"Thanks for the offer to bottle feed but I already got him to nibble on some crab meat." When she saw the disappointment on Abby's crestfallen face, she added, "Don't look so down, you still get to monitor his food intake and…" She puffed out a breath. What the hell. "I guess it wouldn't hurt to make up a bottle and see how it goes. In about three hours he gets transported outside anyway."

"Cool. I'll go make up the formula."

Keegan watched her go and shook her head. She wondered if she had ever been that bubbly and eager. Yeah, she had. At around ten she'd trailed after her grandparents like a baby duckling. It was also around that age she'd put ballet on the backburner for good and decided the rescue center held her future.

So while Cord bought her flowers, Keegan dished out herring and rockfish to her ward of hungry patients. The brown pelican was a little cranky but if he continued to show no signs of parasites he'd be out of quarantine in another week.

The pregnant otter she called Minnie, acted friskier than she'd seen her behave in a week. The young female had been found starving to death and X-rays showed she suffered from scoliosis, a fairly typical ailment due to poor diet.

But today Minnie seemed more playful, swimming around in the water like nature intended.

Around two-thirty Keegan's cell phone rang. Her display told her it was Bran Sullivan. "How's the patient I operated on last night?"

"Alert, better."

"Good. Do you have room for another otter? This morning Clance Hopkins' fishing boat netted one with a laceration to his head, looks like he met up with a boat propeller. I've sedated him, stitched him up and he's ready for transport."

Keegan chuckled. "Since you've done the hard part I'll be happy to take him off your hands. What's his prognosis?"

"Good. CT scan shows his head took a knock but he'll survive with the proper TLC and bed rest. He might have trouble with his vision though."

"How so?"

"The blade caught him right around the eye."

"Damn. Well, we just happen to have an extra bed. Want me to come get him now?"

"If you wouldn't mind, I've got a waiting room full of routine shots and abscesses."

"It's hell being the only vet in town."

"I miss your grandfather, Keegan. I'm an old man. Don't know how much longer I can keep this up."

"Believe it or not I'm trying to find you some help."

"You need to pick up the pace then. Because, girl, I've been ready to retire for two years now. Joy keeps at me about it, too. She wants to take that trip to Ireland I promised her five years ago. Ireland, Keegan. I haven't had a damned vacation in three years and I haven't been fishing since Christmas. I swear Joy would make the airline reservations tomorrow if I could find a vet to take over my practice that quick."

"Oh, no you don't, I've got dibs on any vet who replies first."

Bran guffawed. "Then you better ramp up the effort because I'm seriously thinking of calling it quits by the end of the year."

"Thanks for the warning. I'll call one of those services out of the Bay and see if we might get lucky—maybe find someone looking to relocate to—Mayberry...west coast style."

After a few more minutes of conversation, Keegan hung up and went to look for Abby. She found her in the nursery with Dodger, bottle feeding him again. "I've got to run over to Bran's and pick up another sea otter."

"Want me to go?"

"Nah, looks like you and Dodger have bonded."

"He's adorable, Keegan. Do you think we'll be able to release him back into the wild with his tail cut to ribbons?"

"Depends on how strong it heals. Bran did an excellent job with what he had to work with but let's face it, without the tail strong and without being a hundred percent...he'll have problems keeping up and foraging. Don't worry. We'll get Dodger into nice digs at a zoo or an aquarium. I should be back in half an hour or so. Will you get one of the rooms ready in here for a recovery? He's sedated, but apparently he has a head injury around the eye."

"Oh, poor baby. Don't worry. I'll get everything ready."

Housed in a two-story Craftsman-style house, the Pelican Pointe Animal Clinic had a lot in common with FMRC in that both had been built in the 1940s and both were renovated to serve as a clinic.

But there the similarity ended. Bran and Joy Sullivan had long used their residence as a workplace. Where Porter and Mary had tried to keep their profession separate from their home life, Bran and Joy seemed to fuse theirs together and make it work.

Located a block off Main on Crescent Street, the Sullivan house stood out from the others because of its bright blue-pastel paint job and the fact there were always cars in the driveway and therefore, a parking problem.

The minute Keegan pulled her truck into the crowded area and came to a stop, Joy Sullivan popped out the front door to greet her. The cherubic woman with her red hair turning a stylish gray put a hand to her breast and said, "Are we glad to see you! We were afraid that sea otter would wake up and we'd have to sedate him again."

"I got here as soon as I could. Is he that bad off?"

Joy made a face. "His head's all cut up and—I'll let Bran give you the lowdown on the medical details."

Keegan's heart sank. This sounded more serious than she'd been led to believe. "Well, let's see what we've got."

They walked into a crowded reception area and Joy led her back to the operating room where there on the table lay a very still sea otter, weighing no more than twenty-five pounds with a bandage around his little head.

Keegan also noticed his stomach was wrapped. "What happened there? Bran didn't mention that."

"Gashes around his middle that took forty stitches.

Those will likely give him some pain."

"Okay, then let's get this little guy home before he wakes up."

The three of them loaded the patient into a dog carrier and carted him out to the Ford where they eased him into the bed of the truck, still unconscious. "Thanks guys."

"Call us if he needs anything else."

"Will do." With that she slid behind the wheel and backed out to head for home.

She'd almost made it back to Main Street when she noticed the temperature gauge inching into the red zone. It seemed stuck in the two-forty range and wouldn't budge. And then all of a sudden, the engine light came on, and with it the sound of hissing and spewing.

Coughing and sputtering, she edged the old blue Ford over to the side of the road. White smoke poured from underneath the hood. If she wasn't mistaken, she'd just blown a head gasket.

"I don't believe this," Keegan muttered as she reached into her pocket and dug out her cell phone, punched in a number she knew by heart.

Wally Pierce, the best and only mechanic in town, had cautioned her not two weeks earlier about the poor condition of the radiator. Before that it had been leaking coolant on a fairly regular basis. But at the time she had persuaded him to try adding sealant to fix the problem. Since the miles on the poor old thing already crept close to the three-hundred thousand mark, Wally had been reluctant to use the sealant because it badly needed damn near new parts from back fender to front.

And now it seemed the Band-Aid approach had accentuated the problem because she was stranded—with a sick sea otter onboard.

"Hey Lilly, this is Keegan Fanning. I've got a situation." She repeated her dilemma to Lilly Seybold, Wally's full-time employee, his bookkeeper, and as of last Christmas, the woman he intended to make his wife. The single mom of two kids, Lilly also had a side business, painting. She'd paint anything—from signs to murals to canvas. At one time she'd held down three part-time jobs. To Keegan, the woman seemed perfect for Wally.

After finally taking a breath, she quickly added, "And Lilly I've got a sick animal that needs to be in a secure place when he wakes up in pain."

"Keegan, I'll have him there in fifteen minutes," Lilly promised.

"Thanks, Lilly."

She sat there on the side of the road frustrated that she was so close to the rescue facility she could walk. But she damn sure couldn't carry a sea otter down Main by herself. She could call Abby to help her tote the carrier. The girl would come for sure, but then Abby already had her hands full with a host of other things to deal with. Keegan most certainly couldn't leave the otter in the truck. Because of that she lightly beat her head on the steering wheel. Some days she wished her life was a lot less complicated.

Out at Promise Cove, Cord stepped onto the wide porch and tapped lightly on one of the double front doors just in case the baby was taking her afternoon nap. When Nick came to the door Cord stepped back and motioned for him to come outside.

"I'm sorry, Nick. I screwed up. It won't happen again. I agreed to the counseling, ten sessions. And I have my first AA meeting tomorrow afternoon. I know I have a problem with alcohol. Murphy hosts a chapter right here in town."

Nick furrowed his brow. "Murphy? I had no idea."

"Me either. Anyway, are we good? Do I still have a job, a place to live?"

"You gotta stay sober, Cord. And I won't have you around Jordan or Hutton knowing you're thinking of ending it all. In fact, if you're still thinking like that I talked to Ben Latham this morning. He agreed we'd both check you into rehab. There's a good psychiatric hospital south of here that has a—"

But Cord didn't let him finish. "No. I made a mistake. I admit it now. Ethan confiscated the .22, Nick. And I'm not on any pills. Although right about now if I had a bottle of Excedrin I might be tempted to down more than the prescribed dose."

He rubbed at his throbbing temple.

Nick slapped him on the back. "Will ibuprofen do? Come on inside. Jordan fixed baked chicken and mashed potatoes for supper last night. You get the leftovers."

"The one I missed," Cord muttered and looked down at his feet. "I won't let you down this time, Nick."

"I hope that's true, Cord. I really need to believe you want to change, that you want to get your act together."

And just like that, Cord Bennett decided he'd been given yet another chance at straightening out his life.

Chapter Six

By the time Wally's tow truck pulled up in front of the center and they got the sea otter unloaded and safely tucked into the exam room, it was after four o'clock.

Exhausted from not much sleep the night before, Keegan slid into a chair next to her new patient and looked up to see Wally peering down at her holding a can of Coke in his hand he'd gotten out of the fridge.

Keegan looked up at the lanky, good-looking guy she'd known most of her life. Even though he usually wore his hair down to his shoulders, today he had it secured in the back with a powder-blue bandana.

With Wally's surfer good looks, she had to wonder why they'd never been attracted to each other. They'd grown up two blocks from each other. He'd helped her learn how to ride her bike without the training wheels.

It might've been the four year difference in their ages. Or maybe the fact as an only child Keegan had always considered Wally more like an older brother, someone she could confide in over the years, someone who would listen and take the time to come up with a solution to her problems.

Whether it had been about teen angst or getting through difficult times together at school, they'd always been more like brother and sister.

There was no one in Pelican Pointe who knew her better. "So you're saying the crank-case filled with coolant and the head's warped. You'll have to rebuild the engine. I'll be honest here, Wally. I have no idea where I'll get the money for a new one."

"I know. We'll figure something out. Let me explore

under the hood some more, see exactly what I'm dealing with before I make any kinds of promises. You know, I've still got the old '70 VW bug you can borrow for wheels until I get your truck up and running."

"I appreciate the offer, Wally, but I don't think the bug will work for a rescue. I need something big enough to hold and secure an injured mammal. Besides, I wouldn't want to stink up your little car."

He laughed and rubbed his chin. "The thing is I don't think your patients would hurt it none. Lilly says it already has a 'nice lived in' smell going for it. Remember when we took it up the coast to surf in Monterey and brought back some kind of stinky sea urchin. I think it still lives there—in spirit."

Keegan snorted at the memory, another example of their time spent as buddies. "Oh, my God, I couldn't have been more than fifteen. You were always a better surfer than I was. You were dating, who was it?" She snapped her fingers. "Debbie Harkness. You and Debbie let me tag along with you."

"Like a pesky, kid sister. Yeah, I remember. We couldn't get that horrible smell out of our clothes for weeks."

"Gran threatened to scrub me in tomato juice when I got back, you too as I recall." She punched him in the arm playfully and joked, "I notice you didn't offer me your classic Chevelle."

"Now Keegan, you know, that car's my pride and joy. If you weren't carrying around a smelly seal or two—"

She laughed. "I get it. Thanks Wally, for the offer. If you're sure it'll be okay, I'll take the bug. When are you and Lilly making it official anyway?"

"She's making me wait until June. You'll get your invitation next month. I don't see why we can't just run off to—"

"Men," Keegan interjected, rolling her eyes. "Lilly deserves a nice ceremony not a quickie in front of a justice of the peace. She had to put up with that jackass husband of hers hitting her all those years. She needs the lousy marriage all the way behind her and a formal affair is just the ticket. I heard Jordan's already planning a bridal shower for May out at the Cove."

She caught the concern on his face. "Are you worried about her ex getting out of jail this summer?"

"Early release. Nah, he's already got some other woman dangling on the line, interested in marrying him. He's been corresponding with her through his sister. And he doesn't seem that interested in little Kyra and Joey either." Wally shook his head. "I don't understand the way some men treat their kids. Or why some women are so hard up they'll settle for someone beating them up on a regular basis?"

"It's one of life's mysteries."

"I'm just glad she got out of there."

"Yeah, me too. Okay, what's eating at you?"

"How long have we known each other, Keegan?"

"Ever since you beat up Larry Glover for me after he stole my lunch money."

Wally grinned. "Larry was a bully who liked picking on little girls."

"You busted his nose as I recall." She tilted her head and studied him. "Okay, spill."

"I'm worried about you."

He waved his arms in the air. "This place is overwhelming you. You need a fundraiser. Or I could make another donation—"

"No. You're getting married in three months to a woman with two children who adore you. You're taking on a huge responsibility. You'll need all the dough you can scrape together. You don't need to be donating your vast fortune to this place. Besides, I promised I wouldn't mention your last donation to Lilly. And I didn't. But I'm not going to let you keep doing that, Wally. It isn't right."

He shook his head. "Why is it you're so stubborn, anyway? A donation from a friend isn't going to compromise Keegan Fanning's determination to do things her way."

"Oh, shut up."

"If you won't let me donate then how about doing something special during the street fair, you know, like an open house. It's in three weeks, that's plenty of time to set things up."

"That's a great idea but I may have waited a little too late to plan a special event with everything going on—"

"There's still time. Get the local merchants to donate stuff. I'll be the first."

"If Lilly hadn't snapped you up—I'd marry you myself."

"Yeah. Right. We tried kissing once. Remember?"

She rolled her eyes. "How could I forget? Every girl remembers when a guy tells her a kiss makes him sick."

"I did not say that. I said it felt like I was kissing my sister."

"Yeah. I think my grandmother was sorely disappointed."

"I know my mom was."

"Couldn't be helped. And you have Lilly now."

He grinned. "Who knew? The minute I saw her, we just clicked."

"Must be nice."

"It'll happen, Keegan. Look I gotta get back. I'll bring the bug over tonight, park it out on the street. It'll bring back memories of our youth."

"Right."

"Think about the fundraiser during the street fair."

"I don't know why I didn't think about it myself. Thanks Wally."

"Maybe because you have a crapload of stuff going on right now."

"True. Okay, let's see how much it costs to fix the truck first. In the meantime, I wouldn't object if you wanted to extend your generosity to getting me the parts at cost."

"It's a deal."

"Good because it looks like I won't be going anywhere unless I go on foot," she grumbled as she took the Coke out of his hands and took a long drink.

"I'll let you know tomorrow what I find under the hood."

"Sure, break my heart on a Sunday. Say hi to Lilly for me."

After he'd gone, she checked the vitals on the sea otter she'd nicknamed Jack because he looked a little like Jack Sparrow, the pirate, especially with one eye and half his head covered in a bandana-wrap of gauze.

When he lifted his little head a few inches, she scratched his fur and cooed, "You'll be fine here, Jack. You'll get breakfast in bed for a couple of days and then we'll let you outside in your own pen. How's that sound?"

With that, she left the main building out the back and strolled along the walkway until she got to the porch—and did a double take when she got to the steps.

There on the mat was an oblong floral box, distinctive because it bore a sticker with the logo of Drea's Flowers adorning the baby-blue foiled cardboard.

Her heart did a leap. It had to be a mistake. No one ever sent her flowers.

She slid out the little envelope from underneath the gold ribbon and opened the card.

There scribbled in pen was the message: *Thanks for jumping in the ocean, thanks for getting wet and thanks for saving my sorry ass from drowning, Cord Bennett.*

In spite of her mood, her lips curved into a wide smile right before she muffled a giggle. She picked up the box and went inside. Gingerly, she set the long box on the table by the door and tossed her keys in the collect-all dish.

She untied the ribbon on the box just as Abby stuck her head inside.

"Knock, knock. Someone's got an admirer." Abby wiggled her eyebrows up and down. "Drea brought those over herself. We decided to put them on the doorstep so you wouldn't miss finding them. Surprise!"

"They're from Cord Bennett, the guy I pulled out of the ocean last night, the guy not right in the head."

"Really? Let's see what he sent."

Keegan removed the lid. The minute her eyes landed on the brilliant color against the delicate white tissue paper she let out a long sigh. "Oh, my God, tulips! They're gorgeous. Look at these! They're the most beautiful purple flowers anyone's ever sent me. Okay, they're the only purple flowers anyone's ever sent me."

"Gotta admit," Abby said, "He has great taste when it comes to sending buds."

Like any female, Keegan stuck her nose into the flared petals and inhaled the fragrant blooms before agreeing, "Classy gesture, Cord Bennett, very classy, even if you are crazy as a loon."

Chapter Seven

The organic farm Cord managed and that the Harrises owned, spread out over twenty-five acres of the most fertile farmland California had to offer. Set high on majestic cliffs overlooking the Pacific Ocean and shoreline, the farm Nick and Jordan Harris had inherited from Edmund Taggert the previous fall, had come a long way. With new ownership had come an influx of new ideas. With new ideas and the backbreaking work from one Cord Bennett, Taggert Organic Farms had not just survived Edmund's death, it had thrived.

For one, they had almost doubled their stock of Holstein and Jersey cross breeds from fifteen to twenty-four. More cows meant producing more milk, which in turn, had them serving more customers, and thus, increasing their profits. Greater profits meant they could pour more money back into the farm.

One way was to make the place a totally grass fed operation, rotating pasture land. They also had plans to build stabilized walkways so the cows would never have to walk in mud that might create contamination problems. At one time after he'd first gotten here, Cord had worked with Nick to plan a solar-powered watering system, along with a manure lagoon, and new curbing.

It was all pretty standard stuff for an organic operation.

Early on, Cord had expressed interest in increasing the size of their already vast vegetable garden. They already packaged and sold their abundant crops of kale, spinach, carrots, broccoli, sweet corn, and five different varieties of lettuce, to a variety of health food stores and grocery chains up and down the west coast.

But when it all meshed together it required a dedication needed to keep up with the latest techniques in making sure the stock stayed healthy, the fertilizer methods were current, the certifications stayed up to date, along with doing whatever was necessary to keep powdery mildew at bay.

Good thing Cord wasn't resistant to hard work. Hell, he'd been working in one capacity or another since he was fourteen.

With Silas and Sammy and their cousins not due back until Sunday night, Cord had plenty to keep him busy. After leaving Promise Cove that afternoon, he gratefully settled into his routine, a routine that had kept him hopping for the past four months—and had filled him with a certain amount of resentment.

He could admit that now.

After spending last night in lockup, today he intended to start fresh, maybe get back into what he now considered his element with a new perspective.

He worked the two dozen cows into position and hooked them up to the milking machines in stages, six shifts of four.

Instead of resenting the bovines the way he usually had over the past months, for the first time since starting the job, he had a fresh appreciation for the animals, the smells coming from the old barn, and maybe even the grueling work itself.

He had to admit the chip on his shoulder he'd been carrying on his back since he'd arrived here had prevented him from enjoying the place.

He intended to change that.

Nick had been after him for weeks now to take more of an interest in furthering his certifications, even going so far as to bug him about registering to attend an organic dairy conference in Saratoga Springs, New York, come next winter. He might decide to do all of that now.

He glanced at the schedule hanging on the wall, there specifically to remind him of upcoming events.

Taggert's roadside stand was due to open in three weeks, another aspect of running the place. It fell to him to get it set up and going and to make sure the town knew when it opened. He had yet to see it in action firsthand since he'd barely gotten here last fall when the place had closed for the season. Cord understood that come April to mid-November, rain or shine, the fruit and vegetable stand wasn't just a welcome staple to the town, but a fun one as well.

He'd even been surprised to learn the schools in the area made sure they put Taggert Farms on their list of places to bring the kids on field trips.

The brothers, Silas and Sammy, gave tours of the entire growing process from tending to harvesting the crops. While their cousins, Ben and Marty, who maintained the packing, shipping, and delivery chores, handled that aspect.

That left Cord responsible for every other facet of the business, which meant he had his hand in literally every aspect of growing organic. From exploring the healthiest ways to grow the hardiest varieties of produce to practicing the good cultural habits of the past, Cord had been forced to learn on the job.

And learn he had.

To make sure the farm ran smoothly he had to oversee the greenhouse, the refrigerated facilities, which included the packing and storing, all the while studying things like alternating deep-rooted plants versus shallow. Up to this point, crop rotation hadn't exactly interested him enough to keep him awake at night.

But now, it was something else he probably needed to take a keener interest in. Even though he'd promised Nick and Jordan he could and would see that Taggert Organic Farms kept pace with the competition, up to this point he hadn't exactly given the job a hundred percent. Nick and Jordan had to know that. And yet, they had trusted him with the farm. It shamed him how he'd taken advantage of the very people who had given him a chance when no one else would.

Sure, he'd busted his ass here, but his heart hadn't really been in it. He wanted to change that, too.

He wanted to prove to Nick and Jordan they hadn't made a mistake by taking him in and giving him a job and a second chance. Or maybe this was his third.

Who was he kidding? He wanted to prove to himself he could make changes for the better, a lot better.

He also wanted to invite Keegan Fanning out to the farm for dinner. Even the thought of that though had his heart racing. The asking, the chance at rejection made his mouth go dry because he hadn't contemplated dipping his toe in the dating pool again. Ever. Which, he had to confess, sounded fairly ridiculous now. Did he really intend to remain celibate forever? Because there was something about the redhead that made him itch in that way and made him want to get to know her better.

It was a first for him, a first in almost a year and a half. He'd put any feelings for the opposite sex on the backburner. Until now, all he wanted was to be punished for not having helped Cassie that day when she'd needed him the most.

Earlier, while he'd stuffed his face with Jordan's baked chicken, he'd hinted at a "what if" scenario for a supper menu. If he could sweet talk Jordan into providing a few side dishes he could always throw something on the grill for the main course. He wasn't even sure he could pull it off.

"Sure you can," a voice said from the other side of the milking station. "You're just out of practice."

Cord looked up to see Scott Phillips smiling back at him.

He rolled his eyes. The first time he'd seen Scott or rather his ghost, he'd been staying at the B & B. He'd been sacked out in one of the guest rooms less than twenty-four hours after having been dragged back to California from Houston by a Guard buddy. At the time, he'd been grateful that Jarrod Collins had shown up there to bail him out of jail. What he hadn't admitted to anyone at the time though was that he'd been surly from that point forward.

His friends had deserved better. What he'd given them instead was a big fat nothing for their trouble.

"You know, for a ghost you get around," Cord commented as he leaned over the railing and continued supervising the cows.

"It's true. I get bored easily."

"You're starting to piss me off, bugging me like you have been. You must really get a kick out of popping up like some jack-in-the-box, scaring the hell out of people."

"I gotta say I never get tired of seeing their eyes bug out when they recognize it's me. There's a certain thrill in that."

"You're pathetic or maybe perverse."

"Probably a little of both. Why begrudge me the only fun I get to have?" He waggled his eyebrows up and down. "So, you're interested in Keegan Fanning."

"Geez, a ghost that reads my mind. Do you ever consider how rude that is?"

"Not really since I'm here to offer assistance to the given-up-on-life and the defeated."

"Okay, smartass, what can you tell me about her?"

Ethan says she's rock solid, a hard worker."

Cord shook his head. "All things that are great to know but I was hoping for something a little more—personal."

Scott laughed. "I'm not a peeping Tom for chrissakes. I prefer to think of it as I'm here to enlighten and guide you."

"Whatever."

Scott let out a long sigh. "Right now, she's hurting."

That got Cord's attention and he stood up a little straighter. "Someone's hurting her?"

"No, well, no. But the engine in her truck blew up this afternoon. She's hurting financially, or rather the rescue center is. She's pouring herself into that place just like her grandparents did but, the thing is, they had each other to lean on in hard times. Keegan has no one. She's missing both of her grandparents. She's alone. Things are tough for her emotionally. But she's strong and she's smart."

"What do I have in common with a woman like that?"

Scott narrowed his eyes, frowned. "She loves animals. Look around you, Cord. Do you care for the animals out here on the farm? I don't just mean feed and water them; do you care what happens to them?"

"Of course I do. I bust my butt out here—"

"Why are you always so defensive, Cord? Don't you feel appreciated here?"

Cord puffed out a breath, scrubbed a hand over his face. "Not always. Okay, maybe I'm feeling out of my element here, not exactly comfortable with everyone knowing I tried to—" His voice trailed off. "Your favorite little town is already buzzing about me."

"True and true. But the point is you aren't the only one who ever lost someone close to them. You have more in common with Keegan than you know. Maybe you should look her up on the Internet. The rescue center has a website. Look her up. She's a unique and special person. But I'll tell you this, the last thing she needs is anyone hanging around her that doesn't have his head on straight."

"I start going to AA tomorrow."

"It's a step in the right direction. Can you do it, Cord?"

"I don't know, but I'm gonna try." About that time he heard a car pull into the common area outside the barn. Curious, he went outside to see Murphy step out of his vintage, 1954 Chevy truck.

The five foot tall, fifty-something man nodded his head and walked toward him. "Cord."

"Murphy. I know, I know. I'll show up at three o'clock tomorrow like I promised the judge. You didn't have to drive all the way out here to prompt me. I guess I'll meet my sponsor there, right?"

"Pete Alden's been sober more than twenty years now."

"How'd you both do it anyway?"

Murphy didn't need to ask what he meant. "Ethan

intervened, called me, and then got the judge to agree to let you out if you had a mature, successful sponsor mentor you. That's where I recommended Pete. I've been sober sixteen years now, but Pete's got me beat by five years."

"I had no idea."

"Not many do. Look, I stock all kinds of alcohol at the store, wine, beer, whiskey, the works, but I don't dare indulge in the stuff."

Cord raised his brows. "At all, not even a beer?"

"At all. I used to be in sales and first started drinking just to entertain clients. Later though, it became a crutch to get me through all the sales calls I had with difficult customers. Then I would drink with clients beginning as early as ten a.m. all the while telling myself I needed it to get through the meeting. Sales trips began to take on a party atmosphere. I cheated on my wife—with some regularity. What with the drinking and the cheating it cost me my marriage.

"One day I woke up in a hotel room and didn't remember what I'd done the night before. Nothing. I'd blacked out and it scared the crap out of me. But that still wasn't enough for me to quit drinking. It took getting arrested for public intoxication a couple of nights later for me to see the light, especially when my company had their fill and let me go. The night I lost my job, I went to my first AA meeting."

"So meeting with a bunch of strangers put you on the path to sobriety? I gotta tell you, Murphy, I'm more than a little skeptical. I don't mind telling people my story or saying a prayer every now and then, but I'm trying to picture how either one's going to help me get rid of the past."

"I understand. But once I took that step, I got away from my environment, started fresh here in Pelican Pointe. You can, too. I wasn't looking for a sermon or a lecture either, but my sponsor who was Pete at the time, got me through the cravings. Pete and I are here to do that for you."

"Cravings? I don't have to take a drink, Murphy. I drink to get rid of the memories of Cassie and that day when I couldn't save her."

"Ah, I see. When is your first therapy session?"

"Monday. I've been down that road before, too. I'm not looking for a miracle here, Murphy. I'd just like to get my life back on track. I'm not a bad person, although when I drink I tend to become a different person entirely, get lots of crazy thoughts and ideas running through my head to go with my inebriated persona."

"No one thinks you're crazy."

"Oh, I don't know, last night Keegan Fanning looked at me like I was nuts." He raked his fingers through his blondish hair. "Funny, but two days ago I didn't give a shit what anyone thought about me. Now—I think I want to— get on with my life."

Murphy let out a huge sigh. "Good to know. No more thinking suicide then. That's a start. What are your plans tonight?"

Cord scratched his chin. "I have no plans to take another jump in the ocean if that's what you're hinting at."

"Come over for supper. Carla's cooking a Mexican-style meal complete with frijoles and rice while leaving it to me to grill the steak fajitas. You're welcome to join us."

"I appreciate it, Murph, I really do, but I'll have to take a rain check. What with going to AA on Sunday and my psych appointment on Monday, I've got paperwork to catch up on and that includes getting payroll done by Monday."

Murphy's skeptical look had Cord quickly adding, "I'll be okay. If I start feeling weird, I'll give you a call. How's that?"

Finally Murphy laughed. "Okay, but Carla could always ask Keegan to join us." Cord chuckled. "Am I that obvious?"

"You sent her flowers."

"For saving me from drowning," Cord pointed out. "I think I owe her that much."

Now it was Murphy's turn to chuckle. "Sure you do. Get your head sorted out though before you go jumping into a relationship. I've been messed up, I know from experience."

"Good advice. I'll see what I can do about it."

Just that morning he'd woken in a cell, the night before he'd tried to end his own life. Even he knew he wasn't relationship material. No, far from it. He had a lot to do to get right in the head before he ever took a step toward a woman like Keegan Fanning.

With that, he watched as Murphy waved and got back in his truck, leaving him alone to consider his boring night ahead—solo.

For once, taking Scott's advice, Cord went into his office, booted up his laptop. When the browser popped up, he typed in the name Keegan Fanning and got more than a hundred results.

For a local woman from a little town, she had made an impact. After taking over the center from her grandfather, she had made a reputation for herself at only twenty-six. According to the site, she ran one of the best privately funded animal and marine rescue foundations on the west coast.

After reading all the accolades he wondered again why he should even bother getting to know a woman like that. What would a marine biologist want with a simple man like him? The woman had three degrees for chrissakes.

He rubbed his chin and decided to leave her alone. He'd sent her flowers to thank her for what she'd done last night. That had to be the beginning and the end of it. No matter what itch he felt needed scratching.

Fifteen miles from Taggert Farms, Keegan planned a quiet evening at home alone with her dog, Guinness.

Her list of chores that needed doing was as long as her

arm.

Personal laundry didn't do itself. And the house needed a good cleaning. She'd use her frustration to her advantage and cleaned like a fiend. Besides, it was essential she spend a certain amount of quality time with Tide and Clorox now if she intended to take turns with Abby sitting up with Jack and Dodger later.

After more extensive lab results came back, which showed Dodger still fighting an infection, she had upped his dose of antibiotics and held off moving him to an outdoor pen.

That meant they had three patients they needed to watch throughout the night. And even though the brown pelican had made great strides over the last week, he still wasn't a hundred percent.

As Keegan scrubbed the kitchen sink and counters, sadness came over her. She couldn't help it. She missed her grandparents. She wanted to talk to them, confide in them, share the success stories about the animals, as well as all the challenges.

No one quite understood just how much they'd filled so many voids she couldn't even begin to count over the years. And now they were gone.

When the washer stopped, she threw down the scouring pad and detoured into the laundry room.

Even though Porter and Mary had raised a strong, independent woman, she would've enjoyed spending a night like tonight bouncing ideas off both of them over vegetarian shish kabobs from the grill and a beer.

They had given her a rock-solid foundation from the age of five on, now she needed to use that base to her advantage. She didn't want to let them down because she felt a certain amount of pressure to keep the center thriving and successful in their memory.

Knowing how they both had loved the town, loved the community atmosphere, she felt like she needed to give something back. She wanted nothing more at the moment than to make sure there was still a rescue center around for years to come. To make that a reality, she'd been kicking around a few ideas for weeks now.

And Wally was right. She needed to take advantage of the upcoming street fair and have an open house, take advantage of all the tourists in town. Maybe if she could get new people to tour the compound, they'd see the work that went on there and open their wallets.

When the doorbell rang, she gently dropped the lid on the washer, hipped the door to the dryer closed and jogged down the hall to answer the door.

"Hey, girl, where's your truck?" Seventy-two-year-old Pete Alden asked as he stood on the porch holding a can of Coke he was never without. The man had been her grandfather's oldest and dearest friend. He was more like her godfather, a person who had helped teach her the ins and outs of boating, and on more than one occasion over the past fifteen months, had tried to teach her how to accept, first the loss of Porter, and then Mary.

Pete had been the one she'd leaned on at the cemetery—not once—but twice. "What, no hello?"

"Yeah, sure. What's Wally's VW doing parked here?" He pushed past her into the house.

"On loan. Mine blew a head gasket, engine's toast."

Pete shook his head. "Hate to hear that, but…Wally did warn you. Anyway, I had to let you know that if I help out here in the morning, I gotta take off by three."

"You know you don't punch a clock here, Pete," Keegan said as she followed him into the kitchen, where she watched as he calmly made himself at home by going straight to the fridge and pulling out a replacement can of Coke.

She leaned back on the counter to purposely stare at the guy dressed in a pair of light blue Hawaiian-flowered shorts and an equally bright yellow-flowered shirt. His weathered face, tanned from years of soaking in sun on the water, told her something was up. "Why three?"

"That kid you pulled out of the water last night needs himself a sponsor. I'm it. I gotta make sure I'm at the church tomorrow on time, no dragging in twenty minutes late."

"I guess he didn't stay in jail long."

"Nope. Sent you flowers. It's all over town. Them the buds?" He pointed to the purple blossoms she'd prominently displayed on the kitchen table. "Nice gesture. Considering."

"Considering what? You really think you'll make a difference to him. He seems pretty far gone to me."

"So was I—once. Truth be told more than once. Took several times as a matter of fact for me to finally straighten out my life. Judge says he's willing to try AA and go see a shrink. I'm taking a ride out to talk to him now."

"Really?"

"Want to come?"

"Might be awkward. Besides, I've got towels to fold. Not to mention, as of four o'clock this afternoon, we have three patients."

Pete shook his head. "Pathetic. When I was twenty-six years old I never once sat home on a Saturday night to fold towels. And I sure as hell took the time to have fun every now and again. When's the last time you had a date, Keegan?"

"I have fun all the time. And I dated—" She stopped as she tried to remember the last time she'd gone out. Eyeing the cynical look on his face, she tossed out, "I've put dating on hold. And don't look at me like that. I have other more pressing matters to deal with right now than to spend my time in pursuit of a good time with the opposite sex."

"You don't get away from this place long enough to meet the opposite sex let alone have a good time. There's no figuring young people these days," Pete groused before taking a generous slug of Coke and wiping his mouth with the back of his hand.

"I'll tell you what that boy needs without even meeting him for the first time. He needs a reason to wake up in the morning."

"Everybody needs that. Do you know why he's so

screwed up? Did anyone bother to clue you in? Hayden described the whole spree shooting thing to me last night—in detail. Sounds like the incident is something he's having trouble getting past—in a big way, especially since he was standing at the altar about to marry the woman who got killed."

"Yeah, I know what happened. The whole town knows. In fact, if you ask me drinking is the least of his worries. It messed with his head. They call it PTSD these days. Didn't have a fancy name for it back when I hit stateside from 'Nam. Now they study it. The Internet is full of sites that deal with it."

"It's pretty serious. He'll probably never be the same again."

"No, probably not. I'll go out, report back. Find out how bad the situation is."

"You could stay for dinner. I'm too tired to cook. But I could nuke something in the microwave. I've got frozen veggie pizzas, the good kind Murphy stocks."

Knowing Keegan was a strict vegetarian he knew there was no chance in hell of getting one with meat, but instead of giving her a hard time about it, he simply asked, "The one with the thick crust?"

"Yep. And four cheeses, too."

"Tempting, but unlike you, I've got me a date with Betty Brinker. And Betty promised me homemade apple pie for dessert." He wiggled his eyebrows up and down.

Keegan bumped his shoulder and snickered. Betty Brinker had to be a good twelve years younger than Pete. "Is that what your generation calls it?"

"At least my generation is getting some dessert action," Pete pointed out as he turned to leave.

"Okay, you've got a point," she conceded as she walked him to the door. "But my life is too complicated right now for a relationship."

Before pulling open the door he asked, "You never answered my question. When is the last time you had a real date? I'm not talking about the guy you went to school with that you accidentally bumped into in San Sebastian and spent an hour with him—catching up—drinking coffee." He made a face.

"So I'm having a dry spell."

"Keegan, there hasn't been a dry spell on record like yours since the 1930s. They called it the Dust Bowl."

Keegan playfully tapped him on the arm. "You mean since you were around back then to personally take notes?"

He took her chin in his hand and said, "My tough girl isn't so tough. Keep up that sarcasm and you might convince me that veneer is what's holding you up when it should be someone sharing your life. Just don't sink too far into depression you can't pull out. Porter and Mary wanted more for their girl than that. Got it?"

She leaned over, gave him a peck on the cheek. "Got it. Let me know how it goes with Cord. He's the first man to send me flowers in a decade."

"He gets points for that then. I promise I'll make up my time here on Monday morning for sure. Count on it."

"See ya, Pete. You take care with Betty. Safe sex, remember?"

"Yeah, yeah. Smartass," he muttered as he strutted to his pickup like a man with a woman in his life.

After Pete left, Keegan couldn't settle.

What she should be doing is working on a paper she'd hoped to get published about how environmental pollutants damaged marine mammals. She also needed to block off some serious computer time to write a proposal for the grant to go with the study.

Instead she finished the laundry, checked on Jack and Dodger, medicating both, and then came back to zap her frozen, tasteless, veggie pizza.

As she ate she realized she felt out of sorts. Maybe it was because it was Saturday night and Pete did have a date and she—like so many other Saturday nights in the past— did not. Pete was right. Her lack of a social life equaled a very long drought. She glanced at Guinness. "So what if

I'm spending another night sharing my evening with a bunch of injured and sick animals. They need me," she reasoned.

And God was she feeling sorry for herself or what?

She put her plate in the dishwasher and dug out a bag of popcorn from the pantry. While it popped she knew she needed to get out of this blue mood.

When the microwave dinged she emptied the piping hot bag into a bowl and went off to the living room to settle in front of the TV. She perused the DVDs, slid a disc into the player. The movie Sabrina, the 1954 classic not the remake, was the last movie she'd watched with her grandmother. She sighed and sat down on the couch, letting Guinness curl up at her feet.

During Pete Alden's visit the man had assured Cord he'd have backup if need be.

But after Cord's night spent in county lockup, he felt exhaustion overtaking him. He soon fell asleep in front of the TV at seven-thirty watching the San Jose Sharks take on the Anaheim Ducks. He snored softly until the smell of lilies hit him fast and hard.

The church was hot, stifling. His collar felt two sizes too small for his neck. His head ached, even his feet hurt. Nervous, he glanced at the back of the church for any sign of Cassie. What was taking her so damned long to get ready? he wondered.

He remembered looking into Paul's face, seeing him nod his head toward the back of the church at about the same time the organist decided to start the music.

When he looked down the aisle, there stood Cassie on the arm of her father. She'd taken two steps when a man followed her from the vestibule.

It all happened in slow motion. Shots fired.

Yelling.

Warning shouts that turned into screams of horrible mayhem. More gunfire.

Cord remembered running down the aisle until he felt a burn in his chest. The sickening smell of lilies hung in the air, making him wish for things he would never have.

He woke in a sweat, breathing hard. Afraid to open his eyes, afraid he'd find himself back in that chapel again, Cord lifted his head and finally looked around the room. It was only then he realized the hockey game was long over and they were well into postgame wrap up.

He sucked in a breath, ran an unsteady hand through his hair.

It would be okay, it would all be okay, if he could just stop breathing in the smell of lilies and the iron smell of blood, it would all be okay.

After spending two hours with Humphrey Bogart, Audrey Hepburn and William Holden, watching them light up the screen, Keegan still couldn't seem to relax.

Restless and edgy, as soon as the credits rolled, she popped up and said to the dog, "How about we take a walk?"

At the word "walk" Guinness bounded up, ready to roll. She hooked his leash to his collar and grabbed the mackinaw. They slipped out the front door, the dog with all the energy of a puppy.

Outside the air was crisp and thick with low-hanging, foggy wisps coming in off the water. Even from this distance she could hear McCready's beginning to rock with the live band known locally as Blue Skies. Ricky Oden, its lead singer and founder, was a locally grown boy with Native American roots who had achieved a modicum amount of success with his music.

The town loved and supported Ricky and the four other musicians who made up Blue Skies. The band always made a point to play McCready's on a Saturday night and never took the stage any earlier than ten o'clock. They played until closing or rather until the noise ordinance kicked in at midnight.

Keegan shook her head. A person could set their clock by Blue Skies. She and Guinness crossed the compound and slipped out the back gate, down a walled area that led to the beach. As soon as his paws hit the sand, Guinness started barking.

Keegan turned to see a lone figure of a man sitting on the rocks to her right about twenty yards from the pier.

Unlike the night before, this time he had his long hair tied back and secured with a leather binding in a stumpy ponytail.

"Please do not tell me you're planning another jump into the ocean," Keegan remarked. "I'm really in no mood to dive in and get soaking wet again."

Cord's head whipped up and she saw a flash of teeth. The man really did have a handsome face when he smiled

"Nah, I learned my lesson. No jumping in for me."

"What are you doing here then?" She tried to tell in the dark if his eyes looked glassy enough to be drunk. But what she saw were those same golden-brown eyes with just a hint of the devil in them.

He didn't seem to be intoxicated, but rather sad or maybe thoughtful and brooding.

Not a good sign, she thought. Cautious, she wondered if maybe he had another weapon.

"I came into town to see you. Didn't realize there was a big-ass gate keeping you from the general public until I got to it."

"You came to see me? Oh. Well. I haven't had time to write a card to thank you for the flowers yet. And the gate isn't to keep me from the general public but to keep the animals safe."

She watched as Guinness traipsed over and plopped his butt down near the guy's feet. Obviously the dog remembered him from the night before.

"I didn't make the trip into town to solicit a thank you for the flowers. I drove by your place earlier but it didn't seem right to stop by without calling first, especially on a Saturday night and all. I didn't know if you had company inside or what. And I didn't have your number so—" Although he had found a number for the center on her website, he didn't mention that now. Mainly, because he'd needed an excuse to get out of that house and come back to the scene of last night.

As if he needed something to do with his big hands, Cord reached for the dog's head and gave him a good rubbing behind both ears. "What's his name?"

"Guinness. You know, like the beer. My granddad had a fondness for it. He's the one who named him."

"Figures. I've been on a first name basis with Guinness many times in my life."

She chuckled in spite of herself. "Since you're here, thanks for the tulips. They're gorgeous. You didn't have to do that."

"Sure I did. You saved my life. What did you end up putting them in?" He smiled when he noticed the look of astonishment on her face. "You know what kind of container, vase, whatever."

"Uh, I have this old blue-and-white milk pitcher that used to belong to my great-grandmother. She brought it over from Ireland. I put them in that. Why?"

"Just wondering. Drea tried to sell me a clear vase and I wanted them in a box so you could use your own, whatever it happened to be."

"Really?" She'd never known a man to think that far ahead when sending a woman flowers before. They usually just went with the flow.

"I do appreciate your saving my life whether you want to believe me or not. I got a little crazy last night. Thanks for being where you were when you were and dragging me out, giving me CPR, the whole bit."

Flustered, Keegan leaned up against the rock beside him, furrowed her brow. "You're welcome." She took a couple of deep breaths and filled her lungs with cool, ocean air. "Why'd you do it anyway? Why'd you try to end it all?"

He puffed out a breath. "How much do you know about what happened in Virginia?"

"Pretty much what the town knows. Besides, the first thing out of your mouth last night was the name Cassie."

Cord supposed he had to get used to other people saying her name. "I lost someone I loved. The first person in my entire life who ever loved me back. I guess you could say I haven't handled it very well."

Keegan considered how to respond to that before telling him, "When you put it in those terms I suppose I understand. Although, I don't see how killing yourself is the answer because if she loved you I bet she'd want you to go on, do something with your life other than drink it away."

Remembering Cassie's image from his dream the night before, he said, "Yeah, you're probably right."

They needed a change of subject and fast, so she asked, "You really came all the way to town to thank me?"

He found that funny. "It's a fifteen-minute drive. I didn't spend two hours in my truck to get here. I knew you'd get the flowers but—I needed to thank you in person before going to bed tonight. It's just something I had to do. And when I encountered resistance in the way of the gate and after considering you might not be alone, I chickened out and went for a walk on the beach instead. And here you are, doing the same thing I'm doing on a Saturday night."

"Did you see Pete?" When she noted the surprise on his face, she added, "He mentioned he was your sponsor. He intended to see you before his date tonight."

Cord grinned. "Pete had a date? Good for him." He tucked his hand in his jeans pocket, pulled out his truck keys. "Oh, there's another reason I wanted to see you. A little birdie told me this afternoon the engine on your truck blew, the one you use for land rescues."

He held up his keys. "These are for you." Even in the dimly lit area, he saw her gape in surprise.

Thinking Pete must've mentioned her car troubles, she asked, "What? You rented me a vehicle?"

"No. You can borrow my truck until yours gets fixed."

"You're joking. Why would you do that?"

"Hey, saved my life here…grateful, very. I have all manner of transportation like delivery trucks at my disposal courtesy of the farm. Not only that, several months back, I bought Nick's Harley."

"Nick sold his Harley?"

"He's an old married guy now, a father, with another baby on the way. It was sitting around gathering dust so I bought it. I'm willing to let you borrow my truck until you get yours back. It's simple. Isn't that what small towns do, look out for each other? I'm just being neighborly."

"But…you're willing to let a stranger drive your truck. What if I'm a lousy driver?"

"I've got full coverage." He cocked his head, studied her in general before telling her, "You don't look like you'd be a whack job behind the wheel."

"I'm not. I'm a very good, conscientious driver. I drive all over Santa Cruz County and up and down the coast, never so much as had a speeding ticket."

"Women. See…no problem then."

Again, Cord extended the keys out to her. "It's a two-year-old, silver birch-metallic GMC Sierra parked on the street near the pier. You can't miss it."

But Keegan shook her head. "This is ridiculous; I'm not taking your truck."

"Then you have a replacement vehicle already?"

"No. Yes. I borrowed Wally's VW."

"A bug?" He roared with laughter. "You plan to make your rounds saving marine mammals in a bug? What do you intend to do, store them in the boot for transport? Does that seem workable to you?"

It did seem fairly ridiculous. "Hmm. Okay, I'll borrow your truck but just for a couple of days. Until Wally fixes mine. The guy's really a genius with a motor. I'm hoping he'll be able to repair it and I won't have to pay for a new engine. Are you certain you can use the trucks from Taggert Organic Farms after—?"

"My suicide attempt? Yeah. I'm square with Nick—for now. I use the green one with the logo on the side to make runs into town all the time. It's no big deal."

"It is. A very big deal. I'm grateful."

"Now was that so hard?"

"I guess not."

"Then let's go." He jumped down off the rock.

"Go where?"

"I need a ride back to the farm."

He saw her hesitate, saw a wariness come into her eyes, he didn't like. "Well, hell. For God's sakes I'm not going to get you into my truck and—harm myself—or you either for that matter. There's nothing to be afraid of."

She swallowed the lump in her throat. "I'm sorry." She ran a hand through her hair right before she giggled at the ridiculousness of it all. "I bet that's what every Ted Bundy serial killer tells his potential victim."

He finally grinned, stuck his hands in the air and let out a low, spooky laugh like one of those from a cheesy horror flick. "Mwahahahaha." Pretending to be Dracula with an imaginary cape, he took a couple of steps toward her and added in a low menacing voice, "Come into my web, my pretty. I'll show you all manner of things horrific. Mwahahahaha."

It cracked her up. "You are seriously whacked." When she realized her slip, once again, she fumbled with her regret. "I'm sorry. I didn't mean—"

"But I am whacky, always have been. I'm not sure I've ever been what you would call normal."

In spite of his offbeat sense of humor, he had a self-confidence that said, "I'm comfortable in my own skin no matter what, and I don't give a damn about what other people think of me."

So Keegan sighed and shrugged trying for indifference.

"Well, I can't keep dancing around the fact you did try to off yourself. But come on, Guinness, looks like we're going for a midnight ride with Mr. Nutcase."

Chapter Eight

"**I** draw the line at nutcase. I prefer whack-a-doodle to crazy."

She stared at him. "Hmm, I don't know, Cord. You have this devilish look in your eye that screams, 'I'll try anything once.'"

"Well yeah. Sure. But that means I'm adventurous, bold, daring even, not a nutcase."

One of Keegan's brows rose in challenge. "Jumping into the ocean determined not to swim but go down with the tide is—" She blew out a frustrated breath. "I'm sorry."

"How many times do you intend to apologize? I get you're uncomfortable about it. I'm not exactly proud of what I did last night either."

"It's just—you don't seem crazy now, just a little sad, maybe lost. I can relate to that. I'm still missing both my grandparents and it's been a short four months since my grandmother died."

He remembered what Scott had told him in the barn, reminding him he wasn't the only one who'd lost someone important. "Then I guess I just need to learn how to handle it better."

"I think the word is cope. You need to cope with the loss of Cassie."

"Is that what you're doing—what with losing your grandparents—coping?"

"Sure, I try to stay busy but memories of them are all over the center, the house, the town. I even think about them when I'm in the truck, driving down the road on the way to make a rescue, or listening to Stones' music.

Because let's face it, those are all places and things I remember about them the most."

"Exactly. That's why I left Leesburg. I couldn't handle seeing all the old haunts where we spent so much time together."

They stopped walking and eyed each other. Understanding seemed to bloom.

Once they reached his truck, Keegan tried to give him back his keys to let him drive but Cord shook his head. "Nope. I need to see what kind of a driver you are."

"I still don't feel right about this."

"Getting in the truck with me or my lending it to you? Which?"

"Lending me your truck is extremely generous."

He opened the driver's side door for her—and waited. As soon as she climbed behind the wheel he went around to the passenger side, watched the dog jump into the front seat as if he were right at home riding shotgun and scooted him over, settled in next to him.

Not only did it seem strange to be sitting on this side of his own truck but having the woman and her dog invade his domain felt like he'd crossed some line. Maybe she was right. Maybe this had been an incredibly bad idea.

But when he glanced over at the woman as she stuck the key into the ignition, he stifled a chuckle. Even in the dark he could see she had the most intense concentration on her face. She took the time to adjust the rearview mirror, the side mirror, fidgeted with the seat settings to get it as comfortable as possible and then shot him a lost look.

"Are you gonna drive this thing or have a relationship with it?"

She grinned. "Hey, driving someone else's vehicle is a huge responsibility. And yours is so new with all these fancy gadgets I'm not used to. I have to know where the windshield wipers are and the headlights and—"

"I see that. It's just a truck, Keegan—and fully insured at that."

Finally she turned the key and fired up the engine. When she pulled away from the curb she said, "Wow! Nice wheels. It drives like a dream, not like my old tub at all."

"I've seen that ancient white truck with the FMRC logo on the doors around town. Funny, but before today, I didn't even know what FMRC meant, never even asked. That truck's got to be at least twenty years old."

She snorted out a laugh. "It's almost as old as I am."

"And that would be…?"

"Twenty-six this past January. How about you?"

"Thirty-four last month."

"What did you mean back there when you said she—Cassie—was the only one who ever loved you? What about your parents?" Keegan asked once they hit the outskirts of town and headed into the countryside. "I mean I realize you loved Cassie but surely…"

"Must've been a toddler when I got dumped in San Diego because I don't remember anything about my parents. After that, a series of foster homes came and went in a blur, some good, some bad. Most were indifferent to me. They'd take me in but would always find some reason to give me up."

Poor little thing thought Keegan, as she steadied her eyes on the road. And then something else popped into her head. "That could've happened to me, you know. The foster care thing. My mother dropped me off here in Pelican Pointe and took off when I was five. Instead of dumping me into the system though, she came back here. My grandparents raised me. But she sure as hell could've abandoned me anywhere along the way from San Francisco to L.A. before we ended up here. She wasn't exactly what you'd call—maternal."

"Good thing you had your grandparents."

"Don't I know it?" But he'd had no one. Something about that tore at her heart.

"You got a boyfriend?"

"Uh, no. Why?"

"What's wrong with the guys in Pelican Pointe?"

She chortled with laughter. "Wow, you are a newb. Most of the men and women for that matter who grow up around here—leave, or get married to their high school sweetheart." She thought of Wally. "Or they meet the love of their life and settle down for good in marital bliss."

"Why didn't you settle down in marital bliss? Or up and leave?"

"My life's at the rescue center, being a part of that is always something I wanted. Even when I was in college I interned there, so I never really left." She'd never once considered living anywhere else.

"This is home. At least that's the way it started out. I love the animals, the work, curing them of infections, disease, seeing them get better so we can release them back into the wild or get them into a zoo. It's exciting."

"You have three degrees." When she looked perplexed, he added, "I Googled you."

"You did? Hmm." She wasn't sure what to make of that.

"I know you have an undergraduate degree in marine biology, a master's in zoology, and a PhD in marine ecology. With all that, you should be ten years older."

"You're really hung up on age, aren't you?"

He ignored the comment and added, "You must be a genius or something close."

"I wish. I worked my ass off for those degrees. I had a leg up on everyone else though. Think about it, I'd been around marine life and mammals most of my life. I had a built-in place to intern and work on my degrees, a built-in mentor in my grandfather."

"You graduated high school at sixteen."

When she continued to stare at him instead of the road, he said, "I did the math. You might want to look that way." He pointed toward the windshield and the highway beyond. "I've decided I want to live, remember?"

That cracked her up again. "Good to know. What about you? Did you go to college?"

"Hell, I didn't even stick around long enough to graduate high school. Bummed around for two years working construction then one day I got a burr up my ass, joined the army the day I turned eighteen."

"Is that when you got the tattoos?"

He glanced down at his arms covered by the sleeves of his jacket. "How'd you know—? Ah, you saw them last night. No, the tattoos came much later—after."

"I didn't mean to interrupt. Go on."

"I got my GED courtesy of the military though, served six years before coming back to San Diego. It wasn't until then I got into a community college, studied the basics for a couple more. I joined the California Guard for some extra cash, and then, lo and behold, Iraq happened."

"What was it like, Iraq?"

"Messy."

"Do you feel sad or weird now?"

"Only when you don't watch the road."

She snorted out a laugh. "I'm a very good driver."

"So you keep saying."

"What I meant was how come you felt so sad and weird last night when you—did that? And now you don't? It was a short twenty-four hours earlier."

"I feel sad when I drink so maybe I'll try to find a way not to."

"Do you think you can?"

"People keep asking me that. All I can do is give it my best shot."

"If you start feeling, you know, weird or sad, you could always give me a call. We could talk."

Despite the fact she was driving, their eyes met, albeit briefly. But Cord thought he saw a world of compassion in that fleeting moment. "My first AA meeting is tomorrow. Have dinner with me after, chances are I'll need to unload on someone after baring my soul to a bunch of strangers."

"Really? Why me?"

He laughed. "Might as well be you as anyone else, and besides, you're gorgeous." He leaned over the dog and ran his hands through a few strands of hair. "This is not out of a bottle, is it?"

Taken aback, she almost missed the turnoff and had to quickly brake. Used to driving her old Ford, the brakes on Cord's GMC didn't need anything more than a light tap to bring the truck to a stop. Keegan, however, left her foot a little too long on the pedal and sent the truck into a mini-skid, which threw Cord forward, even wearing his seatbelt.

She heard his intake of breath and puffed out, "Sorry, sensitive brakes."

"Geez, woman, you are a road hazard."

"I'm not used to flattery."

"Well, that's just sad. You have gorgeous hair, a beautiful classic face."

"Thanks," she muttered as she concentrated on completing the left turn and heading west, past the iron gates and down the driveway to the farm. She drove by apple and cherry trees laden down with fruit and past fields with rows and rows of growing vegetation.

The unmistakable smell of freshly turned earth filled the vehicle.

"You wouldn't happen to know anything about growing daisies would you?" Keegan asked. "My grandmother's flowers, they're dying. I don't seem to have her green thumb."

"Daisies are pretty easy to grow. Try adding some fertilizer with phosphorous."

"Really? Okay. You'll be opening the fruit stand before long."

"Yeah. But it's a good thing my life insurance is paid up since I almost ended up part of the pavement."

"Do you always embellish like that?" she teased back.

"Only when I risk life and limb."

She snickered. "You don't seem the suicidal type." When she realized she'd used the dreaded S word, she gasped. "I'm sorry, that sort of slipped out."

"No problem since the entire town is well aware of my little attempt at ending it all I'm sure it won't be the only time someone describes me using that word. I guess you're right, from now on I'll be known as the resident nutcase."

"See? There's that sense of humor. Where was that just a short twenty-four hours earlier when you were considering—?" She stopped, let out a huge sigh. "You seem so—different tonight. Split personality maybe?"

"For one thing, last night I wasn't having a conversation with anyone. In fact, I was in a lousy frame of mind, had been all week. I could feel it building up inside me. I usually can. I went from walking into McCready's just so I could let off a little steam, went from having one drink to feeling like I didn't want to be around anymore."

"Could it be that you find yourself in a new place, a new job, and even with all that, you're still alone? Overwhelmed by your new surroundings?"

His brow tightened. Maybe she'd hit on something he hadn't considered. "I go see a shrink on Monday. I don't know how they got me in so quick. But the judge was fairly adamant about me going. I guess I'll see how it goes. And yeah, I feel lonely sometimes, like I'm lost. That's why the best part of last night—"

"There was a best part to last night?"

"Yeah. As I recall, the best part of last night was when you had your mouth on mine just not exactly the way I would've liked."

That made her sputter out, "Geez, I was trying to get you to breathe."

"And if I'd known you existed before I took that dive into the water, I might've kept my butt on that rock, kept my thoughts to watching the setting sun instead of making it the last one I'd ever see."

She opened her mouth to speak but couldn't form a single thought. Making sure she kept her eyes on the dark, narrow lane, she pulled up in front of the farmhouse that used to belong to Edmund Taggert. The marine layer had parted enough that slices of moonlight cut through the clouds allowing hefty streaks to wash over the front yard and the old porch.

When Keegan cut the engine, they sat there in silence for a few minutes until she turned and said, "You really want to have dinner with me?"

He undid his seat belt, nudged Guinness aside where he could slide into the middle. He leaned in, took her chin. "I should probably mention I'd like to do more than have dinner. But I figure we gotta start someplace." With that, he covered her mouth.

His brush of lips, a taste of tongue made for a nice, easy thrill in the belly. The feeling had her dropping into the kiss, a gentle glide into pleasure, a pleasure long absent. It had been a very long time since she'd locked lips with anyone, least of all a hunky, suicidal ex-soldier.

Cord felt her surrender to the dance of his tongue, felt her body revving up. Knowing he could do that to her, elated him. But at the same time, it felt he might be moving too fast here. Was he really ready to move past Cassie?

He pulled back and admitted, "I'm a little out of practice."

"Mmm," Keegan purred, her eyes drifted up to his. "That was…fine," she finally managed.

"Just what every guy longs to hear…" He chuckled and grinned at her. "…fine?"

"I didn't mean…"

He couldn't stop staring at her eyes. The look of want he saw there ended whatever indecision churned in his gut.

"Let's try this again," he offered as he tilted his head and took her mouth again. This time there was nothing gentle about it.

The sizzle and fire went straight through her system. Cord took her under and she felt like she wanted to float, drift all the way into lust.

When they came up for air, Cord rested his forehead on hers. "Better?"

"Ah, yeah. I'd say it came back to you."

He couldn't help himself, looking at her with that

unmistakable air of desire settled in her eyes, it made him feel lightheaded, almost giddy.

Feeling awkward, Keegan cleared her throat. "How about instead of me coming out here for dinner tomorrow night you come to my place instead? You'll be in town anyway and I could give you a tour of the center. I should probably mention though I'm a vegetarian."

"You don't eat meat? At all?"

"No."

"Not even bacon?"

She chortled. "I'm pretty sure that's a pig. I don't eat red meat, chicken, or fish."

"What's left?"

"Pasta, cheese pizza, an assortment of casseroles. I'm not a vegan; I do eat free-range eggs and dairy. I just don't eat meat."

"How long have you had this condition?"

"Since coming to live with my grandparents. They were vegetarians. They worked around animals, Cord. They didn't believe in eating animals for food. Is it a problem?"

"I've never known a vegetarian before, that's all. Did you mean what you said earlier? If I feel weird, or sad, you wouldn't mind if I called you—to talk?"

"I meant it."

"Good. Then I guess I'll see you tomorrow night."

"Okay."

He chuckled.

"What?"

"I don't really want to get out of the truck and go inside that empty house."

"Then don't. We could talk now. Why don't you tell me about Cassie?"

"You want me to talk about Cassie? Now? We're practically on our first date here. I might be out of practice but I think that's a dating-code violation."

"Normally I'd agree. But earlier you seemed almost happy when you mentioned her. Maybe it will make you feel less lonely."

"Wow, you make me sound like the perfect catch. Not."

"Maybe now is a good time to admit I've been out of sorts myself lately. I don't think this is a perfect scenario for either one of us."

He remembered what Scott had told him in the barn. She too, had suffered loss. He glided a finger down her jaw. "You're missing the people who raised you. That has to hurt."

"I feel like a part of me is gone. That's how you feel, isn't it?"

He nodded.

"There's something else to consider. In a town the size of Pelican Pointe, what if we decide to go out and then it gets awkward when one of us decides to end it. What happens then?"

"Talking about ending something before it ever gets started is…not a good sign. Besides, I've been here four months and I never met you until Friday night."

"Point taken. But that is what you want, right? To date?"

"I was considering it. But you make it sound downright unappealing."

"We could start out slow then…start as friends, maybe."

"Ouch. Friends. Okay, maybe that's all I can handle right now anyway. I could use a friend."

"Then tell me about Cassie. How did the two of you meet?"

He blew out a breath. "I was between tours one and two at the time. The night we met I was helping out a buddy of mine by picking up extra cash working a security detail at a concert in Leesburg, Virginia. My buddy, Paul Angleton, his family owns a security company. Anyway, Paul assigned me to a Third Day concert. Cassie was there that night with a bunch of her girlfriends. She seemed more interested in me than the music. We started talking, exchanged phone numbers. I didn't find out until after it all happened that she had a crazy ex-boyfriend. But then we didn't bump up our relationship until I got back from my second tour. Maybe that's the reason she didn't level with me. But then on my third tour, my leg got fucked up..."

He gave her an apologetic look. "Sorry, I mean my leg was messed up."

"You were injured?"

He nodded. "The same day Captain Phillips died, the same day Nick almost didn't make it to the field hospital."

"What happened?"

"An IED blew up the Hummer we were riding in, out in the middle of nowhere. I wasn't hurt as bad though, not like Phillips and Harris. After all, I just had pieces of shrapnel in my leg. Stupid me, I thought for sure Cassie wouldn't want me now that I was wounded and having trouble getting around."

"But she did."

"Yeah, she did. Anyway, they sent me to this hospital and later determined since I'd already served three tours, I could either re-up and go back to Iraq for my fourth, or I could end my time in the Guard and opt out."

"How bad was your leg?"

"I didn't lose it. That's what I was worried the most about as they flew me out of there that day. I've got some nasty scars though."

"Okay, so instead of coming back to San Diego you went to Leesburg to be with Cassie."

"After my third tour, yeah. And after I went to plenty of PT, physical therapy, my leg began to get better. That's when I asked Cassie to marry me. About two weeks later we moved in together. I still didn't know anything about Robby Mack Stevens though."

"Is that who shot everyone?"

"Yeah. Rob Stevens. Robby. I had no idea the ex was capable of violence of that magnitude."

"If you didn't know he existed, how would anyone

know that?"

"Cassie knew. Turns out, he had been arrested a bunch of times for domestic violence in the past. The son of a bitch hit Cassie on more than six different occasions where the neighbors had to call the cops. Each time she apparently backed down and refused to press charges. That's something she never bothered to mention to me. If I'd known—"

"Ah, and that's why you've been beating yourself up all this time. It isn't just about grief. You're angry with yourself thinking you should have somehow read the guy's mind, knew he planned to pick up a gun, come to the church that day and kill all those people. How long have you been psychic?"

He narrowed his eyes. "I should've done more."

"Like what? How? Find him and go beat him up ahead of time? *Before* the shooting ever took place? Right. That makes no sense."

When he frowned at her, she added, "Cord, that's unrealistic. You can't beat up everyone you think might be planning something. And how would you know to beat him up if you had no idea he existed, let alone had an abusive past. Let's say you had done something, you're the one the cops would mostly likely have prosecuted."

He whooshed out a breath and raked a hand through his hair. "I hate to admit it, but there's logic in there somewhere."

Her lips curved up. "Glad to hear you haven't lost total reasoning powers."

"They'd been dating on and off for several years before I met her. Their relationship was rocky. Turns out he had a bad temper. Talk about Ted Bundy, he was kind of narcissistic; at least that's what Cassie's friends told me after the fact. It seems Robby felt the world revolved around him."

"That's always a bad sign."

"How she could put up with a guy like that—?" He stopped talking, put his hand up. "Enough about this, enough about Cassie, about me. Tell me one thing about you no one else knows."

"Hmm, I'm pretty much an open book."

"One thing. That shouldn't be so hard…for a woman with three degrees."

"Okay. I never wanted to find my mother. Ever. I figure she dumped me, what do I care where she is or what she's doing."

"Wow! Same here. I never tried to get in touch with mine. I thought the same thing; if she dumped me at such an early age, she must not have wanted me."

"Some women just aren't mother material."

"You ever want kids?"

"I suppose if I ever found the right guy. Kids are the next step, right? You?"

"Cassie and I talked about having three."

"I'm sorry, Cord. But you really should get past the guilt. The shrink sounds like it might be your best bet."

"Telling my woes to a stranger—"

"Might possibly prevent you from taking another dive off a short pier."

"The judge says I go, I go. Otherwise, she might lock me up."

"You don't want that to happen."

"Twelve hours in a cell was enough for me. Have you ever gone to one, been evaluated?"

"I took a psych course in college. Does that count? Look, go in there with the attitude you just want to talk. Ever told a story to a bartender? Think of it like that."

"Actually that isn't a bad strategy." He tucked a couple of strands of hair behind her ear and heard her intake of breath in anticipation.

"Now that you know more about me I'll understand if you want to remain just friends. But I have to say—I don't mind moving slow because I want something—more. I know I'm messed up—"

"You're hurting, Cord. You're also not over Cassie."

He ran his finger down the side of her jaw. "I know.

Then I guess it's time I head inside."

She touched his hand. "Taking it slow isn't necessarily a bad thing."

And with those words, he took her mouth again.

It was almost three-thirty when Keegan drove Cord's truck through the gates of the compound. They'd necked in the truck like a couple of hormone-raging teenagers. Her lips were still puffy from his kisses.

She felt almost euphoric.

She needed her head examined.

Because even though Cord Bennett was a sexy, good-looking hunk, his list of problems was as long as her leg.

But wow, did the man ever know how to work that mouth.

Chapter Nine

Sunday found Cord in the barn, as the melodious vocals of Russell Hitchcock singing *Making Love Out of Nothing at All* pumped through the speakers, Cord busied himself with the morning milking.

According to Will Foley, the previous manager, the cows had a fondness for '80s music, especially the bands Air Supply and Journey.

In gratitude, the bovines usually managed to produce double the milk as long as they could listen to their favorite pop bands.

Patting the rump of the one he called Eloise, he gave her head a long rub and said, "Yeah, I know you love his voice, don't you, girl? Well, we aim to please around here, anything to keep you happy, sweetheart."

With the milking done, he moved into the executive offices, a separate building located between the modern barn and the packing facility. The four rooms here had been remodeled to include a break area with the obligatory space for fax and copier machines and up-to-date, high speed Internet connection.

In the administrative offices, the music changed to the Foo Fighters and their blood-pumping song, *The Pretender*. All the while he worked on the books and cut checks for payroll, Cord kept up a steady toe-tapping beat to the song.

There were a dozen other chores he needed to get done before he headed into town though. He'd arranged to have the Miller boy tend to the cows that evening so he wouldn't be forced to come back to the farm before going over to Keegan's for dinner.

Plus the crew, Silas and Sammy and Ben and Marty, were all due back sometime after seven tonight.

And because of that, he knew Taggert Farms would survive in his absence for a few brief hours.

But for now, going on two hours of sleep didn't seem to be a problem.

Because he'd spent four of the best hours in a very long time in the company of a beautiful woman, he whistled while he went about his tasks.

While in the refrigerated warehouse, he checked and cleaned the packaging machines, inventoried the containers, and then headed back to the office and his laptop to place an order for more.

All the while he worked he couldn't get his mind off the redhead. His brain skittered on overload with images of her face, her body, even her witty comebacks. She might be light years out of his league, but…

"She is an amazing individual."

Cord turned his head to look at Scott. "Jesus. Do you have to sneak up on people like that? Couldn't you shout out a warning first, announce yourself in some way? Maybe something like, ghost on deck about to materialize out of thin air, or something."

"Do you realize you're whistling today? You haven't done that since you got here."

"What, now you're keeping track of—? Oh hell, never mind. What's the point in asking you anything? I never get any answers."

"I have no idea. You're the one ranting. I used to come over here as a kid."

"Let me guess, you pestered the hell out of old man Taggert even then. Figures. You're a pain in the ass, you know that, Captain? Go haunt Nick and Jordan. Isn't there someone over at Promise Cove you could scare the hell out of, maybe a not-so-very-nice guest that needs an early Halloween jolt?"

"Nah, you're more of a challenge. Besides, I like pissing you off."

"So I've noticed."

"Why are you so bitchy? Man up. It's an AA meeting not a firing squad."

"I'm nervous. I've never been good at speaking in front of a crowd."

Scott guffawed with laughter. "So that's it? Wait till you see *this* crowd. Relax, Cord. They aren't going to judge you. Remember, they've been where you are now. Most had to hit rock bottom before they sought help."

"Do you ever get tired of being right all the time?

"Not really. I rather enjoy it. And by the way, wear something casual for your dinner date. Keegan's pretty laid back. And like here at the farm, you'll be around a lot of animals."

"Gee, thanks for the fashion advice. Any other tips?"

"I'd suggest you get a haircut, but since it's Sunday and the Snip 'N Curl is closed that's not gonna happen."

In reply, Cord raised his middle finger.

"Now, now, there's no need to get nasty, no need at all. Your hair is too long."

"Says you. I wore my hair military-style since I was eighteen. I'm tired of the look, if I want to wear it down to my ass, what's it to you?"

Scott howled with laughter again. "I'm sensing angst about your trip into town. What's really bothering you, Cord? You can't be this upset over going to one little meeting."

"I like Keegan. I'm attracted to her."

"So? What's the problem? Give yourself some time, don't try to—"

"She's nothing like Cassie."

"And that's a bad thing?"

"Cassie had a high school education, a couple of years of beauty school, blue collar, like me. She worked in a beauty shop, cut and styled hair for a living."

"Ah. Cassie didn't have three degrees."

"Exactly. I mean Cassie was smart in her own way. She knew how to do just about anything with fashion and clothes and hair and nails, but Keegan's—different. She's smarter than anyone I've ever known."

Scott shook his head. "Cord, you really are messed up, you know that? Are you that shallow? Do you think Keegan's that shallow?"

"It's a fact. Doesn't matter what I think."

"Give it a chance, Cord. Give her a chance. If you do, you'll find her number of degrees don't have anything to do with attraction. Besides, you'd be surprised what the two of you have in common."

"Like what?"

"Geez, Cord, you are out of practice. Finding that out on your own is half the fun."

From the moment the alarm clock went off at seven, Keegan didn't have time to replay her make-out session with Cord Bennett. The minute she rolled out of bed, she got pulled into a problem with Jack, the sea otter, still recovering in ICU. The early morning call from Bran had her going over Jack's blood screening results. Bran had tested the otter for a variety of pollutants, bacteria, metals and parasites because sea otters had a tendency to suffer from the elements. Toxoplasma gondii, a dangerous protozoan known to cause convulsions, was only one of the many threats that could result in death.

But there was good news. Jack suffered from nothing more than a mild infection. With a generous dose of antibiotics, a steady diet, and some TLC, he should be as good as new. His eye was a different matter entirely. Only time would tell how well he would be able to see.

Keegan donned latex gloves before filling a syringe with medicine and changed Jack's bandage. She then moved on down the line to Dodger.

Pointing a finger at the sea lion, she said, "You, little guy, are doing remarkably well under the circumstances.

You get rewarded by getting moved outside today where you can splash around in the water for awhile. How's that sound?"

As Dodger lazed on the concrete floor, with what was turning out to be his favorite blanket, a purple towel, she mixed up a bottle with formula, added a good measure of ground fish to it, and watched as he nursed like he was getting his appetite back.

Rubbing his head, she gushed, "Aw, you're just hungry aren't you, baby? Hmm, and love to be bottle fed. Well, it's a good thing we can lavish you with plenty of attention."

At two-forty-five Cord roared up in the parking lot at the Community Church riding the Harley. Fifteen minutes early, his stomach flip-flopped with nerves. Because he wasn't sure what to expect from an AA meeting, his hands were clammy. Sweat seemed to pop out on his brow like bullets flying around him.

When he spotted Murphy ambling across the pavement coming from the store across the street, he stuck his hand up in a wave.

"How do you like the motorcycle? Is Nick missing it much?"

Grateful for something else to talk about other than what was about to happen, Cord unsnapped his helmet. "Nah, Nick's got his hands too full at the B & B to miss riding. Today, he's busy slapping blue paint on the walls of his son's nursery."

Murphy shook his head. "Guess it's nice when you already know it's a boy. I remember when that guy first rode into town riding this thing. He was almost as messed up as you are."

"Gee thanks. But I guess I understand the sentiment." Cord changed the subject. "Nick and Jordan are both walking around out there like they were the only two people ever expecting a baby. For awhile there, I swear Nick was having the same symptoms as Jordan."

The chatter made Murphy realize something. "Nervous?"

Cord nodded.

"Don't be. Remember everyone in this group has been in a dark place a time or two, me included." He slapped Cord on the back. "Let's get it started. It won't be nearly as bad as you think."

With that, Cord followed Murphy into the church, palms still sweaty, stomach still uneasy.

They walked down a small, narrow corridor of Sunday school classrooms. Inside one sat three other men and a woman.

Cord recognized Margie Rosterman and Max Bingham from the Hilltop Diner and the veterinarian, Bran Sullivan. Pete Alden, who had already come to the farm the night before to introduce himself, stood up to shake his hand. "Come on in, take a seat. I think you know everyone here. Whaddya say we get started?" "Shouldn't we wait for everyone else?"

Pete chuckled. "This is it. You make an even six."

"I thought…"

"It's just us. Why don't I get things started? You all know me. Pete Alden. Drinking problem. Been sober twenty-two years now. But there isn't a day goes by that I don't walk past McCready's and wish I could go inside for a drink. Trouble is I couldn't stop at one. If Flynn would let me, I'd drink enough for three people."

Cord listened as each person took turns telling their stories. Scott had been right.

According to their own words, each of them had hit rock bottom at one time or another. They all had painful pasts.

Max had a daughter he'd neglected because of alcohol and was just now getting to know her again after an extended absence in her life. Margie, at one time, fought a major addiction to drugs. Pete admitted to losing his fishing business, not because of a lousy economy, but rather his love for booze. Bran had turned to painkillers during the '90s after he'd hurt his back. Murphy took his turn, explained how his drinking had led to the end of his marriage.

By the time it was Cord's turn, he felt a lot better about his situation.

"Um." Cord scratched his chin. "I guess I won't go into my history because most of you already know it. I have to say this fast. I've recently discovered I'm a different person when I drink. It seems I've been using whiskey for the past year and a half as a crutch. Friday night I got drunk at McCready's. I started feeling sorry for myself. Big time. I was missing Cassie. Real bad. I was in pain. All I wanted to do at the time was make it go away. I decided to end it the only way I knew how—with a gun. It wasn't the first time. I tried back in January, too. The gun jammed. That's why Friday night I got this idea that if I just walked out into the water, let it take me under, I'd be gone. End of pain. End of me. But..."

Cord took the time to swallow hard, nervously ran a hand through his hair and shifted his feet.

"I have a problem. I know that now. I don't want to die. In fact, it's remarkable what can change in two short days. I met someone I like...a lot. She's incredible." He looked at the five pairs of eyes staring back at him. "I guess that's it."

Pete Alden stood up, shook Cord's hand. "Son, that's a mighty fine first step. As your sponsor, you call me anytime you're having a problem, anytime you need to talk."

With his hand still grasping Cord's, Pete leaned in and whispered, "But you hurt Keegan Fanning in any way— 'cause I know that's the someone you're talking about— I'll personally string you up by your balls right on Main Street for the whole town to see. You understand?"

Cord looked down at the older man he had by a good

six inches in height and said, "Uh, yes, yes I do."

"Good." He slapped Cord on the back and added, "Now, you go have yourself a nice dinner tonight with my girl, minus the booze, of course."

Fifteen minutes later Cord stood outside the gate at FMRC. He'd already pushed a buzzer and waited for someone to let him in. Instead of Keegan though, a perky blonde strolled up, hit a button and the gate started sliding on its track.

"Hi, you must be Cord. I'm Abby. Keegan's waiting for you over at the house on the other side of the compound. I'll walk you over."

"This is some place. It's larger than it looks from the street."

"It is. But that's because it spreads out in the back and takes up half a block in acreage. We're very proud of the work we do here but we're quickly outgrowing this space. Keegan won't talk about moving because—mainly because her grandparents made this place—what you see here today. She's sentimental and who could blame her."

Looking around, Cord caught the unmistakable bark of a sea lion. "Is he happy or angry?"

Abby laughed. "Neither. That's Elmer. He just likes to announce his presence with authority."

It was Cord's turn to laugh. "This place is amazing."

"A lot of these animals would die without getting rescued. You like animals?"

"I do. But I've never been around anything so massive."

"But you work on a farm," Abby pointed out.

"It's completely different than this."

Abby wasn't so sure about that. In her book, animals en masse of any kind needed TLC whether they were cows or sea lions. "Keegan wants to give you the grand tour later, so you'll get to see the big picture. It's a remarkable place. I'm so lucky to be a part of it all."

Cord followed her across the compound listening as the perky Abby chatted on and on, listing the animals they had in residence.

She finally stopped in front of a house with a long porch, an old-fashioned swing creaking in the breeze. "Here we go. I'll probably see you later when Keegan shows you around. I'm working the weekend shift. Meanwhile, enjoy your date. By the way, the blue tulips, awesome touch." She gave him a thumbs-up sign as she back-pedaled.

"Is everything part of the public domain in this town?"

"Pretty much. You'll get used to it," Abby muttered over her shoulder. Just as Cord got to the porch steps, the door flew open.

Guinness shot past Keegan so he'd be the first one to get Cord's attention. A smaller man might have been bowled over, but not Cord. He bent down, let his big hands scrub the dog's head and ears. And when he looked up at Keegan standing in the doorway all the tension and stress he'd bottled up fell away.

She was dressed casually in a pair of jeans and a cropped green top, her hair still slightly damp and braided down her back. She looked like the bright spot in his otherwise harried day.

"Hi, I thought I heard voices out here."

"We took the shortcut, I think." He walked up the steps, planted a chaste kiss on her lips, tilted his head downward and stared at her eyes. "Hi."

"Hi. Come on in."

He followed her into a tidy, but lived-in rectangular room with cheery, pastel-blue paint on the walls. The blue blended well with the brown leather sofa and comfy recliner. There were soft feminine touches around the room, pillows frilled with lace and scalloped edges. One entire wall showcased a variety of shells from starfish to sand dollars behind glass and wood. The shells shared the space along the line with a generous selection of books.

"Make yourself at home. Are you hungry? I fixed lasagna." She tilted her head and added, "Trust me you'll never miss the meat."

"I love lasagna. Don't know as I've ever had it without chunks of meat though. And since I'm starving, it sounds great. Need some help?"

"Sure. You could keep me company while I finish the salad."

He followed her into a narrow, sunny kitchen with a breakfast area that faced out onto a well-tended backyard full of yellow and white daisies and herb beds. "You weren't kidding about your grandmother's love for flowers. They're everywhere."

"She always said daisies were just too cheerful to be around and be sad. How'd it go?" She asked as she went to the fridge and got out the makings for a spinach and strawberry salad.

"I listened to everyone's story before spilling my guts to five other alcoholics. Three of whom I would never have guessed had an issue with booze or any type of dark past. And that's all I can say. What goes on at the church stays at the church."

She couldn't help it, she giggled. "You have a way of putting things, Cord. Glad it's over?"

"Yeah. Afterward, Pete told me that if I hurt you, he would…" His brow furrowed and he considered how best to phrase the threat as delicately as he could. He decided paraphrase would have to do. "Let's just say, he would make me suffer."

"That's sounds like Pete. He's like a godfather or maybe an honorary grandfather." She eyed him, suddenly frowned. "Did he scare you off?"

"Honestly? No. Right now, I don't think a Mack truck full of enemy soldiers could do that."

She reached up and touched the side of his face. "Why Cord, that might possibly be the sweetest thing anyone's ever said to me."

She got plates down from the cabinet to set the table.

When she turned around, he took them out of her hands, set them down on the counter. With one arm he drew her into him while his mouth zeroed in on hers. He drew out the kiss, as much for himself as her. Once he got a moan out of her he whispered, "I've wanted to do that since I got up this morning. And if that's the sweetest thing any guy's ever said to you, you've lived a very sheltered life."

"Dating-wise, that's probably true. I realized last night I've been socially-challenged lately."

"A beautiful woman like you, that's—kind of hard to believe." He nibbled down her jaw to her ear. "You're my reward for such a stressful day. Turns out—"

She grinned. "It wasn't as bad as you thought."

"I just kept thinking about you."

"You did?"

"Yep, the entire time I realized standing in front of those five people how stupid I've been acting since I got to Pelican Pointe. I didn't like what I saw. The whole thing was a lesson in humility."

"Will you go back?"

"Sure. I'll go because it's part of my agreement with the court. And, there's a small fear inside, I might slide. I don't want to slide, Keegan."

"Then you won't."

"It feels good to hold you like this," he admitted as he skimmed kisses along her ear.

"It feels good to have your arms around me."

"We did agree to go slow, didn't we?"

"We did."

"I was afraid of that." He grinned before placing a chaste kiss on her lips. "Okay, then you'd better point me to the silverware and I'll set the table because I only have so much control here, Keegan."

"Would you like a Coke? Water? I went to Murphy's to pick up some of that non-alcoholic beer for you, but Murphy told me it probably wasn't a good idea. Apparently it has like a point-zero-five percent of alcohol still in it, and it might trigger something."

He reached over and tilted up her chin. "Thanks. A Coke will be fine. Until I get a better handle on this whole thing, I'll steer clear of any kind of alcohol, and that includes beer. I mostly drank the hard stuff anyway, so beer isn't something I've craved…yet. But you go ahead and have a glass of wine, whatever you drink."

"In front of you, while you're just beginning to deal with this, that would be rude. No. Coke is fine with me, too. You don't drink beer? You might be the first man I've ever met who didn't love his pint."

"Well, I mean, I've indulged in my fair share of six-packs but it was never my drink of choice. Now give me a whiskey—I'm set."

"You learn something new every day. By the way," she pointed to the cheery tulips on the kitchen table. "Those were a very thoughtful gesture and a perfect touch to my day yesterday after coming home from having my truck engine blow up. Finding these on the steps…let's just say, they got my attention. What made you think to send them?"

He put his hands out, made a juggling motion. "Women flowers, they just go together."

She picked up the purple flowers and brought them outside to use as the centerpiece on the picnic table, which she'd already set with bright yellow Fiestaware and navy-blue napkins. The table looked like something her grandmother would've recognized as her "Martha Stewart" side. Most of the time Keegan would make do with a paper plate but with Cord coming to dinner, she wanted to do something special.

Over vegetable lasagna and salad, they delved into each other's past. She discovered Cord at one time had his heart set on becoming a major-league ballplayer. Not unlike many of her male friends had when they were younger, Cord had played little league. But he had moved up the ranks where he'd pitched on his high school baseball team, something that had provided him his only interest in school.

"Let's face it, I wasn't college material. Playing sports is all I had, all I loved to do at the time."

"Where were you living then?"

"By high school I lived in a group home with several other kids, mostly other teens who were just as ready to get on with life as I was."

"No structure?"

"I had structure there but not much else."

Ah, no love or no one to care about the little boy, thought Keegan. "What happened to the baseball career?"

He snorted. "It wasn't much of a career. I made varsity as a sophomore, almost unheard of at the huge public school where I went. Coach used me too much though that first year in the starting rotation. I suffered a bad rotator cuff injury that refused to heal. My arm was done...for pitching anyway. I was pretty good too, could throw a ninety-five-mph fast ball with a decent slider and curve ball at sixteen. But then, it was high school so who knows? I was pretty immature at the time. Like some of my other early decisions in life, when the coach sidelined me, it pissed me off. If I didn't have baseball—what was the point in hanging around school anymore? So, I took off."

He shook his head, picked up his Coke. "I left the home, quit school, found a job in construction, doing mostly grunt work."

"At sixteen you were on your own? Oh, Cord." She rested her hand on his. "You were so young."

"Hey, I grew up fast, especially after I joined the army. The military made a man out of me."

"But you didn't want to make it a career?"

"Hell no. See, it's good you had your grandparents and knew what you wanted to do with your life at an early age. By the way, Abby mentioned I get a grand tour. How about it?"

"Now's good. I'll do the dishes later." She grabbed his hand and added, "I need to check on Jack anyway." When Guinness got to his feet, she added, "Time to go on rounds."

All the way to the main building she went on about Minnie and Dodger and every other animal in residence. It didn't take long before Cord realized, once again, Scott had been correct. Her love of wildlife surfaced in every facet of the place. He had only to look around to see that, only had to listen to the way she talked about each one.

Once inside the hospital, she led him down a hallway to an exam room. She introduced her "patients," first Dodger and explained how he'd been injured. When she noticed the fascinated look cross Cord's face, she couldn't help it, she beamed.

"A shark did that?"

"I'm pretty sure. See the bite marks."

"He's lucky he escaped. Ah, I get it. Dodger dodged a bullet, or in this case a big-ass shark."

"Exactly."

They moved on to check on Jack in his pen, which Guinness had to sniff. The otter had somehow found his second wind and played with a rubber ball while he lay on a bed of towels. Any other dog might have been tempted to take Jack's ball, but not Guinness. He had been trained to share his toys with the injured.

"Would you look at Jack tossing that ball around?"

Captivated, Cord inched closer. "He looks like a little weasel."

"Same family." When Jack started moving his little bandaged head back and forth, Keegan said, "That's his way of saying hello."

"Well, I'll be damned. Hey, little guy. What happened to his head?"

She went into the propeller theory, right along with the slashes along his belly. "Wow, these guys really get beat up in the ocean, don't they? Is it okay to touch his head?"

"Sure. In fact I have to feed him."

"He's so furry and his hands look like little baby mittens," Cord realized.

"Wait until you see them eat." She explained how adult otters fished for things like clams and snails and used a rock to break them open to get what's inside. "But tonight Jack will get a bottle of Pedialyte until he's ready for something more solid."

"Like what?"

"Like ground fish mixed up with his milk."

"Isn't Pedialyte what they feed human babies? Doesn't he need to be in or at least around water?"

"We'll get him there…eventually. He's fine for now. And yeah, same thing they give infants."

"So he's going to be all right? He'll get to go back where he came from?"

"He's better. But not all of them will be released back into the wild. They'll stay here until we find them a zoological solution where they can live safe without fear of being hunted, or injured."

He watched as she put on latex gloves, got out a syringe, and filled it with medicine. "Your bio didn't mention you were a vet?"

"That's because I'm not."

"Why not?"

Her brow furrowed. "What do you mean?"

He watched her change the otter's bandage. "Isn't this exactly what a vet does?"

"In a way, I guess, but the go-to guy in town is still Bran, for now, anyway. Did you know he's thinking of retiring at the end of the year? Which means I need to ramp up my efforts to find a full-time vet for the center."

"Why don't you do it?"

Her brow creased again. "Because I'd have to get into a vet school, get certified—and intern—that's another three years at least."

"But you own this place, why not intern here?"

"I—hmm. That's an idea." She had the undergrad biology degree, didn't she? She had the experience working with mammals. Of course there was that little matter of not having been to veterinary school yet. "I'd have to study to take the VCAT," she stated. "No, it's a crazy idea."

"It's not. Let Bran find his own replacement. As for the center, you're a natural to follow in your grandfather's footsteps right here. Even I can see that. He wasn't just the owner of this place, Keegan. The website mentioned he was a vet. I read his bio, the history of the center. You've been without a vet for almost fifteen months now. You're only twenty-six. It makes sense for you to go that route. If it's what you want…it isn't too late."

Was that what she wanted? Why hadn't she considered that before now?

Watching the interest flicker in her eyes and hang there, he went on, "You already have the degrees, Keegan. You'll figure the rest out."

She pulled off the gloves and ran her fingers along the side of his face. "You know what?"

"What?"

"I'm so glad you didn't die when you jumped into the water."

He stared into her tranquil blue eyes. "Yeah? I'm pretty happy about that, too. Even more so now that I've met this beautiful, gorgeous, and talented female living in the same town I do."

The staffers working at Sandhurst did their best to keep the mentally criminal on a schedule. The routine worked for everyone involved. Medication was doled out at nine p.m. every night. Lights out was rigidly enforced at ten-thirty when staff members began checking for locked doors.

Even though Robby Mack wasn't in a "cell" per se, his windowless room measured a confining ten by ten feet. Every morning someone came to let him out to go to chow. And three mornings a week they trotted him to another building for his anger sessions.

He had gym privileges three times a week. A crafts class allowed him time to play at creating and painting cute little ceramic ashtrays. And when no one was paying attention, he squirreled away whatever sharp, clay shards he could get. Some of which, he'd already put to good use.

When he heard the guard outside his door locking him in for the night, he closed his eyes and pictured Cassie Anne. He recalled the last time they'd been together, the day they'd met at a roadside motel where they'd screwed like rabbits for an entire afternoon. It had been two short weeks before that damned wedding to Cord Bennett. Robby had tried like hell to persuade her to call the damn thing off. But Cassie had been adamant. She wanted to be a bride and nothing or no one could prevent her from becoming Mrs. Cord Bennett.

He laughed at the memory. He'd shown the bitch who had been in control of the situation. He remembered her promising they'd still be able to see each other after the honeymoon. Cord Bennett had been none the wiser, stupid bastard, thought Robby.

He sighed. If only Terri Lynn had a body like Cassie Anne Spearman. It couldn't be helped, he decided. A person had to take advantage of whatever opportunity came his way in whatever form.

Tomorrow, Monday, was the day. Terri Lynn would make good on what she'd promised him. He was sure of it because good ol' Terri thought he had been wrongly accused, therefore deep down, he was a good and decent man.

He'd already promised to show her just what kind of person he could be when he got out of this place.

Because if things went his way, by tomorrow night he'd be heading west and that much closer to Cord Bennett.

Chapter Ten

After they got back to the house, Cord decided they needed music. When he spied Keegan's docking station on the kitchen counter, he went over and picked up her iPod, started thumbing through her playlist.

While she busied herself with cleanup detail, he discovered they shared the same tastes. She had many of the same songs he had. The minute he came across the band, Klimt 1918, he hit play.

They did the dishes together, all the while jamming to *Skygazer*.

"What about you, why don't you become a veterinarian?" Keegan suggested.

"Me? Get real. I've got two years of college. I'm thirty-four years old. I've missed my chance at all that stuff."

"But, I saw how you bonded with Jack and Dodger. You love animals. It shows in your eyes. I've lived around them all my life and believe me they know who they can trust, they sense it."

He shook his head. "See, I didn't even realize sea lions and otters could bond with a human like that."

"So, now you know. You just have to read more, study, learn. Besides, if you're good with animals, the rest you get out of books. I could help you get caught up in no time with your chemistry, animal science, even physics requirements."

"Just because I'm good with them doesn't mean I could ever be a vet. I'd be looking at six years before I got to practice."

"Not if you take advance placement. You could cut some time off of that. And like you suggested, you could intern right here."

"You're dreaming. I'd be almost forty years old, Keegan."

"So? You're really hung up on the whole age thing, aren't you? Grandma Moses wasn't discovered until she was eighty. The oldest college graduate was some woman in Kansas who graduated at the age of ninety-five."

"You're making that up."

"I'm not. Google it. I don't remember her name exactly, but she graduated at the same time as her granddaughter. Age has nothing to do with following a dream, Cord. Besides, good vets never stop going to school to keep up with the latest on diseases and technology. It's a lifelong commitment."

He scratched at his chin. "I do like seeing the animals get better."

"There you go. I saw your face light up around Jack and Dodger. You don't just like animals, you love them."

"I never got to have one growing up, not a dog, not a cat, not even a hamster."

"Look around you here and out at the farm. There are all manner of animals that need your help every single day and every day you come through for them. Maybe that's why you've resisted being here, in Pelican Pointe, so much."

"That doesn't even make sense."

"Sure it does. You've never gotten attached to anything in your life. You think if you do, it will all be taken away. You don't want to risk it. The one time you did—"

Cord's temper spiked. "One psych class and you're analyzing me? How do you come to that conclusion?"

"You're afraid to make that bond because you've been disappointed in the past. Because in the four months you've been here, you obviously haven't been very happy."

He ran his hands through his hair and had to admit, "Until lately, that's true."

"Have you asked yourself why?"

"I know why!" Cord shouted. "I fucked up my life."

"Oh, please. Do you think you're the only person that's ever made a mistake or a bad decision? Let's forget about the little technicality that you were shot. Let's say you did hold back that day and hesitated when it came to charging down the aisle to save Cassie. So what? Man with a gun, firing at everyone. But oh, wait, that didn't happen because you were taken down with two shots as you ran down the aisle trying to save Cassie."

"I kind of like it when you get all jazzed like that. Do you know your eyes get big as saucers when you get all fired up? How do you know all that detail anyway?"

"You aren't the only one who uses Google, Cord."

"Ah."

"I think you're being incredibly hard on yourself."

"You have a beautiful mouth."

"You're trying to get on my good side."

"You bet I am," he said with a grin.

After they loaded the last dish into the dishwasher, when the track changed to the moving song *The Breathtaking Days*, he bundled her up in his arms and they swayed to the music. Soon his dance steps began backing them up into the living room.

Their bodies fit together, long and lean, molded to one. "You're a pretty good dancer for a tall guy."

"Funny, I was about to say the same thing about you. What are you, five-eight?"

"Good eye."

He nuzzled her neck, nibbled an ear. "I suddenly remember why taking it slow sucks the life out of necking."

"You mean there's something on the planet that sucks the life out of necking? Live and learn."

They'd just ramped up testing that concept out when the phone rang. Keegan frowned.

"Who could be calling at this time of night?"

But when she answered, a wound up park ranger said in her ear, "Keegan, this is Steve Childs. I hate to bother you so late but we have a stranded baby seal north of Smuggler's Bay. It washed up about five hours ago and then somehow got stranded on the rocks. All this time we thought we'd wait him out, hoping that maybe the mama seal might come back. But I don't like what I'm seeing. I think he's not going anywhere. And now that I've gotten a closer look at him, I see he's in bad shape. Are you in a position to make a run out here tonight, pick him up? He might not make it till morning."

And that was the problem, wasn't it? How could she turn down a request like that and sleep tonight? She'd seen her grandfather go out later than this, in raging storms, plenty of times to make a save. "What about light? I'll need plenty of light without scaring the bejeezus out of him."

"I'm here now. I'll help with the light."

"Then I guess I'll see you in twenty."

"Rescue?" Cord asked when she hung up.

"Looks like a stranded baby seal. Sorry, Cord. I've got to go."

"I'll go with you."

"You sure? It could take awhile, especially if he's on the rocks, getting to him and all. It might take several hours for me to even get close to him enough to net."

"Are you kidding? I wouldn't miss this. I want to see you in action."

"Good thing I spent the morning loading up your truck with the cages, nets and gear. Let's roll then."

When she grabbed her Raiders cap, tugged it down over her hair, Cord scowled. "A Raiders fan? Just my luck. I've rooted for the Chargers my whole life."

"And for what?" she teased as she plopped into the passenger side of Cord's truck while he got behind the wheel. "At least my team's won Super Bowls."

He grinned. "Ouch. A person can only take so much. But slamming my favorite football team might be the deal breaker."

"Hey, not slamming, it's a fact. Have you guys even

won a championship game in the twenty-first century?"

"Like you guys have been burning the house down lately."

"Yeah, since both had eight and eight seasons last year, I guess it's a draw as to which team sucks more."

With that settled, Keegan directed him through town and up the coast toward a scenic overhang.

"That's almost next door to the farm."

"Yeah, we've seen a lot of seals end up there. It's rocky and hazardous surf but that doesn't stop them from getting stranded at that particular spot."

Twenty minutes later he pulled into a circular gravel lot north of town next to a jeep with the state park logo on the door.

The place was deserted this time of night so when the park ranger stepped out to greet them, he looked glad to have the company.

As Keegan emerged from the passenger door, she heard the pitiful wail of a baby seal pup calling for its mama. "That sounds like a pretty young seal, Steve."

"He is—and noisy. He's not very big, Keegan, and his wail is getting weaker by the hour."

Keegan introduced the two men before heading to the back of the pickup where she retrieved her gloves and netting out of the bed along with a large, rectangular, tub-like bin.

Since the park ranger had already set up floodlights aimed on the steep slope to help them all with seeing their way to the shore below, Cord walked to the railing and peered over. No sand here, no stretch of pristine beach either, just rocks and jutting boulders. He knew for a fact it was a spectacular sight during the day, but all he saw now was a dangerous thirty-foot climb down to reach the bottom.

Steve looked genuinely apologetic. "Sorry Keegan for the late call, but I tried to wait him out thinking he might find his way back in the water or that the mother was just off foraging for food or something and would eventually come back for him. She didn't."

"It's okay. Mothers leave to forage all the time, but something could have happened to her. This isn't the best place to do it either. Maybe she couldn't get back. You'll watch out for her over the next couple of days though, right? This is where she'll likely circle back."

"We will. I'll see to it the morning crew knows about her."

From that moment on, Cord got to see the woman in her element. She was impressive as she first had to hike down the ragged hill.

Once she reached ground level she had to scramble up and onto the finger of land to get to the pathetic little creature, gray in color, marooned on the area jutting out over the water, obviously scared to death—and in distress.

Over the roar of the waves crashing up against rock and cliff, Cord heard her talking to the little guy, trying to calm him down.

"Oh, wow, I knew it. You're just a baby, aren't you, probably less than a week old and underweight? How in the world did you make it this far on the rocks?" As Keegan surveyed the surrounding area, she added, "Or did someone put you here?"

That brought Childs closer. "I thought the same thing. We do get stranded seals here, Keegan, but rarely one so young. Porter Fanning personally rescued probably a hundred or more on these very rocks over the years."

She already knew that and did her best to concentrate on the situation and not on her grandfather.

Childs stood next to Cord below Keegan on the narrow strip of earth dividing the precipice, looking up and added, "This is where he's been barking since I found him about five o'clock this afternoon. He hasn't moved much from this spot. I should've called you then."

"Could someone or something have chased him up here?" Keegan wanted to know. "This isn't a good area for foraging anyway. That's why once seals wash up here, they're usually injured or sick and can't get down themselves. The rocks are too craggy, the waves are too harsh. But something drove him up to higher ground like this. That's for certain."

"I don't see him getting this far away from the water on his own."

"So you think someone purposely drove him up here? Why am I surprised? Hell, some people beat their dogs," Cord tossed in.

"Sad, but true," Keegan agreed.

She gauged her approach, decided on the most direct. "Aw, you want mama, don't you? Poor baby. Well, I don't see mama around anywhere so we'll take good care of you in the meantime, get you some place safe until maybe mama comes looking for you." Behind her she heard Steve ask if he could do anything.

"Nope, I won't even need the netting. He's so small and weak I'll just wrap him up in a wet towel. Cord?"

"Right here," Cord answered as he watched her maneuver into position.

"Do me a favor, give me two of those towels I brought and dip them in the cold water there at the edge, wring them out for me, and then hand a couple up here."

Once he brought them back, she took the cloth and stepped around the pup, approached him from behind. Bending down, she draped it out and slowly, gently, covered the seal's back, then his head. She quickly scooped him up and held him to her chest.

"Aren't you afraid he'll bite?" Cord asked, genuinely concerned for her safety.

"Nah, this guy's too weak to put up much of a fight. Aren't you, Sam? You look like a Sam to me," she cooed as she continued to rub his little head in an attempt to keep him calm.

"Sam, huh?" Cord said as they made their way to the rocky slope. "How do you intend to get him back up?"

"Good question. I guess we use the tub after all, and carry him that way."

Reluctantly she let go of Sam, placed him in the

container and let Steve and Cord heft the weight, take point, carrying him while she brought up the rear. The ascent up took much longer than the hike down. But once they got back to the scenic overhang, Cord pointed out, "Sam if it's a girl, Sam if it's a boy. Good call, you can't lose either way."

"Exactly."

"Every rescue gets a name? Elmer?"

"Yeah. It seems rude not to call them something while they're in our care. And Elmer the sea lion sounds a lot like Elmer Fudd when he barks. He has a bit of a stutter."

Not for the first time that day, he realized they did have a great deal in common after all. When he'd first taken the job at the farm, he'd thought it was silly on his part to name each of the cows. But now, he considered that might just be either a quirky part of his personality or the fun part of his job.

Once they got back to the truck, Keegan transferred the pup into one of the cages, keeping him wrapped up in the wet towels.

"Thanks for coming out, Keegan. I don't know what we'd have done with him if we didn't have the center so close by," Steve said.

"Then it's a good thing we're on call twenty-four-seven, huh?" Keegan cracked.

"Do you think he'll make it?"

"He's dehydrated and very young. But we're good at what we do, so yeah, he has a good shot at growing up."

As soon as they settled back inside the cab of the truck, Cord looked over at her before starting the engine. "You're something. You know that, Keegan Fanning?"

"I am?"

"You are. That cute little guy needs you."

"Cute as a button now but will grow to be so much bigger."

"Really?"

And for the next twenty minutes she filled him in about how the harbor seal, whether male or female, would grow to a minimum of six feet and would most likely weigh close to four hundred pounds as an adult.

The minute she got the seal pup back to the center and into the exam room, she set about assessing his condition. She stretched out her measuring tape, jotted down the necessary statistics on a notepad.

She put the baby on a scale and announced, "Twelve pounds. *Very* underweight."

Cord watched as she performed a physical exam on the lethargic little thing and couldn't help but think how exceptional she was at what she did. He'd bet money the woman didn't even realize she was already one part veterinarian.

After another fifteen minutes or so, Keegan announced, "I'd be willing to bet twenty bucks we've got a female here."

"How can you tell?"

"I can't really—not yet anyway. But look at how tiny she is, not simply underweight but small. And see this light gray color on the underbelly and the spot pattern? That says female to me. But if there's a huge weight gain and the color changes..." Her voice trailed off as she opened a supply cabinet, took out an intravenous feeding tube and began to mix up an electrolyte solution with fish oil.

"That fish stuff smells rank."

"Hmm, shouldn't you be used to all the lovely aromatic smells around animals since you spend part of your day mucking out stalls?"

"Sure, but fish is strong and foul."

"Work around it long enough though, live near the ocean, you get used to the smell." Tilting her head, she sized up the baby seal and decided to forego the feeding tube. From a drawer, she dug out a clean eyedropper. "Let's try this first, Sam."

She filled the tiny cylinder with formula, watched as the baby turned up its nose. "Come on now, Sam. Don't be difficult. It's late and you're starving. Admit it." She kept trying to get her interested in the formula by dabbing the end of the eyedropper at the corners of her mouth. Pretty soon the baby opened up and started sucking the tip. "Now we're talking. Get a taste of this and you might get a bottle of Pedialyte instead of the feeding tube."

Cord glanced around the room. "With four patients on board, you're getting crowded in here. Abby told me on the way in, you guys are running out of space."

"We've had twice this number of patients in the past. And yeah, when we need to, we move things around, scooch together, that sort of thing. Get up close and personal and we're like one big happy family."

He went around behind her, started massaging her shoulders with his lean and long fingers.

"Ahhh, that feels exceptional. You have such big hands."

"You know what they say about big hands," he whispered in her ear.

That got a laugh out of her. "I thought that was feet—and an urban myth."

"Have you seen the size of my shoes?"

"Hmm, you do have large feet."

"Eighteens," he whispered. "Wanna see for yourself?"

"Ah—"

"My feet, see how big my feet are. My, you do have a dirty mind."

"Now you're just bragging."

"That might be the case if I couldn't back it up."

That comment had her swallowing hard, conjuring up that image.

But when he heard her moan at the way he massaged her shoulders, he sighed. "I need to go. Morning comes too early on a farm. Because you couldn't keep your hands off me last night in the truck, I got two hours sleep. Plus I have to drive all the way into Santa Cruz to see the shrink."

"Wait. I'll walk you out." She pulled off her gloves and reached for his hand. "Do me a favor. Don't get all tense about sharing your thoughts tomorrow, okay?"

"Make like he's a bartender. I got it."

"Just be open and honest."

They walked out together through the front door of the center where Cord had left his motorcycle parked on the street. Before they reached the bike, Cord grabbed her around the waist and hauled her up against him. "I want you, Keegan. There's no point in playing the guessing game or taking it slow."

She ran her fingers though his long blonde locks, pulled his mouth down to hers. "Haven't you figured out by now, my evil plan is to leave you wanting me until you can't think straight?"

He crushed his mouth to hers. Instant lust spiked. The belly hungered for so much more.

"I'm pretty sure that evil plan needs revising." He moved kisses over her jaw and let out a low growl. "I know, I know. We're waiting for me to get my head on straight."

"That and for you to move past Cassie."

"Same thing, honey." He tucked a loose strand of red hair behind her ear. "Look, why don't you plan to come out to the farm tomorrow night for dinner. I'll beg Jordan for some of her infamous cuisine and we'll see how it goes from there."

She figured after the session with the psychiatrist he would need another sounding board. Well, it was a start at getting him to open up about the emotions that had to be bombarding his brain right now.

"Okay, it's a date."

"Our third." He wiggled his eyebrows up and down. "The history of the third date is a classic for a reason."

She actually giggled. "You're a funny guy, you know that, Cord?"

"So I've been told."

She watched him straddle the Harley, rev up the engine. And watched him drive off with a bit of an attitude—and knew instantly the reason why.

Cord Bennett already looked like he was sweating bullets about his appointment tomorrow with the therapist.

Chapter Eleven

Monday morning staff shortages and another injured, beat-up pelican brought in from a man who lived south of town and who had found the bird along the roadway, kept Keegan hopping. Plus, she had preparations to make for the busload of school children due to arrive that afternoon for a field trip.

Porter Fanning had always been a fanatic about the welfare of the animals. He believed half the battle was educating the public. Whether bird or mammal, it was never too early for show and tell and to get kids interested in preserving wildlife.

Because of that, she particularly loved it whenever she got an opportunity to show off, not just the center or the animals, or the state-of-the-art hospital, but her staff as well.

Their number might be few, but those she had were passionate about animals. She couldn't ask for more than that.

There were, however, precautions to take to make sure the two hours the kids spent on the premises went smoothly and any safety issues had been dealt with properly before the children ever stepped off the bus.

When she spotted Pete, she all but did a happy dance down the middle of the compound. "Thank God, reinforcements!"

"What's up?"

"We're slowly reaching capacity." She gave him a quick rundown on the patients, and brought him up to speed on Minnie, the pregnant otter. "My guess is we'll have a new baby before the week is out. That means we need to transfer her to the tide pool. Today."

The tide pool was the closest thing to their native environment that the rescue center could offer the mammals, mimicking what they had in the wild.

In this case, much like the hospital, Porter Fanning had spared no expense. Spanning fifteen feet across and thirty feet in length, the rounded enclosure had steep rock formations on the sides complete with a railing and a glass enclosed observation deck for viewing.

But now, she watched Pete scratch at the thinning hair on his head. He always liked to give her a hard time about her go-team enthusiasm, and today was no exception.

"I'm gone two days and miss all the fun, or rather Keegan's idea of fun. I swear you get that zest for this place just like Porter and Mary did. The center changes day to day and you seem to be the only one that can keep up with all of it."

Since they were about the same height, she dangled an arm off his shoulder. "You always say that. And you know I've got great people around me who make it all come together. You're one of those."

"When they show up. They're volunteers, Keegan. You need to find more go-getters like Abby."

"Come on, Pete. Don't drag me down this morning. We haven't had a baby sea otter born here in more than four years. Minnie's time is close. And you spend ten minutes with Sam, I guarantee it'll bring you out of that mood you're in. Wasn't Betty cooperative this weekend?"

"Woman wants to get married. To me!"

Keegan laughed outright. "The nerve of some women. What is she thinking to want marriage from you?" But Pete was too far gone to see the sarcasm or humor in her words.

"My thoughts exactly."

"So you had a fight with Betty and want sympathy from me. Nope. Not gonna happen." When she saw Pete's genuine deer-in-the-headlights look, she softened a little. "You gotta leave your past behind at some point, Pete. Do you care for Betty?"

"Sure I do. But marriage, Keegan? The last time...I don't want to talk about it. Betty yapped at me all last night enough for two people. Just tell me where you want me to start. I need something to do."

"I want you to keep an eye on Minnie and then go spend some time with the baby seal."

"Shoot. I guess with the baby seal we'll be opening fish school before long."

Fish school meant they had to teach the babies how to recognize and catch their own supper, eat what they caught because otherwise the mammals didn't have a clue how to do it because mama wasn't around to instruct them in the art of survival. If not for fish school they would never make it back in the ocean.

"Most definitely," Keegan agreed as she walked Pete to where Minnie played in her own pen. "But as soon as Russell gets in she goes to the tide pool. Abby's in the main building occupied with the sick and injured."

"I thought Abby worked all weekend. She usually gets Mondays off. See this is what I'm talking about. What happened to Tina?"

Tina Drayton was another volunteer from Scotts Valley. "Tina had car trouble. But she'll be in before the field trip gets here. And you know Abby. Russ calls in late so she foregoes her day off to come in, knowing we have a busy Monday ahead."

Pete shook his head. "You really need to talk to Russell. What's his deal now?"

Keegan rolled her eyes. "Apparently he has girlfriend issues this morning."

Russell Dennis was a retired, tattooed, former merchant marine, a great addition to the staff of volunteers but around town he had a reputation as a major ladies' man, even though the guy was pushing fifty.

"What you mean is Russ sweet-talked some gal he met at McCready's last night into hitting the sheets with him but come this morning he couldn't get her ass out the door fast enough and had to call in late."

Keegan laughed. "That pretty much sums it up."

"Mark my word, one day that guy's gonna mess with the wrong woman."

"Did you really threaten Cord if he hurt me? We only just met Friday night under very unique circumstances."

Pete gave her a withering stare. "Yeah. Right. You gonna stand there and tell me you guys aren't moving faster than a runaway freight train. It's all over town. And yeah, I thought it was the proper thing to do and all by telling him straight out, like it is. Your granddad would've wanted it that way. Know what else? He'd have been proud of me, too."

Pete rubbed the stubble on his chin just thinking about yesterday at the church. "The boy went white as a stick a chalk when I mentioned I'd string him up by his balls."

"Ouch! I'd be sorely disappointed if he didn't. Threaten harm to the balls and we're talking a serious reaction from a male every time."

"Now the male knows what happens if he gets stupid. It's only fair."

She leaned over and gave Pete a peck on the cheek. "But you're his sponsor. You're supposed to be supportive and make sure he stays on the straight and narrow."

"That's right. And I'll do everything possible to make sure that happens. But when it comes to you, you're my first priority."

"Aww, Pete." She patted the bald spot on his head. "I love you, too."

Cord had his own Monday morning problems at the farm. One of the workers cut his hand on a fence rail and had to be transported to Doc Prescott's for stitches. The wrapping machine malfunctioned in the packing house and shut down production for two hours before Marty had it fixed.

Cord started to worry about getting to Santa Cruz on time and being late for his appointment. But after handing out the payroll checks, he borrowed one of the farm trucks and headed to his fifty-minute session with Dr. Tony Pontadera with time to spare.

It turned out Tony wasn't male at all, but rather a curvaceous, raven-haired, forty-six-year-old single mother who spelled Toni with an i.

Toni Pontadera was in the process of raising two sully teens. Both boys seemed determined to test, not only every inch of a mother's patience, but her vast knowledge of the mental health profession as well. Her kids had always been her priority. But sometimes her thriving private practice had to take top billing.

Such was the case this morning when neither boy wanted to get up and go to class. She'd had to get tough. She'd reminded them both she had a new patient onboard, which meant she could not be late. Her sons giving her grief today was not an option. The life of a career-minded, single mom was rarely a walk in the park.

In her twenty years in the business of therapy though, Toni Pontadera had seen her fair share of PTSD victims. It was her specialty. She'd been treating victims suffering with the disorder as old as seventy who had dealt with the horrors they had experienced in Vietnam to victims as young as fifteen, a girl who'd been snatched off the street not five miles from her office door.

Anyone exposed to psychological trauma might experience flashbacks, depression, anxiety, anger, fear, or have problems with various addictions including alcohol, drugs, or sex. All exhibited an inability to cope with what had caused them pain in the first place.

With a certain professional curiosity she used to size up all of her new cases, she eyed Cord Bennett over the folder and the data sheet he'd filled out.

Despite the man's David Beckham facial features, she detected an intense set to his jaw, not to mention the "I want to be anywhere else look."

As she always did, she perused the info Cord had provided and then asked the usual background questions.

The yes or no answers she got were fairly typical from a reluctant man who did not want to be sitting in front of her answering what he considered dumb questions about a very sticky problem.

But when she looked into his eyes, she saw real uneasiness.

And because she was a no-nonsense type woman, the eyes got her attention. "You survived a spree shooting where you lost the woman you loved just eighteen months earlier, is that correct, Mr. Bennett?"

"Yeah."

She noted his leg bouncing up and down nervously and stated, "You're very anxious today, aren't you?"

"Yeah."

"Why?"

"I don't really want to be here."

A laugh snuck out in spite of the seriousness of the topic and the professional demeanor Toni so wanted to convey. "No kidding. But Mr. Bennett surely you understand that jumping in the ocean with the intent of drowning isn't exactly normal behavior, is it? Not only that, but the same night you were arrested for public intoxication and in possession of a weapon. You understand that's a huge red flag for law enforcement, for the people who care about you, those who are worried about you, right?"

"Yes."

"Friday, the night you decided to act on your depressed state, you had been drinking heavily?"

This time he simply nodded.

She sighed, getting patients to talk initially was always a challenge, some more than others. "Our sessions are only fifty minutes long, Mr. Bennett. Where would you like to start? Perhaps back at the beginning?"

Cord huffed out a ragged breath, rested his hands on his

jiggling thighs and admitted, "I don't know where to start. I've been messed up for so long, I've lost me, the way I used to feel, the way I used to approach doing things. I'm not me. It isn't like me to give up on anything, but without Cassie, I've felt…lost."

Toni nodded and softly prompted, "Tell me about that day."

For the next thirty minutes, Toni listened as Cord went over every detail leading up to his wedding day. Even though he described the events that morning when it came to the actual time and place of the shooting…he faltered. He recalled how hung over he'd been from the rehearsal dinner the night before, how badly he'd felt out of sorts at the church.

And then he blurted out, "Maybe if I hadn't had so much to drink the night before—I might've been able to react quicker, wrestle the gun away from the son of a bitch, stop him from firing so many rounds—something."

"I see. Do you think that's realistic? That you could have stopped the shooter? With your military training do you think that was logistically and tactically possible from where you were standing at the altar? How many steps were you from where Cassie stood with her father, Mr. Bennett? Was it feasible for you to run all the way to the back of the church to lunge for the gunman?"

At that moment, the timer dinged signaling their session was over.

"Okay, we'll leave it right there for now. But you might consider your answer because we'll pick up right here on Thursday. You do realize the court scheduled twice weekly visits, don't you? We can always add to the ten sessions once we get a feel for how it's going."

"Yeah, twice a week for five weeks, I know."

"Are you sleeping well, Mr. Bennett?"

"Sometimes, sometimes not."

But when she reached for her prescription pad, Cord shook his head. "No pills. You realize I have a problem with alcohol? I'm battling two fronts here, doc. Depression and the need to drink so I don't think about Cassie, about that day."

"Ah, yes, it's in the file. I could start you on sertraline, fifty milligrams." When he simply stared at her, she clarified, "It's generic for Zoloft—for the depression—and very affordable. Even though I see you have a very good insurance plan, I think sertraline is a good place to start. If it doesn't work there are a dozen other drugs we can try."

"I guess. Is it effective against depression?"

"Very. It does have some side effects though."

"Like what?"

"Some patients report headaches, nervousness at first until the brain gets used to the drug."

"You mean the chemical?"

"That's right." And because this patient was thirty-four years old, she thought he deserved to know. "And some have reported a drop in their libido." She ripped off the paper from the pad and handed him the prescription.

Terrific, he thought as he took the piece of paper, stared at it. "That's a lot of damned side effects, all of which sound a lot worse than what I'm dealing with now."

"Depression is not something to ignore, Mr. Bennett. And had you not jumped into the ocean, had you not been carrying a weapon, I wouldn't even think about prescribing you antidepressants. But since we can't change either one of those events, I'll see you on Thursday at one o'clock. Now scoot."

The minute Cord got outside and walked to the truck he'd driven in from the farm, he almost collapsed next to it.

He'd survived the first appointment.

Talking about that day always brought pain and anger to the forefront at the senseless deaths he'd witnessed firsthand. Lives had been lost that day, not just Cassie's, but her father, her maid of honor, one of her cousins, and two of their guests, all on Cassie's side of the family, of course.

Cord had lost no family that day because he had none.

Only Cassie. Cassie had been the only person he'd ever considered his family.

And look how that had turned out?

The tragedy should never have happened. If he'd acted sooner, done something about Robby before their wedding day…

He scrubbed a hand down his face.

Dr. Pontadera's question hung in the back of his head as he slid behind the wheel. Could he have reached Robbie Mack in time that day to prevent all of it from happening?

He raked shaky fingers through his hair. Not likely, he thought now. Not likely at all. He might not be a brilliant man with a college education, but he was smart enough to know Robby Stevens had been standing too far away to have done anything at all, except stand there and watch as the son of a bitch shot seventeen people that day, killing six. He could see that now. Why hadn't he been able to see that before today?

It seemed incredibly stupid to have put the blame on anyone other than Robby Mack. For months now he hadn't been able to see that. It wasn't like him not to be able to sort through a problem and deal with the solution. But for the past year and a half, he'd had difficulty with the outcome.

And now, he realized he'd had no control over the entire incident.

He had to admit talking to the shrink hadn't been as bad as he'd imagined. He'd done his best to follow Keegan's advice and think of it as a casual exchange of his story, stranger to stranger. Once he got going, for the most part, it had worked.

He turned the key in the ignition, deciding almost immediately he needed to call Keegan and tell her the deets on how the visit had gone. But if he called now what would he have to talk about later when she came to dinner?

That hadn't been a problem Saturday night or for that matter last night. Their time spent together had been chock full of interesting conversation, a lot more than a "one night get to know you" session. In fact, he hadn't wanted it to end.

And if he knew anything about women, Keegan had been reluctant for him to leave, too.

He wanted her in spite of all the reasons it was a bad idea. He had no business getting involved with anyone right now.

And what about taking the antidepressants? Did he really want to travel down that road? Did he even need the meds? He certainly didn't want to start taking anything that slammed his libido, not when he wanted to take Keegan to bed.

As he pulled out of the parking lot, he decided he'd try the damn pills mainly because he wanted to get better. He didn't want to be depressed anymore. He wanted to do everything he could to feel normal again.

So he'd take the damn Zoloft and see what happened on that score because he wanted to beat this thing.

As he headed back to Pelican Pointe, he thought of spending another evening with Keegan. And he couldn't hold back the wide curve of his grin.

He hit the gas in anticipation.

Just as labor was unpredictable for most expectant mothers, so it went with pregnant sea otters. Around one-thirty that afternoon, surrounded by a group of first graders peering into the tide pool from the upper deck, Minnie darted back and forth in the water acting more energetic than usual.

Noting the change in behavior, Keegan alerted the crew via walkie-talkie and her entire staff gathered to watch Minnie as she darted around the water several times preparing to give birth.

Sure enough, a quick twenty minutes later, the baby

popped out to plenty of oohs and aahs from the kids. They watched in fascination as Minnie nestled the little guy on her belly and immediately began to lick and clean her newborn pup.

The children were all full of questions and curiosity.

"Is it a boy or a girl baby?" asked a little brown-haired moppet, clearly awed by the experience.

"My mom had a baby last Christmas and she weighed, um, eight pounds. How much does this baby weigh?"

"Right now, about two pounds, but before long she or he, will grow big and strong."

Another little girl wanted to know, "Will they get to go back to the ocean?"

"That's the goal, to release them back into the water. Before that though, we'll tag them with microchips so we can keep track of them."

"Will it hurt?" asked a little boy.

"Only for a second. Do you have a dog?" His head bobbed up and down in reply.

"Does he have a microchip so that when he gets lost you'll be able to find him?"

He rubbed his nose in an upward swipe with his hand and said, "Yep, my mom says we gotta make sure if Sebastian gets lost we can find him again."

"Exactly. It's like that with otters."

They were all clearly disappointed when the teachers, with help from a couple of volunteer moms, started trying to round up the kids and get them back on the bus.

"I'm always glad when that's over," Russell snarled as he watched them tromp through the tunnel and away from the tide pool back to the bus.

"Why?" Keegan asked.

"Because you never know what the little rug rats will do from one minute to the next."

"Not kid-friendly, huh Russ?" Keegan asked because she knew Russ. The man might've been rough around the edges, but he had a solid heart inside when it came to the animals. Russ couldn't stand to see one suffer.

"Friendly enough. One or two is fine but I don't like it when there's a passel to keep up with, like today. You miss one, and who knows where it might be heading for trouble."

"These were pretty well-behaved. We gave them quite a show today, one they won't forget."

Russ eyed his boss. "Here tell about town you've got yourself a boyfriend. That nutcase that runs Taggert Farms sent you flowers."

Keegan put her hands on her hips and pointed to Russ's chest. "You, do not repeat gossip around me. And from here on out, you do not get to call Cord Bennett a nutcase!"

"Crazy in the head is what he is. You be careful, Keegan, never know what that kind will do."

"Stop it! I don't believe you. Gossip is all it is. Are you aware he survived a spree shooting? Have a little compassion for chrissakes. Cord Bennett is in a bad place right now and I won't stand here and listen to you calling him crazy." Having made her thoughts known, she stormed off.

Russ and Pete exchanged looks. "Testing the waters there, Pete, I'd say she's more than smitten."

"Yeah," Pete agreed, rubbing his chin, considering the situation. "That's what I was afraid of."

Chapter Twelve

Around seven, Cord heard his own truck rumbling up the long stretch of paved road that led to the house. He could tell it was his by the hum of the engine. A little nervous, he threw down the dish towel he'd been using to wipe up the mess he'd made on the counter and hurried to the front door to flip on the front porch light.

By the time he stood on his planked wooden portico, he got to watch her climb out of his truck, walk around the hood with a wide grin on her face. She'd taken the time to put on makeup, even eye shadow. She wore a dark green sweater dress—over black leggings—and looked like a fashion model walking the runway instead of tromping over a gravel driveway.

Her long legs ate up the distance fast. She planted a quick kiss on his mouth. He stood there speechless until he finally managed, "Wow! You look—wow!"

"You're such a sweet-talker, Cord." She sniffed the air. "What are you cooking? Whatever it is smells delicious. I'm starving."

She might look like a model but she ate like a regular person who didn't obsess with calorie intake or ration her food.

"Jordan dropped off a pot roast." He quickly held up his hands. "I know. But when I told her you were a vegetarian, she brought over a casserole about thirty minutes ago. Something she called paella primavera. I'm keeping the thing warm. It has rice and tomatoes and a bunch of other veggies. I told her it sounded like it was right up your alley."

"I could've made do with a salad and some soup.

Jordan shouldn't have gone to so much trouble. She's pregnant."

"And loves to cook," he added. "Jordan insisted, Keegan. She says she's used to preparing vegetarian dishes for her guests who don't eat red meat."

"Well it sounds yummy. Anything I can do to help?" she asked as she took in the room. The walls were paneled, which dated the entire place. It looked like something out of the'70s. A green-and-tan striped sofa dominated what could only be described as a purely male environment. A well-worn recliner sported a piece of duct tape proudly worn on one arm as if covering up a war wound to the leather. There were sports magazines stacked neatly on a coffee table that reminded her of a doctor's waiting room. If not for the 55-inch flat-screen TV and the laptop computer sitting on the ottoman, she might've thought she'd gone back in time to Archie Bunker's living room.

But the area was tidy as a nun's convent.

Cord waved his arm in a backhand motion and said, "Don't judge me by the décor. Every item is a leftover except for the flat-screen, courtesy of the man who lived here."

"Taggert." She didn't feel the need to tell him the man had also died in this very room so she started moving into the dining room.

But Cord had other ideas. He nipped her around the waist and brought her up against his chest. He sniffed her neck. "You smell great by the way."

"I know. I took a shower and everything." Amusement danced in her eyes. "For once I tried to smell like a female and not the animals I work around."

He couldn't help it, he laughed. He cocked his head, swung her out giving her a long look. "You're a lot taller tonight. You almost come up to my shoulders. Almost."

"It's the boots."

"They make your legs look longer."

"I'm no fashionista but I'm pretty sure that's the idea."

"Hmm. You are the most unpretentious woman I've

ever met."

Her eyes went wide. Those blue spheres speared straight into warm brown. "Really? Why do you say that?"

"Because you're gorgeous—and yet—you don't act like it." It hit him then. Maybe it was her small town upbringing but Keegan and Cassie were polar opposites. Why should that appeal to him? Shouldn't he be looking for a replacement for Cassie on all levels?

He shook himself out of his funk and noticed she was frowning. What was wrong with him anyway? Here he had a hot female standing in his house and he was back in the past.

Keegan's mind had been trying to figure out what kind of women he'd known before if he thought she was unpretentious. She didn't dare bring up Cassie though. For one, it seemed rude, and the other, she really didn't want to make him sad tonight.

He looked almost cheerful. Because of that, she went another way. "We had a baby today."

"Minnie? Aw, I wish I'd known. Why didn't you text me?"

She shrugged. "You had a full day what with going to Santa Cruz. How'd it go with the shrink anyway?"

"It took me awhile to open up. *He* turns out is a *she* in her mid-forties, Italian. She seems like a decent person. She had pictures of her kids hanging on her walls. I liked that about her."

He kept her hand in his as he tugged her along into the kitchen.

"Once you opened up, did you feel better?"

"Some. She got me to realize there's nothing I could've done to stop Robby Mack that day. But—"

Keegan held a finger up to his lips. "When you stop beating yourself up, maybe you'll understand there's nothing you could've done to stop him that day from doing what he did."

"I know." He picked up the dish towel, used it as a potholder to take the roast out of the oven. He lowered the temp and slid in the pan to warm the rolls.

"Are you sure you won't be upset if I eat the roast? It has baby carrots and potatoes."

She laughed. "I could eat the veggies, Cord. But it's entirely up to you what you put in your body. It's a personal preference for me. I won't eat animal meat." She glanced around the kitchen. "What can I do to help out?"

"Got everything covered. Jordan even brought over some iced tea."

"Then point me to the right cabinet and I'll get the glasses."

"The one over the coffeemaker."

"Got it." She scanned the counter, took in all the food, enough to feed ten people. "Looks like Jordan thought of everything. Are we expecting a crowd?"

He grinned. "She did kinda get carried away. But who am I to complain? She put this all together for me today after I mentioned it to her on Saturday, knowing I wanted you to come for dinner."

"Saturday? But how did you know we'd—click—like we did Saturday night."

He reached over and ran his fingers through that red, silky mane of hers. "I don't know, a feeling I guess. Friday night I looked up into your face, saw those eyes, your drenched hair and—I wanted to get to know you. I haven't wanted to get to know anyone, Keegan, not for a very long time."

She stepped into his space, reached up, brought his head down.

His arms encircled her. He took his time nibbling on her jaw and ear before working his way to her mouth. He tasted. He savored. "We get started, I won't want to stop."

Her breath backed up in her chest. The man knew how to make her heart race. "I better get the ice."

He chuckled. "Like that's going to put out the fire."

"I'd say we both need to bank the heat—for now anyway."

After Keegan filled up the glasses, she turned and

watched as he took the rolls from the oven. She crossed the space and went over to help stack the bread in a basket. When their fingers touched, she could almost swear a lightning bolt vibrated between them. It was all she could do to make it to the dining room.

He took down candles from a buffet, set them on the table and lit them to flame. He hit the lights and shadows danced along the wall.

They sat down to dinner with the unmistakable hint of desire hovering on the fringes.

But over the meal, his pot roast, her rice dish, they tried small talk to cut the sexual tension.

Once he went into the details about his visit with Dr. Pontadera, the lust ebbed. Nothing like talking about your psych problems to kill the mood, he thought. But after about five minutes of sharing, he divulged, "She prescribed me Zoloft."

Keegan's brows arched up in surprise. "Really? Did you take one?"

"Yeah. And it's one of the reasons I'm nervous and my head is pounding. This after taking only one pill, Keegan. It kicked in about an hour before you got here. Right now, I feel like I want to jump through the plate glass door."

She reached over and put her hand on top of his. "It'll take some time for your brain to adjust to the chemical."

"It has a long list of side effects." He ticked off all of them except for the libido issue. The drug certainly didn't make him want Keegan any less. At least not yet it didn't.

"There has to be another antidepressant that doesn't have you wanting to jump through the plate glass."

"God, I hope so."

With that, Keegan switched gears. "As always, Jordan's food is in a class by itself, culinary genius."

"There's apple pie for dessert."

Keegan patted her stomach. "Maybe later. Right now, I couldn't eat another bite." Cord tugged on Keegan's hand, placed a kiss on her palm, moved to her lips. "I'm seriously considering having you for dessert."

Her breath hitched.

He liked seeing that nervous flicker in her eyes, got a kick out of feeling her pulse jump at the prospect of going to bed with him.

"Tell you what, why don't we take a walk. I'll take you on a tour of the farm. I know it's already dark outside but—"

"Sounds like a great idea," she agreed, almost too quickly.

He chuckled. "Honey, you look like you'd've agreed to meet the devil himself instead of that progressing into the bedroom."

Her heart skidded in her chest. She had to reel in her emotions because she knew Cord was nowhere near ready for a relationship. Sex, Lord, yes, but he wasn't ready for anything else. And that prompted the question. Was she ready for the "just sex" scenario? "Now you're reading my mind?"

He felt her bristle and added, "I'm reading your body language. Come on." He urged her up and out of the chair. "You like animals so we'll start in the barn."

"You nibble on my lips, get me all worked up, and now, just like that, you want to show me cows?"

He grinned as he grabbed a flashlight from the kitchen drawer. "What I'd like to show you neither one of us is ready for so we need to find something else to do." He brought her hand up to his lips again, placed a kiss there. "The last thing I want, Keegan, is to get you mixed up in my problems."

She ran her hand down his cheek. "How'd you get so understanding? Most men would be pushing me."

"Maybe I'm not most men."

She was beginning to consider that possibility.

Once outside on the pathway, he told her, "And I don't want to mess this up."

"Why?"

He tilted her chin up and covered her mouth. The kiss played out until he said, "Let me ask you something. Are you willing to go back inside right now and spend the night with me?"

Exasperated, she rolled her eyes. "You aren't ready."

"That's what I thought. If I touch you again like I did in there, we might not be so sensible. When it comes to getting you into my bed, I want no second thoughts on either side."

"Maybe I'll be the one to get you into bed. What about that?"

"You might as well know now, I'm highly susceptible to sweet-talk and the lure of a beautiful woman."

Even in the dark, he could see she rolled her eyes. He let out a laugh and yanked her up against him. They walked like that hugged up to each other until they got to the barn. He swung the huge door back and let her lead the way inside. He hit the lights and the huge space lit up revealing rows and rows of stalls on either side, each containing various sizes of stock.

"Evening ladies," Cord said in his most charming voice. "I brought you a visitor tonight." He went to the sound system on the wall and turned down the steady stream of music. Tonight it was Journey. Steve Perry's tenor serenaded them with *Open Arms*.

Keegan sent out a giggle at the music. "Journey? That's so—"

"Eighties? Yeah, I know. I started out by reading Hayden's notes from the previous manager and wondering how the hell cows could like listening to this stuff. But I hate to admit it, Air Supply and Journey really gets us more milk."

"The right kind of music increases milk production twofold. I read about that," Keegan commented, all the while appreciating the fact he talked to the animals as if they mattered, just as she did.

She walked down the aisle until she got to a very pregnant heifer. "She looks like she's due any day now."

He went over to the cow and rubbed its ears and head. "I'd say another two weeks. Huh, Priss? And before you ask that's short for Priscilla."

That prompted Keegan to go into a detailed account of Minnie's new baby, and how Minnie had delivered the little guy in front of a bunch of curious school kids.

"And?"

"And what?"

"What'd you name him?"

"Oh. Bumper." Because she saw that questioning look form on his face, she added, "The little guy likes to bump the edge of the pool with his head. It's like he's already showing off."

All at once, Cord spotted Scott hanging out at the other end of the barn door. It pissed him off.

And when Keegan saw him look over as if he were startled at something, then annoyed, she followed his gaze. When he continued to stare in that direction, she noted his face had completely changed.

He had such a caught-off-guard, irritated look in his eyes she finally asked, "What's wrong?"

"In a million years you'd never believe me."

"Try me."

Cord stuffed his hands in his pockets and leaned his boot on the rail of one of the stalls as if thinking, deciding whether or not to confess.

"Come on," Keegan prodded. "What's wrong? The way you're acting is only making me more curious."

"What the hell, you already think I'm nuts anyway."

"I do not," she claimed. When his intent look lasted a little too long, she admitted, "Okay, maybe at first I did but that was before I'd gotten to know you. The last couple of days I've reassessed your whole situation."

"You aren't put off because half the town considers me a nutcase?"

She gave him a sympathetic look. "I'd say, more like seventy-five percent." She bumped his shoulder in a playful attempt to coax him out of thinking about it.

"Ouch. Then I guess there's no harm in going for ninety-nine point nine. By any chance did you know Scott

Phillips?"

"The Guard soldier from Pelican Pointe who was killed in Iraq? Sure. He used to help my granddad around the center during his summers, even went on a few rescues with him as a teenager."

"You've heard the stories then." It wasn't a question.

"That he's running around haunting the town and certain people see his ghost? Yeah, I've heard the stories. Who hasn't? Rumor has it Ethan, our own wannabe local author, is working it up from a fictional angle in a book while Wade Hawkins is writing about it from a nonfiction standpoint."

When he continued to gape at her, the implication finally sunk in. "Wait. You mean you see Scott here, now?"

"He's standing right over there at the end of the barn with Myra?"

"Myra?"

"One of the sick heifers separated from the others because she's on antibiotics right now."

"I see I'm not the only one who thinks up cute names for the animals. Wait, does that mean Myra has to go to the slaughterhouse?"

Cord sent her a mortified look. "None of these girls are headed to the slaughterhouse. Taggert Farms sets precedent on that score. They may not be able to give milk once they go on antibiotics due to organic certifications but we have an arrangement with a family farm in the San Joaquin Valley. They take the cows that have minor infections. They'll come get Myra next week."

Relieved to hear that, she studied him. "Was that precedent in place when you got here?"

"No."

"Ah." And that, Keegan thought, said it all and spoke volumes to the man's values.

She looked up and down the stalls, settling on the barn door at the end—and didn't see a single soul anywhere. "Do you still see him? Is he still here?"

Cord nodded his head in Myra's direction.

"So, Scott Phillips haunts Taggert Farms...and you? Why? I can understand you because you both served together and you ended up here in Pelican Pointe but—"

All of a sudden he caught the glint in her eye.

Now, his demeanor changed from serious to teasing. No longer hesitant to discuss Scott, he found he was delighted at her reaction. He decided he liked the idea of yanking her chain a bit. "Not everyone sees him. Maybe you just don't have what it takes to imagine a ghost existing in another realm."

"Are you saying I lack imagination?"

"I'm saying you're too serious-minded to believe in the notion that ghosts walk among us. A biologist like you wouldn't consider it plausible."

"But you have seen him multiple times?" Keegan asked.

"Sure. When he isn't in town or at the cove, he's around here most of the time, bugging the hell out of me about something. He tried to stop me from—" It suddenly wasn't as funny as he'd thought.

Keegan's mouth dropped open. "Scott was with you Friday night? And you did it anyway? Cord, that's—not good."

"Crazy?"

She blew out a breath and ran nimble fingers through her hair. She started to pace. "You see Scott and he talks to you, tried to talk you out of going in for that swim." It dawned on her then. "Wait a minute. That wasn't the first time you tried, was it?" She turned to face him.

He swiped a hand across his chin, suddenly reluctant to tell her more. But watching her eyes fill with dismay, he decided to come clean. "New Year's Day. I'd been here about a month. I didn't like it very much. I missed Cassie. I was alone and—depressed. I took out the .22 and held it under my chin. The gun misfired."

Cord watched Keegan go white, watched as her lips parted as if she wanted to speak but had trouble forming the words. Her hand though, flew to her mouth.

His jaw tightened. He saw for real the panic in her eyes and wondered how he could have even considered ending his life without much of a fight. What if he'd been successful? Twice now he'd tried and failed and realized he never wanted to put that kind of look on Keegan's face ever again.

"Do you really want to die, Cord?" She sucked in a breath waiting for his answer, afraid what it might be.

"No."

She blew out a breath. "Are you absolutely certain of that? Does this shrink know you tried twice?"

"She knows. That's why I agreed to try the goddamned pills. Zoloft, Keegan. As of this afternoon, I'm taking Zoloft. That's how serious I am about getting better. You think I want to feel depressed? You think I want to feel like shit about things? I hate feeling different than the old me."

To his surprise she stepped closer, put her arms around his waist, laid her head on his chest. "I don't want you to die, Cord. You're kind. Do you know how rare it is to find someone who is as much an animal lover as we both are? You're so funny and warm and thoughtful. You have so much to offer life. Don't do that again, Cord. Do you hear me? Promise me, okay? If you ever feel down like that again, will you, at least call me, text me, something? Does Ethan still have—?"

"Yeah, Ethan took the .22. I'm not getting it back." He tilted his head down and took her mouth just because he needed the contact. He gnawed on her lips and then rested his head on hers. "I don't want to die anymore, Keegan."

"Then I guess we'll have to make sure you don't do anything stupid."

Thanks to plump Terri Lynn's devotion to him,

Robby Mack Stevens had a makeshift weapon in his pocket, a blueprint of the hospital's entire layout in his head, and a gutsy plan for freedom.

Tonight, it was now or never.

He stretched out on his single-sized bed and waited for the night guard to make his rounds. The slow-witted orderly usually checked the door at approximately ten-thirty before taking his evening break to go outside and smoke a cigarette.

At ten forty-five, feeling that he'd waited the obligatory fifteen minutes for the staffer to keep to his routine, Robby Mack made his move. He stood up on his bunk and lifted off the ceiling tile he'd been working free for the better part of eight months. It took him three tries to boost himself up into the opening.

Once up and in, he slithered on his belly along the crawlspace until he got to an area he knew for certain to be outside the security perimeter. He took out the flathead screwdriver Terri had smuggled him and set to work on prying up the metal plate. It took him ten minutes to unscrew the bolts but with the last one, he took a good hold on the heavy flap and lifted it up and to the side. He swung his legs into the opening, braced his arms on each side and dropped down into the office of the administrator with a thud.

For several long seconds he listened for any movement outside the door.

When no alarm sounded, Robby Mack simply walked behind the desk, unlocked the window, slid up the glass and climbed out into the night.

He kept to the side of the building, along the shadows, as he made his way through the grounds. Keeping his pace brisk, he walked across the parking lot designated for employees only. He spared a glance up at the night stars and hoped like hell that stupid bitch was where she was supposed to be. Because with any luck, they'd never know Robby Mack Stevens had slipped away until time for breakfast the next morning. And the hospital certainly would never miss their March employee of the month, Terri Lynn Cranston.

He had such plans for Terri Lynn. And after spending the last year and a half locked up, he intended to take his time.

When he spotted Terri's blue Honda, he made a promise to himself. Never again would he allow anyone to have control over how he did things, tell him when to eat, or when to take a piss. No more spending his life locked up especially with some trained gorilla forcing him to do things he didn't want to do. Anger management classes my ass.

Not even inside a loony bin would he let anyone boss him around.

Next time, he didn't intend to give up his freedom so easily without a fight.

Chapter Thirteen

With his crew gone for the day, Cord felt out of sorts. Left alone, the quiet pulled him from the prospect of a boring Tuesday-night television lineup to the peace of outside.

It was a nice evening, or it would be as stars were just now beginning to pop out and glisten. Restless, he started to walk. Over rolling hills and through rows of crops, it didn't take long before he realized for the first time that week, those old feelings of inadequacy, of not being able to save Cassie, started inching up his spine.

Despite the unrealistic aspects, it didn't take a genius to know he needed to get out of here—and do something— talk to someone, his sponsor, Pete, Murphy, preferably Keegan.

Keegan. He needed to see her.

Digging his keys out of his pocket, he headed to one of the trucks and to town. If Keegan was busy, he'd find someone else to talk to, shed this mood before he did something he really didn't want to do.

On the drive to town, he'd sent a text message to Keegan. When he pulled up in front of the center, she was waiting for him.

"I just got a call from Clance Hopkins. He runs a fishing business. He netted a sea turtle about an hour ago. I've got to go get him, Cord. He's got a piece of plastic bag stuck in his mouth. The turtle, not Clance," she explained breathless, before adding, "Come with me."

"Sure," Cord agreed. "A turtle, reptile, right?"

"Right. Good thing we rescue anything in distress."

"Truck or boat."

"We're taking the boat. It's faster for one, and two, Clance isn't coming in for the night. He's almost fifteen miles out."

Cord hurried after her, through the compound, and around back to where the path was well-worn, a shortcut to Smuggler's Bay that led right to the boat.

"What about Guinness?"

"He's staying here. I don't want to scare the turtle. Guinness is great most times, but he can get unduly excited around certain animals. " She tilted her head in his direction. "You don't get seasick, do you?"

"Never have. I'd make a good sailor."

"Good because it's a little too late to take the seasick pills. And the patch takes awhile to work, too. We don't have that kind of time."

Keegan dug out her cell to give Bran Sullivan a heads up. "Hey Bran, standby tonight, will you? I've got a leatherback coming in after ingesting plastic. I don't have many details but I'm on the way out now to get him."

Before Cord could ask anymore questions, they were boarding the *Moonlight Mile*. There, Keegan was all business. She re-checked her GPS coordinates for Hopkin's location at sea, and then digitally charted the course for the Ruby Tuesday.

They were underway in a matter of minutes.

"I'm sorry, Cord, I know you wanted to talk. But this is something I have to do."

"No need to explain. Besides, this is better. It's a beautiful night. I just couldn't be at the farm tonight by myself. I started getting antsy."

Keegan reached out, took his hand. "I was a little out of sorts tonight, too. Today was my grandmother's birthday. She would've been seventy-five."

"Why didn't you say something?" He moved to her, wrapped her up. When her arms went around his waist, when he breathed in the smell of her hair, he knew this was what he'd needed.

"I guess, like you, I wanted to see if I could get past a

rough patch alone. I thought if I stayed busy, it would be enough. Turns out, when things quieted down tonight, I got sad and more than a bit sulky."

"Same here. I was okay as long as things were popping during the day and I had problems to solve. Once everyone left though, I found myself in a funk."

She laid her head on his shoulder and decided, "I think both of us have to find our own way through the grief process and beat this to come out the other side. I'm glad you texted me, Cord."

"Why, Keegan? Why didn't you tell me how you were feeling? You could've called me, too, could've let me know today might be a problem. I would've come. Why didn't you?"

"Because…I didn't want to add to your problems."

"Don't do that. I'm a big boy, I can handle things." He lifted her chin. "It's a two-way street. You need to learn to reach out and so do I."

"Lean on each other? It's a deal."

They'd gone perhaps twelve miles out when the *Ruby Tuesday* came into view. Keegan throttled back on the motor to slow her speed. She reached for the radio. "This is *Moonlight Mile* to *Ruby Tuesday*. I've got you in sight. Are you coming to me? Or am I going there. Over."

A few minutes of silence and then she heard Clance's voice. "This is the *Ruby Tuesday*. Fishing's pretty good tonight. You stay put. Don't want you scaring off the fish. We'll bring him to you. Over."

"Roger that. What've we got, Clance? What's his condition? How big? Talk to me. Over."

"Definitely a leatherback. Looks like to me he's choking, Keegan. I'd say he weighs about a hundred pounds or so, he's not that big, but big enough that we'll need to use a harness to transport him to the launch. Over."

"Roger that. Sounds like a sub adult. Bring him over then, Clance. I'll get the tub ready. We'll try to get him some help. Over."

While they got busy preparing the container, a large

bin, Cord asked the first of a series of curious questions. "Why'd he eat a plastic bag?"

"To a leatherback swimming around in the water, plastic bags look just like jellyfish. They love jellyfish. But they chew on the bags, ingest them, it clogs the intestine. They can't pass the plastic. They die. Plastic isn't biodegradable. Once it's in the ocean, on the beach, it's there forever until we pick it up, get it out of the water or the nesting places for good."

"I never thought of plastic one way or the other." But he was beginning to think there was a great deal he hadn't considered about the dangers posed to wildlife, both on land and at sea. "So he's swimming around, and he nibbles on plastic. Where do you suppose he was headed?"

Keegan took out her binoculars, scanned the water for any sign of Clance's launch. "They cross the Pacific to feed in Monterey Bay where the jellyfish are abundant."

"Wow. Really? That is so cool."

She grinned at the comment. He was like a ten-year-old, fascinated with learning more. And it warmed her heart. She'd been around plenty of guys who could've cared less about one little sea turtle. But, here was Cord seeming to lap up every little tidbit. "I've got Clance's launch in sight. They're rowing over, instead of using the motor."

"No scaring the fish."

"That's the idea."

"Aren't you upset that the turtle ended up in a net from a fishing boat?" To him, she seemed remarkably calm about the whole ordeal.

"Well, as long as there's a market for fish, and there is, Clance Hopkins has every right to make his living on the water, fishing for swordfish or white fin, shrimp, you name it. In fact, Clance is one of the good guys. I know some fishermen, who would've just tossed the turtle away, let him die, or just killed it outright when they got the turtle onboard, but not Clance."

"So turtles get caught all the time?"

"U.S. regulations require a TED, Turtle Excluder Device onboard commercial fishing vessels. But they still get hung up now and again. Look, think of it like this. Clance isn't responsible for the turtle ingesting the bag. We're all on the hook for that. But if Clance hadn't found him in his net, he'd have died for sure. This way, the turtle gets a second chance at living."

And another reason she didn't eat fish, Cord reasoned before he asked, "What happens once we get the leatherback onboard?"

"Keep him alive if we can. Get him back to the center ASAP, run some diagnostics, see if Bran Sullivan can remove the plastic—surgically."

"There's nothing boring about your life, you know that, Keegan."

She laughed out loud. "I guess not. Oh, look, they're about fifty yards out. Let's get ready."

The fishermen made sure the harness secured the leatherback as it hooked around his middle before hoisting it out of the side of the launch and over to the *Moonlight Mile*. The waiting container Cord and Keegan had already filled with plenty of water made sure the turtle could maintain his natural swimming motion while in transit.

Cord's first look at the reptile told him the huge leatherback labored to live with the eight-inch piece of white plastic bag dangling from its mouth. "That's a good sign, right? Maybe it didn't get too far in and get swallowed any farther along the digestive tract," Cord commented, hopeful.

"Poor thing. He's just a baby, too."

"You're kidding? He's huge."

"Trust me they get way bigger than this. Be glad he isn't nine-hundred pounds."

While she radioed Bran, giving him their ETA, Cord stood next to the container peering in, fascinated. "We can't remove the harness."

"Not yet. Not until we transport him to the center. Amazing creatures, aren't they?"

"The flippers are huge, and look, no claws. See how hard his shell is and thick, this must be his layer of fat. They must use that for insulation in the cold water."

"Perceptive. Just one reason they can adapt to living in either the waters of the Arctic or the South Pacific."

"And they're endangered?"

"They are, every year fewer and fewer show back up to nest on the beaches, although lately, they are making a comeback of sorts along the Atlantic seaboard, and the tropical waters of the Caribbean. But every time we humans take over a beach, develop another resort or subdivision, we're pushing out the wildlife that used it before we did for their natural habitats."

Cord shook his head. "Is there anything you don't know?"

She grinned. "You know what, Cord? I'm beginning to think you must be easily impressed."

"Yeah? And I think you're incredible. What do we name him?"

She grinned. "You pick."

"He looks like a Haggerty."

"Haggerty?"

"He looks beleaguered and haggard. He's been suffering some."

She opened her mouth for an acerbic comeback, but it caught in her throat. She took in the line on his forehead, decided it was rare to find a man who cared that much about naming a turtle. So she breathed in the night air and said, "Haggerty it is then."

Once they got back to Smuggler's Bay, Keegan motored the *Moonlight Mile* into position where they worked on securing the lines.

Bran Sullivan greeted them on the dock. Cord noticed Bran seemed to know exactly what to expect, almost as if the two of them, Keegan and Bran, had done this many times before.

Bran waited with a gurney, an oversized one, to transport the leatherback to the center. Using the harness, they were able to hoist the turtle into position on the portable litter, and finally secured it in place.

Once that was done, all three of them used some serious muscle to load the metal litter into the back of Bran's truck.

While Bran drove the couple of blocks to the center, Keegan gave him a rundown on the reptile's condition.

At the back door, they unloaded the turtle and wheeled him into the hospital where Cord watched transfixed, as Bran and Keegan went to work.

"You staying?" Bran asked a wide-eyed Cord.

"I'm not leaving unless you kick me out," Cord replied.

"Got a strong stomach?"

"I guess we're about to find out."

Comfortable using Porter Fanning's medical facility, Bran got down to business. "Keegan, I'll start an IV with the sedative, you grab that chart over there and make some notes for me."

Bran washed up for surgery while Keegan weighed, measured, took blood samples, and documented everything. "Even though his weight is one-thirty-eight, he's still considered a sub adult."

Then an idea formed.

"Cord, there's a video camera in the cabinet over there. Dig it out and let's get this procedure on film for posterity. Unless you're queasy?"

He gave her a withering stare. "Geez, I guess you guys forgot I've been through combat. Remember? Seen worse than this with humans trying to kill each other."

"Okay, then. Show me what you've got."

So Cord chronicled the event while Keegan and Bran took X-rays and found a massive length of plastic obstructing what looked like the turtle's entire digestive tract.

"But no tumors," Keegan surmised as she studied the black-and-white image with her hands on her hips. "And no internal bleeding either. He's relatively healthy except for the extra baggage."

But just as with any surgery, there was always an element of risk to the patient, even if the patient in this case was a hundred-and-forty-pound turtle. Anesthesia could prove as deadly to the reptile as the foreign material.

Once Bran cut into the intestines though, it wasn't difficult to spot the obstruction. "There must be fourteen inches of plastic here," Bran relayed.

"Might be easier to get to if it weren't for all his backward spikes that help him swallow food. What're you going to do about the plastic stuck in those?"

"I'll have to maneuver over one spine at a time."

And because of that the procedure took almost three hours digging the foreign substance out of every crevice. But the good news, Bran was able to remove the entire length from his digestive tract.

Later, after the vet had gone home, Keegan and Cord sat on the floor of the exam room, sipping on a can of soda, both of them exhausted.

"You can't say I don't know how to show a man a good time," Keegan tossed out as she leaned back against the wall.

Cord busted out laughing. His legs drawn up, his hands poised above his knees. "You have a unique idea of fun then. But I'll go you one better. You really took my breath away, watching you in action tonight." Cord tucked a strand of loose hair behind her ear, and grew serious, considered the still-sleeping patient.

"Will you release him back into the ocean?"

"Probably. You saw the X-rays. It took some time but Bran got it all out even though it clogged up his throat and system. Because of that, Haggerty will be able to eat all the jellyfish that swims his way."

"It's amazing what you guys did."

"Hmm, we had some help here tonight, Cord. You were pretty amazing yourself."

"Me? I just watched."

"No, you definitely did more than that. And it got my mind off my grandmother. Did it help you?"

"Being with you, yeah, it all clicked away. But I was very close to the edge tonight and you pulled me back, Keegan."

"I think maybe we pulled each other back tonight, Cord. Maybe the pros know what they're talking about. Maybe it just takes time for the loss to—become less at some point and—more bearable."

"Yeah, maybe so." But it sure didn't hurt knowing an amazing marine biologist who loves helping out wildlife any time it's in distress.

Chapter Fourteen

By Thursday morning the pain in his head felt like a heavy-metal band had set up a drumming that steadily increased to the pounding and intensity of a sledgehammer.

Sitting in Dr. Pontadera's office holding his aching head in his hands, Cord admitted, "This is like no other headache I've ever had before. This, after taking only four pills, is like someone drilled a hole in my head. Look, I'm going cross-eyed the pain is so fierce. I can't concentrate, can't focus, can't get the pain to ease up long enough to think straight. Then there's the nervousness. I feel like I'm crawling out of my skin."

"Obvious side effects from the sertraline. We'll try something else. There's Celexa which comes in an inexpensive generic. I told you we have all manner of meds we can try to get you over this shaky hump in the road."

She ripped off a prescription from her pad and handed him the paper then went to her desk, took out a bottle of ibuprofen. "Here, let's see if we can dull that headache."

When she sat back down, she wanted to know, "Did you give anymore thought to what I asked you on Monday? Was it logistically realistic that you could've reached the shooter that day in the church?"

"I thought about it. And there is no way I could have gotten to Robby Mack in time. But that's not the—"

Toni held up a hand. "No, for now, it *is* the issue. Let's stick to reality not what you think you should've done or what should've happened. How's that? I should've invested heavily in Microsoft, but as you can plainly see, I didn't."

When she saw his brow furrow, she added, "Don't give me that look like I'm comparing buying stocks to losing the woman you loved that day. I'm not. But do we agree here, Mr. Bennett, that there's truth, what's real and then there's fantasy, what happens up here." She held two fingers to the side of her head before continuing. "What we think should've happened is in no way a correlation to reality? Do we agree?"

"Yeah. I'm starting to believe that sooner or later the son of a bitch would've done something awful, whether it was our wedding day or much later after the fact. I had no idea the guy was that violent, okay? Cassie never leveled with me about any of it, about how abusive he'd been with her in the past."

"There you go. You can't fix something, Mr. Bennett, if you don't know it's even broken. You have to at least admit Cassie either didn't feel it was important enough to share with you, didn't suspect this man posed such a problem that way, or—"

"She had other motives."

Toni arched a brow at that remark. "Why do you say that?"

"She knew the man had hit her in the past. She knew how violent he was. She could've at least gone to the cops, reported him. She didn't."

"Ever?"

"Ever. There were no reports on file. I know. I checked myself once I recovered enough to poke around on my own."

Toni tilted her head to study his face, his eyes. She thought they might've touched on a nerve for the first time and she intended to pursue it. "How would you describe your relationship with Cassie? You knew her what, for several years, right?"

"I loved her. I would've done anything for her. She was the first woman I felt that way about. Sometimes she could make me crazy though."

"How so?"

"She liked to play head games sometimes. Okay, a lot."

"Really? So Cassie is the first woman you ever loved but she was somewhat deceitful? Hmm, tell me something, Mr. Bennett." Toni bit her lip, tapped the end of her ballpoint pen on her lip as if deep in thought and asked, "Did Cassie profess her love the same way you did? By that I mean, was she as enthusiastic about telling you she loved you? Was she affectionate, demonstrative, or did she hold back?"

"How am I supposed to answer that?" Cord puffed out a breath in frustration. "She was the first family I ever had! The first person I ever truly loved. Don't you see? I couldn't protect the one person who loved me."

"Hmm." Toni chewed on her lip again. "But you didn't exactly answer my question or describe your relationship there, Mr. Bennett. Do you feel that Cassie felt the same way about you, that the feeling was mutual, that she would've done anything for you? That the love was equally returned? I'm asking you to think back, to delve into your relationship."

Cord looked away. "Not exactly. She could be manipulative when she didn't get her way."

"Ah." Now they were getting somewhere, Toni thought. "In what way was she manipulative?"

"Basically, she called all the shots. If she didn't want me hanging around my buddies after work, she'd pitch a fit if I even mentioned going for a beer with them. Because I wanted to make her happy, I didn't see my friends all that much."

"You gave up seeing your friends? Totally?"

"Yeah, pretty much. And she didn't like me going anywhere unless I checked in with her a couple of times a day, either. I thought it was, you know, normal. That this is what it was like to have a family, someone who cared. I thought, okay, she's worried about me, she wants to know where I am every minute of the day so that she knows I'm okay."

Toni didn't like what she was hearing. "But?"

"I've been thinking—"

"It sounds like she isolated you from your buddies, the ones you'd known for such a long time in the Guard, friends and relationships you'd nurtured over the years. It sounds more like she wanted to be in control all the time. Was she possessive, Mr. Bennett?"

"Yeah. She could be that, too."

"What made you tell me this?"

"I've been thinking I might've put Cassie up on a pedestal, one she didn't exactly deserve."

"Really? How did you come to that conclusion?"

"I met someone recently. She's nothing like Cassie. It makes me realize—"

"Oh, Mr. Bennett, you're in a bad place right now to start a new relationship. It is way too soon for something like that."

"That's what everyone keeps telling me, but this woman is grounded, loves animals. She's a marine biologist. Can you see me with a woman like that? A scientist?"

"Does this scientist lord her education over you, throw it in your face, so to speak?"

"Not at all. In fact, she's the most down-to-earth person I've ever met. She thinks I'd make a good vet."

"A veterinarian?"

"Yeah. Because I like animals so much. No one even picked up on that before."

"So, she's grounded, confident, encouraging, sounds like all the qualities any man would admire in a woman."

"She's amazing. I'm...attracted, first time I've been attracted to anyone in two years." He ran a hand through his hair in a nervous gesture that said he was uncomfortable talking about sex and Keegan.

"Nothing wrong with attraction. What's bothering you...exactly?"

"You said it yourself. I'm not in a good place to start a relationship. But one head isn't exactly on the same wavelength as the other when it comes to Keegan. That's her name, by the way."

Toni nodded. "To be sexually attracted to a strong, intelligent woman like Keegan is a natural thing."

"I don't want to mess this up though. She's incredible."

"I take it this is recent?"

He nodded. "Don't laugh but she's the one who pulled me out of the water that night."

Toni's mouth dropped open. "You're kidding?"

"Nope. Jumped right into the Pacific Ocean and saved my ass, gave me mouth to mouth, the whole bit."

"So you haven't had time to take it to the next level yet?"

"No. I'm beginning to see the beauty in getting to know each other first. But physically it's been almost a week and it's…getting tougher. Every time I'm close to her I want to—"

"You've been celibate now for—?"

"A year and a half. I haven't wanted to be anywhere near another woman. Not like that."

"Until now."

"Exactly."

"And you're starting meds that have you worried about your libido?"

"I'm bothered by it, that's for sure. But so far the pills haven't lessened my wanting her."

Toni smiled. "Then we'll make sure the meds don't get in the way of that happening."

While Keegan went about her morning routine, cleaning enclosures, taking care of her list of patients, she couldn't help but think of Cord. She knew it was merely a matter of time before she gave in and slept with him.

In spite of his messed up life, those golden-brown eyes of his drew her into their depths. She didn't even want to consider all that sexy longish hair, or the way he kissed. And the man adored animals as much as she did. Who was she kidding? He was getting harder and harder to resist.

Images of him had kept her up three nights in a row.

Since Monday night when they'd both been amped and ready to jump each other, she'd done nothing but visualize how he'd look out of his clothes. Not a good sign she'd be making it through the weekend without ending up in the sack with him. Okay, so no one would be nominating her for sainthood anytime soon. But then, sainthood was so overrated.

If she wanted Cord what was the big deal? A twenty-six-year-old woman who knew her own mind had a right to lust after a good-looking guy, didn't she?

Plus, she'd given up caring what the town thought about him. He wasn't crazy. He had issues, yes. But then didn't everyone? And since those issues were the result of a traumatic incident in his past, an incident so horrific it would undoubtedly make the sanest person depressed and maybe even think about ending it all. Losing someone you loved in such a violent way had to cause issues in dealing with anything major in the immediate future.

And didn't that include relationships?

A buzzer went off in her head. *Warning. Warning. Big red relationship flag.*

But as long as she was aware of his past, what to look out for, as long as she considered the pitfalls, she could assess their future together, if they had one, that is.

She needed to think about getting Cord into bed as nothing more than a simple release, a mechanism that might make them cope better. Something they both needed right now to get them through a difficult time.

As far as Keegan was concerned the town should be a whole lot more supportive. She'd like to see them go through that kind of traumatic event and see how they came out the other side.

With that settled in her mind, she left her patients, threw a load of towels into the washer, and made her way into the miniature space she used for an office. She picked up the phone and dialed Wally at the service station.

When Lilly picked up, she asked, "Any news on my truck?"

"Wally's finishing up right now. You should have it back by this afternoon. You're lucky, Keegan. Wally was able to rebuild the engine. Have you thought anymore about having an open house during the street fair?"

"It's a go and one of Wally's best ideas. I should've thought of it last year. I called the elementary school yesterday and Mrs. Monroe's first-grade class agreed to draw posters and decorate buckets we can set around the center for donations. The idea is for visitors to crack open their wallets or checkbooks and drop in generous donations along the way when they see our adorable resident animals. Will you be setting up a booth this year?"

"Are you kidding? I was the first one to sign up and pay my entry fee this year. I'm not as nervous as I was last time. In fact, I'm looking forward to sketching portraits for the whole town."

"It's strange but I think I'm looking forward to the street fair, too. My grandparents used to get such a kick out of showing this place off. I guess I better get used to doing the same thing." And if the open house was a success she'd have a center to show off through the summer months.

After hanging up with Lilly—she set out to see how Minnie and Bumper were doing—and wondered if she could keep the center running another six months without a major philanthropist stepping forward to save Fanning Marine Rescue.

Chapter Fifteen

Even though Deputy Sheriff Ethan Cody's assigned territory included Pelican Pointe, he didn't really have an official office in town. He didn't need one as long as he could rely on his home office, the space where he tried to write at least a thousand words a night. At this rate, he had to admit, he might finish his first novel before he reached forty.

Sometimes it sucked that his personal writing space had to double as the law enforcement command center. But then he could often slog through notifications here and forego having to make a lengthy trip into Santa Cruz.

Because of that he relied on technology that kept him connected to the sheriff's office and took up a stingy corner of his desk to keep in touch with his superiors in an official capacity.

So when his fax machine began spitting out a paperfest, he didn't pay much attention. After all, Thursdays could be just as busy as Fridays, which easily produced a certain number of routine BOLOs, or Be On the Lookouts. At any given time BOLOs might pertain to teenage runaways, missing or endangered persons, stolen vehicles, escaped cons, or any armed robberies that had occurred within a hundred-mile radius.

But as Ethan shuffled through the papers and the lists, a familiar name jumped off the page. Robby Mack Stevens had escaped from his comfy digs at some Virginia state mental hospital.

Three days ago Robby Mack had flown the coop. And now it seemed a hospital worker was missing from Sandhurst. A woman by the name of Terri Lynn Cranston hadn't been seen for three days. To Ethan Cody's mind, Robby Stevens should never have seen the inside of a mental facility with such lax security.

Despite the three-thousand-mile distance, Ethan couldn't help it. He got that weird vibe in his gut that spelled trouble. Could Stevens be headed his way and to Pelican Pointe?

He needed to find out everything Cord knew about the man. Grabbing his keys off the counter, he headed out the door to tell Bennett.

Given such a head start, Ethan knew Robby Stevens could be anywhere in the country by now. But his gut told him the man might have unfinished business with the town's newest resident.

Not only that, his second sense told him there was no chance Terri Lynn Cranston would ever be found alive.

Robby Stevens had himself a brand-new ID. His driver's license now read John Gold. He also sported a trendy new appearance, what he called his California look. He'd bleached his black hair a white blond, like a surfer dude, he thought now, sparing a glance at himself in the mirrored wall behind the counter.

He'd gotten himself a new pair of contact lenses which turned his baby blues a dazzling shade of green. And thanks to the credit card he'd stolen from Terri Lynn's purse, as well as the tidy sum he'd cleaned out of her savings account, he had a brand-new ride.

He took a bite out of his eggs-over-easy and stared out the window of the greasy dive just off I-80 near Walcott, Iowa, where he'd stopped to grab a quick breakfast. The sleek Mustang sitting in the parking lot went a long way to convey his persona. He'd paid cash for the sporty, blue convertible in Morgantown, West Virginia, before he'd ever made the turn to head west.

He crammed in another bite of hash browns and decided it was a damned shame he'd had to get rid of hefty Terri. He hadn't counted on the bitch having such a skillful mouth. Who would've guessed the mousy woman had been capable of giving him the best head he'd ever had? Certainly he hadn't. That had been a nice surprise, a very sweet surprise. But then he'd been locked up for a year and half. That had to count for his overreaction to Terri's services. If he'd known the woman could work that luscious mouth of hers, he would've made a move in her direction two months earlier right after she'd started to work at Camp Sandhurst.

As it was, he had rushed his technique. His charm had been a little rusty. It had taken longer than he thought to wine and dine Terri in a confined environment. At one time, it wouldn't have taken so long to bend her to his will. Ah, well, he thought. He doubted anyone would ever find her body. Knowing her final resting place though, there was something comforting in that.

Cord stood in the cherry orchard enjoying the late afternoon sun, the way it angled through the branches, and wondered why he hadn't noticed before how beautiful the farm could be in the spring. From where he stood he could smell the ocean. He inhaled the scent of the blossoms, tilted his head up to look at the crystal blue sky. He felt a joy he hadn't known in almost two years.

He did his best to get his mind back on the subject at hand. They were having a meeting of sorts as Silas went over his plans to hire more pickers to harvest the springtime crops.

At the sound of a car though, Cord spied Ethan in the distance getting out of his cruiser. For some reason, all the pleasure drained from his body. His gut tightened. He continued to watch as Ethan made his way across the landscape. The deputy looked all business, his walk brisk, his face official.

"Cord."

"Ethan. What's up?"

Ethan eyed Silas. "I need to talk to Cord. Could you give us a minute?"

"Sure," Silas said. "I'll catch up with you later, Cord. We need to go over setting up the roadside stand soon anyway."

After Silas walked off, Ethan turned to face Cord. "I guess there's no good way to say this so I'll just pull off the Band-Aid in one fast yank. Robby Mack Stevens escaped from Sandhurst Mental Hospital Monday night. Three days ago, Cord. And there's a female, a member of the staff, gone missing right along with him."

"Son of a bitch," Cord snapped. "I knew giving that bastard a cozy hospital room instead of prison was a huge mistake. I told them so, but no one listened." He stormed off a couple of steps before storming right back. "They believed he was sick in the head. It was an act. I told them that, too."

"Preaching to the choir here," Ethan said agreeably. "He has a three-day head start though. May try to leave the country somehow, maybe head to Canada or Mexico, or maybe pick a country with no extradition." He tried to make the theory sound convincing.

Cord studied Ethan's face. "But you don't think so?"

"I'm here to officially warn you to be on the lookout, that's it. But you of all people know what this man is capable of doing. Plus, you are the one person he wanted to kill that day but survived. That fact may not sit well with him right about now. If it comes down to making sure you're gone for good—he might decide to head this way— with the intent of finishing you off."

"Okay, what exactly do you want me to do about it if he finds me? Stand behind a cow for protection and throw a rock in his direction. You confiscated my damned gun, even a peashooter would do some damage if aimed in the right place."

Ethan shook his head. "Yeah I did, and you don't get to throw that up to me. I'm not even going to address your state of mind at the time. To get the gun back you'd have to petition the court, go through the judge."

"Goddamn it!"

"But she won't give it to you, Cord. Not until you've completed your mandatory sessions with the shrink. I know that for a fact."

Cord raked both hands through his hair. "Okay. Okay. But if Robby Mack is out there looking for me, I'll be more than happy to give the son of a bitch a second chance. I'll even be the bait. You just make sure you cover my back in the process."

"And what about Keegan? Where exactly does she fit into your being the carrot at the end of the stick?"

"Shit."

"That's what I thought. Are you two—? None of my business but under the circumstances—"

Cord eyed him with a certain amount of derision before interrupting him. "There's only so much I'm willing to share—even with the law—even with you. I'm not getting Keegan mixed up in all of this crap. Robby Mack doesn't even know she exists and that's the way I intend to keep it."

"Good luck with that," Ethan retorted. "Last time I tried to tell a woman what to do with her heart, I got married. Look, I know what you're going through. You seem to forget that piece of shit Dochenko sent a hit man after Hayden not six months ago."

Cord had heard all about what had happened last fall when Luka Radovan had shown up to kill Emile Reed aka Hayden Ryan now Hayden Cody.

Because he'd already taken a plea deal for a long list of offenses, Luka was serving time somewhere out of state in a maximum-security federal facility. It hadn't taken long in custody for Jeremy Dochenko's head lackey to agree to testify against his former boss.

Cord's jaw tightened. "Keegan deserves someone who doesn't have my long list of problems and Robby adds one more."

Ethan nodded. "Like I said before, good luck with that since Keegan Fanning is every bit as hardheaded and stubborn as my wife. Look, I printed up flyers with Robby Mack's face on them. I'm distributing them all over town. Everyone will get a good look at him and be aware he's on the run."

Ethan offered one to Cord. "This is his last known mug shot the night Leesburg PD booked him."

Cord snatched the paper out of Ethan's hand and stared long and hard at the man who had single-handedly ripped his world in two.

"Yeah, I'm familiar with what he looks like," Cord muttered. Hadn't he spent too long reliving that scene at the church, seeing the man fire his weapon over and over again in his dreams?

"You go ahead and plaster this up and down Pelican Pointe for all the good it will do." It wouldn't matter, Cord thought. Nothing did. Because he'd learned the hard way, he could count on no one but himself when it came to stopping Robby Mack Stevens.

But once Ethan took off, Cord wandered around the orchard, stalking his past. Just when things had started to look somewhat promising, Robby Mack had decided to resurface. Why did his life have to be so complicated right now? There was no way he would involve Keegan in this. He kicked a clod of dirt with the toe of his Danner work boot and sulked.

"Seriously. You're thinking of cutting things off with her now?"

Cord whirled around at the sound of Scott's voice. "Fuck you. I'm in no mood to have a conversation with a dead guy right now, okay?" Cord stared down Scott's ghost who was every bit as much a solid form as he himself was. Despite his tough persona, seeing Scott always gave him a jolt, one he would admit to no one. But right now he had other more pressing matters to focus on than a ghostly apparition.

"You think I want to break it off? Hell, I want her more than I want my next breath of air. But I'm not putting her in the line of fire if that son of a bitch comes looking for me. I'm not taking the chance. Robby Mack is crazy."

"He will, he'll come for you."

That stopped Cord in mid-mad. He narrowed his eyes. "You know this for a fact? What? Are you psychic now, too?"

"He's headed to California."

Cord ran shaky fingers through his long, loose locks. "Fine. I need to go talk to Keegan. The sooner I get this over with the better."

And with that, he stormed off to find an available truck.

But before Cord reached the vehicle, Marty came running up to him. "There's a man waiting for you inside the office, says it's important he talk to you."

Because Robby Mack's face popped into Cord's head, he pulled out the flyer, showed it to Marty. "By any chance is this the guy?"

Marty shook his head. "No way. This guy is almost as tall as you are, maybe a couple of inches shorter, graying sandy blond hair, not as long as yours. He looks like he's about fifty or so. Says for me to tell you he's your father."

Chapter Sixteen

By the time Cord reached the executive offices, he'd worked up an already serious head of steam. Storming inside, he took two steps and stopped dead in his tracks. Even from ten feet away—he gaped at what could only be described as an older version of—himself.

Marty's description was spot on. The man stood at least six-two with the same streaky blondish-brown hair as Cord. The only difference was that the stranger had fringes along his temples edging toward gray. He wore jeans and a simple plaid shirt. His boots were worn and scuffed and the big-ass belt buckle at his trim waist told Cord he considered himself a cowboy.

The guy seemed nervous as he stood in front of the desk waiting, and clutching a tan Stetson in his hand.

Fidgeting, the stranger turned at the sound of Cord coming into the room. Cord saw him tuck his hands in his pockets, a gesture that seemed oddly familiar.

Cord saw the man swallow hard. Their eyes met. The same gold-flecked brown stared back at him. Cord finally managed to speak. "What the hell is this? Who are you?"

The man stretched out his right hand. "Douglas Gabriel Bennett's the name. Most people just call me Gabe, though. I've been looking for you close to ten years now."

Cord glared at the outstretched hand. "Why?"

"Didn't the guy tell you? I'm your father. Your name is Cord Douglas Bennett. You were born February 22 at Mercy Hospital in San Diego. You weighed eight pounds two ounces. You have a purple birthmark on your left shoulder shaped like the state of California. I sure had me a big baby boy—once upon a time," Gabe finished in a husky voice with tears in his eyes.

The jolt of surprise and unease turned to resentment. Cord hardened his heart. "Yeah? Well, these days anyone with access to the Internet can look up basic statistics which brings me to the next question. Where the hell have you been the last thirty-four years?"

"It's a long story."

"Ain't they all?" Cord replied with a sneer. "Look, I don't know what your game is or who sent you but now is not a good time to play me. If it's money you're looking for—"

"I just want to talk. I came down from Fresno for the day, took off from work as soon as I got the word where you were. I hired one of those private investigators some time back to locate you. You've been a tough man to find."

Even though Cord wasn't buying the man's story for a minute, he planted his butt on the corner of the desk and felt the need to point out, "Me? I've been right here in this same spot for months now."

"Try years. I've been looking for you since I got out of prison."

Great, an ex-con, thought Cord, just what he needed. Well, his luck in the family department had always sucked. Why would now be any different? "Uh-huh. What were you in for?"

"Murder. Look, I just want to get to know you, maybe take in a ballgame every once in awhile or go get a meal together. Give me ten minutes of your time."

Cord looked at his watch on purpose, letting an air of indifference surround him. He wasn't about to admit the man had him all kinds of curious. With the mask firmly in place, he offered, "Ten minutes and then you're out of here. Start talking, make it quick. I was just on my way into town."

"Social services took you from me when you were ten months old."

"A fine testament to your parenting skills I'm sure,"

Cord fired back.

"No. I was seventeen at the time. Your mother, she was sixteen when she died. Someone killed your mother, Cord, came right into the little apartment we had at the time—this little place—a hole in the wall really over on Sea Ridge Drive in Pacific Beach. Anyway, when I was at work, someone came in and stabbed her to death. You were just a baby, asleep in your crib when it happened. Walked in that morning and you were crying, looked like you had been at it for hours and hours. I found Tammy's body lying in a pool of blood in the kitchen. I called 911. The cops immediately thought I did it."

"Did you?" Cord asked, still skeptical about the whole thing.

"No! I would never have hurt Tammy. I loved her. We were just kids ourselves trying to raise a baby. But they arrested me anyway and put you in foster care. I never laid eyes on you again after that, not till today."

"When did you get out of the joint?"

"Ten years this May."

"Paroled?"

"No. They finally matched DNA from Tammy's crime scene to some guy that used to live in the same complex. I spent over two decades locked up. But I was exonerated, Cord. Check it out if you don't believe me."

"Oh believe me, I intend to. I'll make calls starting with Ethan Cody, our deputy sheriff here in town."

But Gabe didn't seem daunted at the idea of being checked out by law enforcement. In fact, he straightened his spine a little more and claimed, "I've been looking for you ever since I got out. Private investigator discovered you'd never been adopted. Turns out, you were still Bennett. Found out you went into the service. But then after three tours of duty in Iraq, he never could get a bead on you...until now."

"Yeah? Lucky me. Well, it was nice meeting you. Look, I've got an errand to run so if you don't mind..." He didn't have time for a faux family reunion especially today. Breaking it off with Keegan came first and would likely take everything out of him. But now it seemed, he had to work in some time to have a face-to-face chat with Ethan Cody…again.

Cord stood up, his big frame almost eye-to-eye with the stranger. He held out his hand for the first time and stated, "Thanks for stopping by. You be sure to drive safely heading back to Fresno."

"You don't believe a word I've said here, do you?"

"No. I don't."

"All right. Let's go get us one of those DNA tests. There's got to be a lab near here that'll do it. I'll even foot the bill. It'll prove to you I am your father."

Cord shook his head. "I'm trying to be polite here and not throw you out on your ass but, like I said before, right now is not a good time. I've got things to do."

"This isn't over."

"Actually, it is. I'll walk you to your car."

To prove his point though, Gabe Bennett picked up a pen from the desk and started scribbling on a scratch piece of paper he'd pulled from his pocket. "Here is my address and phone number. You let me know when you get your head out of your ass because I am your father."

And with that, the man clomped out of the room.

On the drive into town to see Keegan, Cord considered what the man had told him. Sure, it was a great sounding tale with all the elements of a good scam. But that didn't mean he had to fall for it. He'd get Ethan to check out the man's story, find out more about this Gabe Bennett. The nerve of some people, showing up out of the blue, and expecting a person to believe a wild lie like that.

But before he checked out Gabe Bennett, he needed to see Keegan and explain that things could not move forward between them. Not with Robby Mack Stevens out and loose on society.

A little after four, Cord pulled up in front of the rescue center. He sat behind the wheel of the truck with a sinking feeling in the pit of his stomach, trying to work up the nerve for what he had to do.

When the sound of a car horn brought him out of his reverie, Cord glanced up, only to see Keegan getting out of his truck and jogging up to the driver's side door. He took a deep breath and stepped out onto the pavement.

She was a little breathless like she'd just run a mile. Her hair, all that red gold glistened in the sun. She had it braided down her back and the long tail hanging down bounced whenever her head moved. He hadn't seen her in two days and yet he wanted to nibble down her neck and devour her.

He banked his lust, remembering why he'd made the trip in the first place and why he had no business nurturing the idea they could ever be together.

"Hey, what are you doing in town? Wally's done with my truck. You get yours back. I was just about to call you and head out to the farm, drop it off. How'd your second visit with Dr. Pontadera go?"

He breathed in her scent, which was a mistake. He would've been better off had he not. And then he blurted it out before he lost his nerve. "I need to talk to you."

She didn't like the sound of that. Plus, he seemed edgy. "Okay. Let's take it inside the compound."

He followed her through the gate and continued on through the grounds to her little house, away from the prying eyes of her staff.

She was about to head up the steps to the porch when he grabbed her hand. "I think it's better if we stay out here." The minute she stopped her progress, he dropped her hand as if it hurt to touch her skin.

Now Keegan was sure something was wrong and asked, "What's this about, Cord?"

He shuffled his big feet. "I can't do this."

She swallowed hard. "Do what?" She was very much

afraid she knew.

"I'm not ready."

"Okay. Then we'll slow it down." If it got any slower they'd need a respirator.

"No. I— That won't work either. I need to make sure you understand. I'm in this bad place right now and I...I don't want it rubbing off on you. You deserve better. I'm not ready for a relationship. Everyone keeps telling me that and today it finally occurred to me how right they are."

As he droned on and on about how the two of them were never going to work together as a couple because of his situation, she watched his eyes. Those dark eyes pierced her heart. And then she realized all that stuff coming out of his mouth didn't seem to be heartfelt or said with any sort of conviction.

His mouth was moving but the words didn't reach his eyes.

Without considering the consequences, she reached out, grabbed him by the shirt. "You want to walk away? Fine. But know this, you better move those big-ass feet of yours right now or otherwise— I want you Cord Bennett! Inside! Now!"

Cord stepped into her space, nipped her around her waist, lifted her off her feet and up into his arms. He made his way up the steps until he got to the barrier of the door where, one-handed, he all but kicked in the wood.

They moved into the living room, their bodies joined in pure heat. Hungry mouths ate at each other, ravaged.

They began to tug at each other's clothes. She inched up his T-shirt. He reared up, yanked it off himself.

She moved over him to unsnap his jeans—slid down to the floor—bringing him with her.

But he stilled her hand. "Not yet. It's been too long for me. Let's get you there first because I guarantee it won't take long for me."

So they rolled. Hands groped. Fingers took turns finding curves, hard muscle, and degrees of soft flesh.

She ran her hands along powerful shoulders, lean abs and down across the scars on his chest. At her touch, Keegan heard him suck in a breath. But she only smiled at the ugly ridges and leaned in to spread kisses along the jagged edges.

But when it got too much, he switched their positions and took the time to break contact long enough to help her wriggle out of her jeans. She jerked her sweater up. He tugged it off—threw it against the wall.

Her lace panties became airborne.

Their mouths fused together like molten metal. Immediate, adept fingers flicked the front clasp of her bra, toyed with a breast. He took a peak into his mouth, suckled. His tongue slicked warm and wet over the other.

All that creamy flesh made him want to savor each bite until he put his lips to better use and skimmed down skin already slippery damp.

He sampled belly and then nibbled thigh.

A thin slice of ginger-colored hair drew him inward. Wild hunger drove him to taste all of her. He put his tongue to work, back and forth, in and out.

And when she moaned his name triumph soared through him like the sweetest concert he'd ever heard. Their eyes locked. He watched desire build in layers until she fractured into ripples of blue crashing waves.

Then his fingers spanned the searing heat. He noted desire blossoming again in her eyes, the way it turned them a deeper sapphire before glazing over, completely doused in pleasure.

Once more they rolled.

This time she came out on top. She covered his mouth. Once more he felt her body yield to his. It still awed him he could do that to her.

She leaned over him, glided her tongue along his neck, over the tattoos on his arms, his once-wounded chest, and the rippled muscle of his belly. When she reached the waist of his jeans, she finally worked down the zipper. Cord lifted his hips and watched as she slid off his pants, then boxers.

The minute both went flying through the air, she straddled him. A nibble and bite along his torso had him groaning in urgent need. She brought him into her, slick and hot. They rocked, bucked. And with that, he grabbed her hips, doubled his effort and took them both into the blissful curl of release.

Loose and lithe she whooshed out, "I'll move in a minute as soon as I find an ounce of strength."

When she collapsed on top of him, he confessed, "I can't feel my legs."

"The floor has to be hard."

He busted out laughing. "Oh, baby, I guarantee you it isn't the floor. You drained me. Wow!"

She started to move but he held her in place. "Not yet." He nuzzled her neck then let that curtain of copper hair drape across his chest. "I want to stay like this a minute more."

"Why? So you can break up with me?" Her eyes danced with a generous mix of amusement tinged with a hint of resentment beginning to take shape. "Told you I'd be the one to get you into bed."

"Hmm, I must've missed the bed part. No. That thing earlier—I do need to talk to you—later. Right this minute I want to say thank you."

"What?" Her head popped up and she realized he wasn't joking. "You want to thank me? You asshole—"

When she started to move, he held her in place, calmly rubbed her back. "Just listen to me for one second, will you? Because of you, this bad place I've been in for so long has lifted."

She immediately softened. "Really? You think so? For real? You feel better about things?"

"Yeah, I'm coming back to myself—I feel better

because of you, Keegan. Not because of pills or talking to a shrink either." He stroked her hair, placed a kiss on her forehead. "You made me want to live, really live, not just exist, not just take up space somewhere, but live."

For a few moments, she couldn't speak. She ran her hand down his cheek and told him, "And you made me a better person."

That's the last thing he expected her to say. "Me? How so?"

"You made me see what I want."

"What do you want?"

"You—in my bed."

Later, they were still bundled together between the sheets when Cord glanced down at Keegan's left shoulder and noticed the dainty little splat of color there. No more than three inches long, it decorated her skin in bright red and blue-green. He ran his index finger over the outline. "What do we have here?"

"Oh, that. I call her Ariel."

"You didn't tell me you were such a badass. It's a mermaid. The first time I saw you, I thought you looked like one."

She leaned over his chest. "It's the red hair."

"Mmm, I love having my hands in all this." To prove it, he combed his fingers through the locks.

But then she abruptly sat up like she'd just thought of something, breaking the moment. "Okay. Spill. What was bothering you when you first got here? Whatever it was, it put you in that dark place again even briefly, didn't it?"

He told her about Robby Mack.

"He's out? But…how can that be? He killed six people," she reasoned, tossing him a look of pure horror at the knowledge.

"The state of Virginia labeled him crazy because of

several psych evaluations. As a result, he got a pass to some place called Camp Sandhurst. I didn't want you on his radar."

"Ah. I see. I mean so little to you that giving me up isn't a problem. You can do it, just like that." She snapped her fingers.

Suddenly, he reversed their positions, covering her body with his. "That's not true. I'm trying to keep him away from you."

"See, you're doing it again. It isn't up to you to protect me, Cord. That's Ethan's job. Besides, don't you think that's for me to decide? You don't even know he's headed here. He could be anywhere."

Okay, so maybe Ethan had recognized her stubborn streak long before he had. Right now though, this minute, the last thing he wanted was to bring Robby into the picture or to think about Ethan and Scott's warning.

Instead, he twirled a lock of her hair between his lean fingers. "That isn't all. A guy showed up this afternoon out at the farm claiming to be my father."

"What?" When she realized he was serious, she tossed back her head and howled with laughter.

"You're taking this a helluva lot better than I did."

"Oh, Cord, when you have issues, you don't mess around. Do you ever do anything half-assed?"

That had him chuckling. "Come to think of it, I guess I don't."

He stayed for supper. They ate vegetable tacos laden with red and green peppers, avocado, cilantro, and plenty of lettuce and tomato.

As he chomped into one, he wanted to know, "How do you make these things so tasty?"

"It's a Fanning state secret."

"You really grew up eating nothing but vegetables?

Come on, in your rebellious teen years, didn't you ever sneak a hamburger? Ever eat a tuna sandwich?"

She tossed him a grin and shook her head. "It isn't that unbelievable. My grandparents worked around fish all the time. I didn't look at it as food for humans. I guess they made a conscious choice and I followed. I always thought it was odd though that granddad's best friend was a fisherman who made his living netting fish."

"I wished I could've gotten to know him, your grandmother, too."

"They'd have both loved you."

"Why do you say that?"

"Because you show such a keen interest in the wildlife. Hey, after we eat, what do you say we go release Haggerty back into Smuggler's Bay?"

His eyebrows rose in surprise. "It isn't too soon?"

"Not at all."

"Haggerty's able to eat?"

"Oh, yeah. In fact, the sooner we get him back where he belongs, the sooner he'll forget his ordeal and go right back to swimming for Monterey Bay and chowing down on jellyfish."

"Okay, then let's do it." He pushed back from the table, stood up. "I gotta see Haggerty in action."

Russ and Pete helped them muscle the reptile onto a plastic tarp they used as a bottom before wrapping him up in the netted sling for transport to the truck. It took all four of them to load the net into the flatbed of the pickup.

Cord got comfortable behind the wheel while Keegan settled in beside him. They started off down the street toward the bay, bringing Haggerty closer toward his freedom.

Once they drove to the wharf, they still had to get Haggerty out of the bed of the truck and down to the sand. For that, the four of them got the turtle into a square tub. Dragging the container wasn't an option. So Keegan and Cord took one end, Russ and Pete the other. And together they carried the bin the rest of the way.

They plodded through the sand, until they got to the water's edge.

It was nearing sunset, in Keegan's mind, a perfect time to release.

They set down the tub, struggled to lift up Haggerty out of the container, and then placed him on the beach where he immediately waddled the distance to what was left of the damp shoreline, probably no more than three feet.

Cord grabbed his camera phone and hit video. "Who says turtles are slow? Look at him go! What an awesome sight!"

Flippers pushed Haggerty forward until he reached the water. Once he hit the surf though, he began to drift into the tides. It didn't take long before he was far enough out to paddle. Soon, he picked up speed and that's when Haggerty took off for real, swimming for all it was worth.

All four of them watched as Haggerty disappeared into the waters of Smuggler's Bay, never even coming up for air.

Pete and Russ exchanged looks but it was Pete who stated, "Bet that big boy is in Monterey by tomorrow night." He slapped Russ on the back and nodded his head toward Cord. "Want me to take your truck back to the center?"

For an answer, Cord dug in his pocket. "Sure. We'll walk back." He tossed the keys to Pete who caught them in the air.

"Well, I gotta go clean up and go see Betty. She's holding supper for me." When Russ continued to stand there looking out at the bay, Pete took him by the arm. "You've still got pens to clean."

"What's the rush? Look at that sunset!"

But Pete shook his head and whispered, "You ever heard of being a third wheel, Russell?"

"Sure I have but—" Finally getting the hint, Russ grinned. "Uh, see you guys later. Don't do anything I wouldn't do."

Keegan waved them off and plopped down where she

stood. Cord though kept a watchful eye on the tides for another couple of minutes until finally he realized Haggerty was gone and dropped down beside her.

"My first release," Cord puffed out. "Is it always this exhilarating? I'm not sure what I expected. It's kind of sad, but then joyous at the same time that we did something that made him all better so he could live."

Keegan simply smiled at his enthusiasm. The man had a way of putting things that made her heart zing. He probably didn't even see the parallel between Haggerty and himself. They'd both been given major second chances.

"Yes, there's always that little twinge of sadness to have to say so long, but right there with it is the moment you know you did something right to get them here. I remember my first."

"Tell me."

"I must've been no more than six when granddad and gran released a sea otter I'd grown fond of, right here on this very beach. That day I watched Ariel wiggle out to sea and was too young to know the joy she must've felt at getting back into the water."

"Ariel? I'm seeing a pattern here."

"I was six. I'd made my grandparents sit through *The Little Mermaid* at least a dozen times before the sea otter ever came to the center. The night they released her, I cried my eyes out until they both explained to me that Ariel needed to go home, back to her family in order to be happy."

She turned to meet his eyes. "How did you do it, Cord?"

"Do what?"

"How did you go through so much of your life all alone? At such an early age, too?"

"I had no choice, Keegan. No one bothers to ask a kid if they want to get dumped into the system and grow up in all these different homes."

She laid a hand on his cheek. "But if this Gabe Bennett

is telling the truth, if he's your father, whether or not you accept him as such, that's a choice."

"It's a little too late for—"

"Don't say that. It's not. It's never too late. Don't close yourself off from family when it's offered, Cord. That would be incredibly immature. And you are many things but immature isn't one of them. Impulsive, yes, but—" She stopped when she realized how she sounded. "I'm sorry. I didn't mean it to sound preachy."

He planted his hands in the sand and leaned back on them for support, finished watching the sun dip into the water. "Yeah, but the guy could be the world's biggest liar. What if—"

"That's why we'll check out his story." She let the subject drop then because he seemed a little blue about it. They sat there on the beach, both pensive, enjoying the sun setting into a glimmering sheen of ocean while the tides danced in and out around them.

All at once, he pulled her to him, ran his long fingers through the braid she'd so painstakingly worked on not an hour earlier when they'd finally decided to crawl out of bed for food. He raked the tresses so they loosened and draped around her shoulders. "God, I love having my hands in your hair."

"Show me again."

And when they got back to the house, he did.

Cord spent the night.

And the next morning after breakfast, they finally made their way over to the Cody house.

In the living room they went over Gabe Bennett's story with both Hayden and Ethan to get their take.

"It's easy enough to check," Ethan reasoned.

"But why would the guy bother to come all the way to Pelican Pointe with a made-up story like this one? What would he have to gain?" Hayden wanted to know.

"And how'd he know Cord's date of birth and the birthmark thing along with all that other stuff if he isn't the real deal?" Keegan pointed out. "I mean who would make up that part about prison and murder."

Her gaze shifted to Cord. "Maybe that's the reason you were never adopted. No one wanted to take a chance on offspring that had a murderer for a father. Think about it. That had to be a stigma the boy could never shake. Gabe wasn't cleared until a decade ago."

"Sounds like something people might use to factor into their decision when looking at the boy they select for adoption," Hayden agreed.

"It makes sense. The child's history, his background, would definitely come into play if people looked into it, especially if they were considering making him a permanent member of their family. You have to admit there's an element of authenticity to Gabe's story," Keegan proffered. "He knew personal deets no one else would. I didn't even know about the birthmark on his back until—" She caught herself and smiled. "Well, until very recently."

Cord grinned and picked up her hand, gave it a kiss.

"The birthmark does look a lot like the state of California. The man got that right," Keegan said, her lips curving widely in Cord's direction.

"You're kidding? Uh, could I see that?" Hayden asked.

But Ethan rolled his eyes and stated, "Could we focus here? That too, is easy enough to come by. You ever been in an online chat room, Cord? You ever get wound up, and reveal personal details like that about yourself to a total stranger? Say, on a dating site of any kind?"

"Not that I remember. And I haven't dated in a really long time, until now."

"Still, it could be some kind of Internet scam. Happens all the time. People unload personal info in cyberspace like it was the safest thing in the world."

While Ethan ticked off every online con he knew about,

Keegan studied the funny look on Cord's face. "What are you not telling us, Cord?"

He met her eyes. How did she always seem to pick up on little nuggets everyone else missed?

"He looked like me."

"What? How so?"

"Same build. Same eyes. Same hair coloring but graying at the temples."

"Well, that is interesting." And something he'd left out entirely—until now. "Ethan, how soon will you be able to check this guy out?"

"I can do a criminal background check on him in five minutes."

"Then let's do it," Cord suggested. "After all this time, I need to know."

And it was a long fifteen minutes later before Cord had his answers.

Chapter Seventeen

Cord decided a trip to Fresno made the most sense. After the way he had practically thrown the guy off the property it was the least he could do. He needed to meet the man again and it had to be face-to-face, man-to-man.

Keegan had agreed to go with him, mainly because he didn't want to do this alone. He'd done enough in his life by himself. He wanted, no, he *needed* her there with him for what might prove to be a heart-wrenching process.

They spent the trip talking about the circumstances that had brought Cord roundabout to Pelican Pointe and how his father had been a mere three hours away the entire time.

"What are the odds of that, Cord? I mean, six months ago you'd never even heard of our little town, didn't even plan on coming back to California at all to live. And now—"

"And now I'm on the way to talk to the father I'd given up on two decades earlier. Since I was ten years old, I figured no one wanted me. Now I know why. Those families probably looked at me and said, 'no way am I taking a chance on a kid whose father murdered his wife.'"

Keegan nodded. "It's not fair to the child, but then, that's how people think."

"Turns out, this guy spent a decade looking for me. Wonder why the Captain never mentioned that?"

She studied him as he focused on the traffic. "The Captain? You're saying you think Scott Phillips should've somehow mentioned this to you during one of your many talks? Why?"

"Don't look at me like that. I told you he spends a lot

of his time these days out at the farm. Yesterday afternoon he tells me he's certain Robby Mack is headed out west."

Keegan puffed out a breath. "Was that the definitive thing that made you come into town to break up with me? Scott scaring you into thinking this guy is on his way to get you?"

"No, I'd already decided it was the right thing to do."

"Says you."

"To keep you out of harm's way, I'll do anything."

She decided to drop that line of conversation since it would more than likely lead to more tension they didn't need at the moment. Instead, she elected to go with a lighter tone. "Maybe I should take the time to research more about hauntings, find out why Scott's here bugging you and doesn't seem to want to move on or something. Maybe we could see what Wade Hawkins has to say, maybe even mention it to Ethan."

"Why? That's all I need is for the entire town to think the nutcase is making up ghost stories along with everything else."

"That's where you're wrong. Other people have seen him, too. Sometimes when I go into the Diner, there is a group sitting there in the booth talking about it—him."

He picked up her hand and placed a kiss on the palm. "I haven't told you thanks for coming with me."

"How could I not? Even though to tell you the truth I feel a little like a third wheel. But I figure if you were a girlfriend in the same situation who asked me for a little support when meeting the father she didn't know, I'd be right there anyway."

"Okay. I guess there must be logic in that statement— somewhere." His eyes twinkled in mock delight. "I'm just glad you said yes."

"Well, they say the world is a small place. I figure you leave Leesburg and end up getting into a fight in Houston, which caused you to get locked up. That incident prompts your friends to come get you and haul you back here to a town where you really don't want to be. Why here?"

"Yeah, because it just as easily could've been San Jose. That's where Ben Latham lives, another buddy from the Guard."

"You have to admit, it's odd."

"Odd? I should be so lucky. My life just keeps sliding along the path to *Ripley's Believe it or Not*."

Forty-five minutes later they pulled into Fresno. Cord hit the GPS and put in the address Gabe Bennett had written down on the piece of paper. Another twenty minutes and they were headed down a street in the old section of town.

Gabe Bennett lived in a two-bedroom, postage-stamp-sized house with a slab foundation nestled among tall elms and sycamores dotting an old residential street with manicured lawns.

Cord pulled into the driveway behind a Dodge pickup parked in front of a carport and stared at the nine-hundred-square-foot house.

"I know you're nervous, but it'll be okay. You already know he looked you up because he wants contact so there's no second guessing that part of it."

Before he could answer that, the front door flew open and Gabe Bennett stepped out onto the speck of a porch. He waved a big hand and motioned them out of the truck.

"Here goes nothing," Cord mumbled as he scrambled out of the pickup.

This time, Cord was the first one to extend his hand. "I guess I owe you an apology," he said as the other man pulled him closer into an embrace.

"I don't blame you, not really. It's an unbelievable story on all counts. But you checked it out, or you wouldn't have called, wouldn't be here." He turned to focus on the tall redhead. "And who is this?"

"This is Keegan Fanning."

"It's nice to meet you, Mr. Bennett."

After the two shook hands, Gabe said, "Well, come on inside, no point in giving my neighbors more of an eyeful than they deserve."

As soon as they got settled on a well-worn sofa in the small living room, Gabe disappeared into the kitchen. They heard dishes clattering before he returned with a tray that held a pot of coffee and sandwiches.

"I couldn't eat a thing," Cord told him. "I'm a little nervous."

"So am I. But I thought you might be hungry after the trip." The older man wiped his palms on his jeans. "You must have a ton of questions. There's something I want you to see."

Gabe walked over to a cabinet, brought out an old photo album with a red-and-gold cloth binding. "Of course, I lost everything after they arrested me. Most of what belongings were worth keeping ended up with Tammy's sister, Tara Dover. About a year after I got out, after they cleared me of the murder, Tara got in touch, sent me one of those emails. Told me she was sorry she'd thought all this time I'd done it. She felt so bad she sent me a few things that were Tammy's. This photo album was one of them."

Cord sucked in a breath and took the book he handed off.

"Isn't much, I know. Couldn't be more than thirty-five pictures in there at most, all of which were taken by two teenagers in love. But it's worth a look because it's all I have left of her—and you. It was all I had until now."

With sudden clumsy fingers, Cord lifted the heavy cover. For the first time in his life his eyes landed on a photo of his mother. A very young blonde, wearing her jean shorts and white blouse, smiled for the camera as if she didn't have a care in the world.

"Wow, she was beautiful."

"Oh, she was that. I took that picture the day she turned sixteen. We'd gone over to Coronado for the day. Had us a picnic, went swimming, made love, probably made you that day, if truth be known."

In spite of his thirty-four years, Cord's hand flew to his lips and his eyes grew moist. He tried to blink away the tears by pressing his lips together until they turned white. He desperately fought to control his emotions.

Keegan reached over and laid her hand on top of his. "Why don't you sit down, Mr. Bennett and tell us more about Cord's mother?"

"Sure. If you'll stop calling me Mr. Bennett, I'll tell you a whole slew of stories."

But just then, Cord abruptly stood up, excused himself to go to the bathroom.

When he was out of the room, Gabe took the opportunity to pry a bit and asked, "You care about him?"

"Of course I do, I wouldn't be here if I didn't."

"Why isn't he happy?"

"He's had a difficult time lately."

"How so?"

"You should ask him yourself. It isn't my story to tell, but his."

"Okay. Then look out for him, will you?"

She thought she should explain how new their relationship was. "Mr. Bennett, we're just getting started." But looking into his eyes so much like Cord's she decided the lines on his face showed genuine fatherly concern for his son. So Keegan added, "I'll do my best."

The minute Cord came back in and sat down, Gabe took that to mean he should pick up where he had left off.

"You should know, Cord, Tammy wasn't just pretty— and tall—tallest girl in our sophomore class—that girl could've easily been a model. Tammy was the sweetest person I ever knew. She had a way about her, loved animals and you, Cord. She loved you, loved being your mother. She might've been young but she had a powerful amount of love stored up for you. She used to sing this song to you, what was it called back then? Ah, I remember now, *You Light up My Life*."

Gabe chuckled. "Sappiest damn song if there ever was one. But your mother loved it. She'd sing it to you and dance around the room with you on her hip."

As Gabe began to reminisce about other things, other

times, the awkwardness of the moment, slipped away.

Cord and Keegan stayed for supper and took the sandwiches Gabe had fixed outside in the backyard to the picnic table.

When Cord saw Keegan pick off the ham from between the pieces of bread, he smiled and told Gabe, "You ever met a vegetarian, a person who never lets meat pass their lips?"

"I've heard of them. Can't say I ever met one though." Gabe's eyes twinkled just as Cord's did in pseudo scorn.

Cord grinned. "Keegan is one. That's why she's taking off the ham and leaving nothing but the cheese and bread. She doesn't eat red meat."

"At all? Well I'll be damned," Gabe said in continued amusement.

"At all. I'm thinking she has the right idea." And with that, Cord picked the meat off his sandwich, as well and took a huge bite. "Mmm, turns out, I love cheese sandwiches."

"Your son is not a vegetarian. In fact—" Keegan started to explain.

"But I'm rethinking that whole red meat from animals thing," Cord admitted and winked in Keegan's direction.

During the meal, Cord listened to his father as he went on and on about Tammy Lynn Bennett, who three weeks shy of her seventeenth birthday, had died at the hands of a man named Carl Manning.

"And he's in jail, right?" Cord asked.

Gabe nodded. "Locked up in San Quentin, same place I spent twenty-four years."

"An innocent man," Cord finished. He looked over into eyes so like his own. "What is it you do for a living?"

"Well, now, I sued those people in San Diego that wrongly had me locked up. They settled with me for a sizeable chunk of money. I took it and started a contracting company. I help put up office buildings around town."

"And you're alone now?"

Gabe shook his head. "Met a woman sometime back.

Her name's Polly. She's got me over quite a few rough spots. We don't live together though. Look, I'll never forget your mother, Cord. She was the first woman I ever loved. And then, I had you. There was a time I didn't think I'd ever find you."

"What do I call you?"

"Whatever you want?"

Cord scratched his ear. "Never had a father before. I might try dad at some point. But—the word sounds foreign."

"Then for now, Gabe will work just fine."

Outside Cheyenne, Wyoming, John Gold's blue Mustang got caught speeding by a highway patrol officer named J.T. McDaniel. John Gold kept his cool as he handed off his fake driver's license and waited while the cop ran the plates through his computer.

John Gold had no doubt this was a test. That's why he fought the urge to start the car and hit the gas. He could take off, but the new ID had to pass scrutiny at some point. He knew he should've bought a gun at the same time he'd purchased the new car. He'd remedy that little mistake first chance he got.

Gold kept a watchful eye in his rearview mirror for any indication the gig was up. But when the officer came walking back to the car without having drawn his weapon and handed him back his license along with a ticket to sign, he knew the ID had been well worth the five grand he'd paid for it.

As he calmly added his John Gold signature to the paper without a fuss, he grinned to himself, listening to the cop politely tell him how to pay the fine. The minute the guy slid back inside his cruiser, John Gold turned the key, put the car in gear and took off continuing to head west along I-80, making sure this time he kept the sports car at a legal seventy-five miles per hour.

Chapter Eighteen

A spring storm threatened to mar the annual spring Pelican Pointe Street Fair, a three-day event sandwiched between Christmas and Memorial weekend and always scheduled for the third week of March over a Friday, Saturday and Sunday.

They had already cordoned off one end of Main to the other and detoured traffic around to Ocean Street. Workers were even now slaving away to make sure the booths were ready to go by morning.

Even though the fair created traffic congestion in a town with less than three thousand people, it also brought in much-needed cash from the surrounding towns without waiting for the start of the summer tourist season to begin.

A parade on Friday morning, complete with area high school marching bands and homemade floats, would kick off the whole thing.

Old and new RVs and truck trailers towing carnival rides and portable booths for food vendors began showing up as early as last Sunday as they fought for space along Ocean Street. It was the one time of the year parking became a major headache.

At the rescue center, Keegan and Pete had already spent a busy Thursday morning tacking up No Parking signs and stretching rope from the front gate to the main hospital building reminding visitors that they'd have to find someplace else to leave their vehicles.

Their own open house was less than twenty-four hours away. Keegan had spent a week working up handouts describing each of the animals they had in residence, specifically Minnie and Bumper and Jack and Dodger. But the flyers also covered general information on sea otters, sea lions, harbor seals and California brown pelicans.

The kids could get their pictures taken with the various mammals. Sign up to adopt a marine animal. Play with a miniature aquatic replica, built by local carpenter, Troy Dayton. Receive a coloring book printed courtesy of Murphy's Market featuring marine mammals. And thanks to other local businesses, register to enter for prizes. Up for grabs were things like key chains, books about mammals and bookmarks bearing the Fanning Marine Rescue Center logo.

All in all, it was ramping up to be a demanding three days. She'd have to remember to give Wally a huge hug for coming up with this idea.

Good thing Keegan had a full staff onboard. Pete, Russ, Abby, and Tina had two new raw recruits. They'd drafted Connor Davis and Jason Broderick to be their gofers. The boys had turned out to be as eager as Hayden had described.

Several blocks over, vendors went about setting up tents and booths despite thunder booming overhead.

In spite of overcast skies and the chance of rain, Keegan opted to forego pulling her truck out of the compound and instead started to head over to the Diner on foot. She hoped if it did decide to open up and pour, the bad weather wouldn't hang around for longer than twenty-four hours.

Her staff had put their hearts and souls into making this event a success. They'd been briefed on the right way to bring up donations into their assigned tours. They'd spent hours training to handle the mammals in front of a packed house. In other words, they'd worked their asses off. At this point she could only put her faith in her team and the generosity of strangers.

She was about to step off the curb at Main and cross the street when she spotted a familiar man zigzagging his way through the vendor tents. He lifted his face up to the storm clouds as if to study every movement, every rumble.

Keegan's heart did a double beat as he turned, spotted her and raised his hand in a neighborly wave. Before she could get her mouth to work, she watched the man vanish into thin air.

She swallowed her shock.

Scott Phillips. She'd seen with her own eyes, Scott Phillips, as he took a stroll along Main Street. Scott Phillips, the solider who had died in Iraq two years earlier.

She turned around and dashed back to the center to get her truck.

At the same time Keegan tried to overcome her shock, Harold Boedecker and his son, Drake, bobbed on the lip of Smuggler's Bay in Harold's twenty-foot fishing boat, *Orion's Song* under overcast skies, hoping to catch enough striped bass for their supper.

On the south side of the bay, the craggy shoreline gave way to patchy stretches of beach dotted with scrub brush and low hanging juniper. Drake squinted into the distance, watched the rise and fall of the tides and commented, "Dad, do you see that? Over there. What is that hung up in that low-hanging cluster of cypress?"

Harold narrowed his eyes. "Can't make it out from here. Eyes aren't what they used to be. Let me grab my field glasses." He reached in his bag, dug out the binoculars, held them up, and adjusted the focus where he could see what his son had spotted.

"Shit. Start the motor!"

"Why? What do you think it is?"

"That's a floater for sure."

"No way. Let me see the glasses."

Harold handed them off to his son and shifted to pull the cord on the motor himself. "We need to get closer. If it's a body—"

"But there's no one in town missing. Gotta be a

tourist," Drake reasoned, eyeballing the ballooned form hung up in the cypress trees, rising and falling in the white caps.

While Harold steered them through the choppy waves, he began taking a mental inventory. There were only two people in town unaccounted for and had been for several months back. After stealing in excess of half a million dollars from the bank, Kent Springer and Sissy Carr had snuck off six months earlier in the dead of night. Police choppers had searched up and down the coast for three straight days looking for any sign of Kent's boat, *East Money*. They hadn't turned up a single thing.

Closing the distance, Harold decided that from the looks of the bloated body, it appeared to be unmistakably female. At least the bleached, blonde hair on her head indicated that much.

But eyeing the corpse, Harold said to his son, "Drake, there ain't much left here. But I think we might've just found Sissy Carr." Harold scratched his scruffy chin. "Even if it ain't her, Ethan's gonna have himself a shitload of paperwork."

Drake drew his phone from his pocket, held it skyward as fat drops of rain began to fall. "Getting a weak signal on my cell."

"Good. Let's call her in."

And with that, Drake punched in Ethan's number.

Cord had several issues to deal with at the farm, issues he couldn't avoid before he headed to Keegan's for the night. While he straightened out a problem with a supplier via email, the image of Keegan, and what they had done to each other the night before, popped into his head.

Lately, he didn't seem to be able to go an hour without thinking about her. He didn't doubt for a minute they were moving faster than Jeff Gordon in a race to capture the checkered flag at Daytona. But they weren't hurting anyone. He needed her. And she needed him. It was as simple as that.

As he listened to the rain beat down on the barn roof— he hadn't understood what a dark place he'd been in—not until escaping it. He certainly hadn't known just how close he had ventured to the edge without ever coming back. That is, until he'd met Keegan. She made him want to keep that light glowing inside he'd thought was gone forever and never lose it again.

He took care of other work, checked on delivery schedules, made sure orders were updated. The calendar on his desk reminded him he hadn't had a drop of alcohol in three weeks.

He hadn't missed an AA meeting or a trip to see the shrink. He'd gone three for three each Sunday afternoon and six for six every Monday and Thursday to hash out his past with Dr. Pontadera. He'd kept every appointment and his promise to the judge. He'd been on his new medication now for two weeks without any horrible side effects, no headaches, no nervousness, and no drop in libido.

He had to admit the sex couldn't get any better. And how in the world had he gone a year and half without it? An earlier visit to a grief counselor would've probably been the ticket. It was his bad luck he'd passed that up. Instead he'd opted to waste a lot of valuable time he'd never get back, time he'd spent picking fights with anyone willing to slug it out, and generally feeling sorry about his situation.

Having Keegan in his life was nothing short of a miracle.

When he heard a car drive into the common area outside the barn, he went on immediate alert. He picked up the pitchfork from beside the door and peeked outside.

To his surprise he saw Keegan make a run for the porch in the rain. He called out to her so she'd know he was in the barn instead.

"Hey, what're you doing here?" he yelled.

She wheeled on her heels with Guinness in tow and he could tell even from this distance she was upset. When she started running toward him, he dropped the makeshift weapon and took off.

She all but collapsed in his arms. The dog circled them twice and then loped off for the shelter of the porch.

"What's wrong, Keegan? Did you see Robby Mack?" He noted the look of distress on her face and shook her shoulders a little to get her to answer him.

"What? No. I...I saw Scott," she announced. Out of breath, she related what she'd seen.

"Is that all? You scared the life out of me. I told you about Scott. What's the big deal?"

"Well, excuse me. But the first time you see a man who's been dead two years standing right there in the middle of the street around other people calmly going about their work, you get a little unnerved."

"I see that."

"Cord, he was twenty feet in front of me looking up at the sky, watching the storm move in just like a regular person might, the joy on his face spoke volumes."

It was the snicker she heard that had her punching his arm.

"Ow! What was that for?"

"You laughed at me."

He stifled a chuckle. "Who me? I thought something terrible had happened. You looked like you'd seen a ghost. Oh, wait." He did laugh then. He threw back his head with a howl of laughter, and it bellowed upward into the storm.

Then his head whipped around and their eyes met, he wound her wet hair around his fingers and said, "Don't you have an umbrella? This rain's freezing cold." He ran his hands up and down her arms in a weak attempt to warm her up. "You look so beautiful wet though." He started to spread kisses along her face, licking at some of the drops. "You're shivering."

But in spite of the downpour and the cold they didn't

move from that spot as they stood wrapped up in each other. She whispered his name and the husky sound did him in.

"We better get you out of your wet clothes."

"And you. You aren't even wearing a jacket."

"It's not that cold." He was burning up for her. Together they slogged up to the house.

Guinness greeted them with a bark and a wag of his tail as he eagerly waited to get inside.

Once in the living room, Cord went over to the fireplace, started stacking logs for a fire.

But when he turned around Keegan was already shedding her clothes.

He watched as she pulled up her sweater, shimmied out of her wet, black leggings. By the time she got down to panties and bra, he dragged her against him. "Hot shower. Now."

She undressed him on the way down the hallway, and sticky wet, they both bumped up the water to hot. While they waited for the spray to heat, they created their own steam, skin-to-skin.

Once they stepped into the narrow stall, foreplay had reached the frenzy stage. Here, fingertips soaped, slick and fast, while hands traveled up and down over curves and valleys. Impatient for each other, he backed her up against the tile and drove himself inside.

Glorious color framed her senses. Keegan dropped her head back and rode the crest, full out and hard.

Cord quickened his pace, drove them both until they shattered together in golden circles of light.

She ran a hand down his face. The minute she could speak, she told him, "That just keeps getting better and better…every time."

He grinned. "I'm making it my personal mission to make up for lost time."

Later in the kitchen, wearing one of his oversized T-shirts and a pair of sweat pants, she rolled out her own dough for spinach, tomato and cheese pizza.

When he didn't grumble too much at the prospect of eating a vegetarian pie for dinner, she knew they were progressing into a comfort zone of sorts on both sides.

"I won't hold you to putting your meat-eating days behind you."

"I meant what I said at Gabe's. I'm beginning to see the advantages."

"For real? Most people don't."

He cocked his head. "Haven't we had this conversation before? I thought we established, I'm not most people."

She sighed. It was true. Cord Bennett had to be the strongest person she'd ever known. What he'd been through as a kid had to be tough, and yet, it seemed to her as though he'd put that early disappointment from life behind him. It was the memory of Cassie he had trouble letting go of.

As Guinness spread out in one corner of the kitchen, as rain continued to beat down outside, Cord gathered up their wet clothes from the living room and stuffed them into the washer.

He couldn't help it. The sense of domestic bliss struck a happy chord with him. Somewhere in the last three weeks, he'd turned a corner.

He glanced over and stared at the woman at the counter, throwing together a meal. Was there anything the woman couldn't do?

"Who's on duty tonight at the center?"

"Pete and Russell. God, I hope they don't kill each other," she groaned, as she removed the piping hot pan from the oven.

"They don't get along?"

"Like oil and water. One's a leftover from the sixties, the other still tries to live the life of Tony Manero in *Saturday Night Fever*."

"Sounds like they have more in common than they know."

"Oh, they do, but it would take nothing short of torture for either one to admit it. How's Pete working out as your sponsor?"

"He's okay. I haven't had to call him so all we do is share a little bit more of our past each Sunday afternoon. Some of it is pretty raw. Why?"

"I guess he shared what happened to his wife?"

"You know about that? Of course, you do. You've known him your whole life."

"Just about."

"I'm not supposed to talk about what's said at the meeting."

"It's okay, you don't have to. I wasn't even living here when it happened. But I've heard Pete talk about it, cry about it, blame himself, sitting right there in my grandparents' kitchen. Apparently, Pete had a terrible drinking problem back then that resulted in him driving drunk one night out on the Coast Highway. He walked away from the accident without scratch. His wife, Cheryl, wasn't that lucky. He was devastated. I guess the six years he spent in jail sobered him up."

"Twenty-two years of sobriety. Do you suppose I'll make it that far?"

She gave him an incredulous stare, anger bubbled at the fringe. "You will if you want to. No one but you can make it happen, Cord."

He went to her then, lifted her chin, met her eyes. "It's a struggle I want to win every day. I don't have an option."

"I know. But some days I don't like seeing you have to fight so hard."

He had to swallow twice before he got his mouth to work and get out what he had to say. "This is a demon I have to take down. If you feel it's too much, if you feel you want to walk away, tell me now. I won't hold it against you." He held his breath and waited for her answer.

"Why? Why are you always so willing to give me up, let me walk away just like that?"

He rested his head on hers. "It's anything but easy. But I don't want to drag you down. I'm no prize."

"Stop saying that!" She shouted. "You're the most amazing person I've ever met."

"Come on—"

"You've been through a lot in your life and you're so strong and sweet." She slumped against him. "I don't want to walk though. I'm no quitter."

"Thank God. It's tough, I know." He rubbed her back. "There's no quick fix. I wish there was."

"I'm not looking for that. I just want to help and I don't know how."

"You said it yourself. It's up to me. Most days, it's just up to me."

That night snuggled up in bed, Keegan woke to a noise coming from somewhere inside the house. Glancing at the clock on the nightstand, the digital alarm clock told her the time was five minutes after two. For several long minutes she lay there not moving, listening. Maybe she'd imagined the noise. After all, this was her first time spending the night in his house, a strange place, a strange bed.

When she heard what sounded like the closing of a door, she jabbed Cord in the ribs and whispered, "Cord, Cord, wake up. I heard something. I think there's someone in the house."

With his eyes still closed, he mumbled, "It's probably nothing, just an old house. Go back to sleep."

"No! Cord, wake up." She shook him harder.

This time the unmistakable sound of a door closing from some other room was more pronounced.

Cord's eyes fluttered open. He bolted upright and in one fluid motion reached for his jeans. Staggering a bit to pull on his pants, he hopped on one foot before groping in the dark for the baseball bat he kept hidden under the bed.

Keegan on the other hand, threw a blanket around her

shoulders and followed him out into the hallway. She wondered why Guinness hadn't so much as barked.

Together they both tip-toed into the living room and tried to avoid making the old floor squeak beneath their bare feet.

Standing in the front room, they both heard what sounded like footsteps on the old porch. Cord went to the window and pulled back the curtain.

Outside the rain had stopped. Drifts of moonlight streaked down in wide swaths from porch to barn. Cord spotted a form in the shadows.

"Stay here," he murmured.

"Not on your life. You go out that door, I go with you. I heard something inside here. Don't even bother telling me I didn't. I'm not staying inside alone."

"Fine. But keep behind me."

Cord flipped the lock on the front door and sighed when it creaked open. They stepped out onto the wooden porch as a unit struggling mightily with the old planks not to tip their hand. Cord gripped the bat tighter as he prepared to move down the steps.

But the old slats groaned in protest and gave away their position.

At the sound, the shadowy form looked back over his shoulder at the house and lifted an arm in greeting. Guinness stood next to Scott, wagging his tail in happy welcome.

"Oh, for chrissakes," Cord said aloud at the same time he loosened his grip on the bat.

"What," Keegan asked bumping into him from behind.

"It's Scott."

She peered around Cord and there, standing in the middle of the yard, was Scott Phillips. "Good grief."

"That's what I said. Ghosts may not need their eight hours, but we do," Cord shouted in furious clipped tones.

Scott stepped out into the moonlight with a huge grin on his face, took a few steps closer, as did the dog.

"Sorry, didn't mean to scare you."

At his approach, she couldn't help it, her mouth dropped open.

"You guys go back to sleep. Don't mind me. I'm just restless tonight."

Cord charged down the steps doing a slow burn only to growl when his bare feet hit the damp, gravel driveway. Hopping around on one foot, chunky bits of rock bored into the soles of his feet, which infuriated him all the more.

He marched right up to where Scott stood, got in his face.

"Goddamn it, you scared the hell out of us! It's one thing to haunt the grounds during the day. It's another to scare the wits out of people when they're trying to sleep."

Like any good apparition, Scott threw his head back and roared with laughter. Then his face sobered and he held up his hands in peace. But that only lasted a couple of seconds before he started guffawing all over again. "Sorry. But…if you could only see the look on both your faces."

Cord ran a hand through his hair in exasperation. "Get out of here. Go haunt someone else for a change!"

"Okay, okay, I'm gone. But no one makes a better sentry than I do. Who better to be on the lookout for Robby Mack?"

That caught Cord off guard. "And I'm the one seeing a psychiatrist?" he muttered as he made his way back to Keegan still standing on the porch a little in awe of the entire exchange.

Chapter Nineteen

"**I** still say we need to talk to an expert," Keegan argued the next morning at breakfast. "Find out why he's still earthbound."

Cord dropped two pieces of bread into the toaster and said, "Listen to you, it wasn't that long ago you thought I was nuts."

She cracked eggs into a bowl and explained, "That was before I actually saw him. Seeing him was different. Has he ever done that before? Come in and out of the house like that, doors opening and closing? That was unsettling."

He gave her a withering stare. "Rattling chains like the ghost of Christmas past you mean? The first night I spent at the B & B he managed to scare the bejeezus out of me. Had me thinking I was back in the drunk tank. Then when I took the job here, that first night, he bugged the hell out of me. I almost packed up."

She dumped the egg mixture into the pan. "Hmm, interesting. Maybe he's focused on you for some reason. Maybe he knew you were in a bad place and wanted to help in some way." She picked up her coffee cup off the counter, took a sip, considered. "When did you say you tried to, uh, when did you…uh, pick up the .22 and it misfired?"

Cord turned to stare at her. "New Year's Day. You think he did something to the gun so it wouldn't fire that day?"

She finished with the eggs and divided them onto two plates. "Can ghosts do that? Do they have the ability to fiddle with a tangible object? I don't know. I'm thinking out loud here. Think about it. Was he around New Year's

Day—the day you tried to—?"

"Kill myself," he finished. "It's okay to say it. According to Dr. Pontadera I have to own it. Twice."

They sat down at the table to eat, both thoughtful. There were a few minutes of silence, of trying to figure it all out before Keegan finally supposed, "Okay, so maybe you get here, he sees how depressed you are, a former buddy in distress, grieving, and he hangs around you for safety reasons, protecting you—"

"From myself."

"I think I'd like to have a talk with Jordan. What exactly is the proper protocol for bringing up a woman's dead husband into a conversation?"

"I don't think you should. She's six months along. Nick will have your head if you upset her."

Keegan sighed. "You're right. Well, it was just an idea." She glanced at the clock. "And I'm running late. In less than an hour I open the gate to what I hope is hordes of people willing to donate to a good cause and keep the center going for another six months."

"Are things that bad?"

"It takes a lot of money to run a rescue center like this. Without the generosity of people who love animals I'm afraid we'll have to close our doors by summer if I can't think of some way to keep donations up."

"I've got some money saved. Nick used to be an investment banker. When we were in the Guard together, he set us all up with investment accounts. Turns out, Nick knew his stuff."

Keegan smiled. "You know something, Cord?"

"What?"

She ran a finger down his face. "I adore you. But I won't take your money, a reasonable donation, absolutely, but anything over one hundred dollars is forbidden. You and Wally have generous hearts."

"Wally? Wally at the service station? You and Wally?" A little spurt of jealousy circled his heart and he did his best to tamp it down.

"Friends since kindergarten. Absolutely. You know, Wally and Lilly are getting married in June, don't you?"

"The cute brunette who works at the station? I didn't know that, but I'm glad to hear it."

"And it was Wally who suggested the open house. I might've thought of it if I hadn't been so down in the dumps lately since losing my grandmother that I haven't been able to think straight."

"Ah. I'm sorry, honey. Go on. Go have a successful open house. I'll get the dishes."

"Are you coming in later?"

"Sure. How can the newcomer afford to miss his first Pelican Pointe parade?"

"But you were here at Christmas. We put on a helluva Christmas parade."

"I don't know what I was thinking but somehow I managed to miss that."

She laughed and kissed his cheek. "Aw, it's just a matter of time before you get used to the ins and outs of small towns. Make sure you make it by ten. I'll save you a front-row seat. Plus, I'll buy you lunch. We're selling bag lunches donated from the Diner."

"Sounds yummy."

"Anything for a buck," Keegan teased as she called to Guinness before dashing out the door, already going over in her head the dozens of things she had to do to kick off the open house.

But when she got to her truck, she automatically scanned the grounds for Scott Phillips. And couldn't help wondering why the man's spirit refused to leave this place or the town.

It wasn't until Keegan got to work that she heard the buzz about how Harold and Drake Boedecker had found what they believed was Sissy Carr's body floating in the bay.

"Wow, where's the body been all this time?" Keegan asked.

"Sounds like maybe ol' Kent and Sissy didn't get along as well as people thought they did. I always said they couldn't last too long without one of them killing the other."

"You seriously think Kent had something to do with killing her?"

"Sissy had a mouth on her. Kent had a temper. Bad combo," Pete stated.

"Does Ethan think Kent did it?"

"Ethan's been tightlipped. But he does want to talk to you when you get a minute."

"Me? Why me?"

"Because he knows you patrol these waters more often than the Coast Guard."

"Luckily, I never stumbled across anything like that. I've seen dead dolphins, a shark or two, even a whale once wash up on shore, but never, ever a dead body. I'm glad it wasn't me that found her."

"There you go. That's all he wants to know."

From that point on, Keegan put Sissy Carr out of her head.

There were last minute things to prep. After going over everything with her staff a second time, Keegan made certain the animals had been fed and treated for their ailments and as ready for visitors as she could get them.

To her amazement, people started lining up at the gate before nine a.m. Parents brought children. Grandparents brought their grandkids. Turns out, teenagers vied for one-on-one, face time with the animals the same way a three-year-old did.

Because of the steady stream of visitors, there was no sitting or standing idly around watching the parade. The staff had to put that off. In fact, all the activity kept every one of them hopping from one end of the compound to the other.

So when Cord arrived, Keegan put him to work.

While she played tour guide, he acted as information director, pointing the way to the observation deck so they could see Minnie and Bumper in action. He also handed out information packets and at one point, he even took turns manning the camera to take pictures of the kids with the mammals.

He found delight in watching each kid's reaction to the playful, animated sea otters, especially when the animals amused themselves with a ball or a rock. Drawn to the antics, the children stared in fascination as Jack, who had a fondness for his little rubber ball, lay on his back and tossed it back and forth in his furry, little mittens.

Three weeks of TLC had the little ball of fur healing nicely and very energetic. Jack would never go back in the wild though. His eye had been injured too severely to know if he could see well enough to forage for food on his own, although everyday Jack got better at learning the basics in that department, too.

And as always, Minnie and Bumper were crowd favorites, especially when mom nestled her baby boy on her tummy. But when she groomed the fur of her three-week-old pup, Cord could tell the kids were pulled in for good.

During a break between tours, Keegan looked up and spotted a very pregnant Jordan Harris pushing her toddler daughter in a stroller down the middle of the compound.

Even though she still wasn't sure how to pursue the line of questioning about her former husband, Keegan headed her way.

"When's the baby due?" Keegan asked cheerfully.

Jordan rubbed a hand over her belly. "June tenth. And before you ask, it's a boy."

"You read my mind."

"Most people want to know. And Nick is so hands-on with everything. I'm pretty sure he sent out an email to half the state of California." She paused to look around at the crowd and commented, "The center is absolutely bursting at the seams today, busier than I've ever seen it."

"It is. I had no idea we'd have such a huge turnout."

"The town wants to support the center, Keegan. Sometimes they have difficulty showing it."

"I'll say one thing, this time they really came through for me. We put this thing together on a shoestring. Wally and Murphy were instrumental in getting prizes out of most of the merchants but it was Wally who was able to pry open Ferguson's wallet. And you know Ferguson. I swear that man is tighter than Scrooge with his money or giving anything away for free."

Jordan smiled. "Go ahead, say it, the man's a major tightwad. He rarely has a sale at the hardware store."

"Are you feeling okay what with the pregnancy and all?" Keegan asked, feeling a little awkward at the question.

"So healthy and happy I'm full of nothing but bliss these days. Two years ago, I was miserable and could only dream my life might turnaround. Now—" Jordan stopped, stared at the younger woman. Keegan wasn't exactly subtle. "What's on your mind? I recognize that look in your eye."

Keegan puffed out a breath at her own uneasiness. "Well, I don't know how to say this, but—twice now I've seen Scott, big as life—last night he was wandering around the farm."

Laughter glistened in Jordan's eyes. "He scared you? That man can be such a pest. Since last fall, I see him around The Cove all the time. He comes and goes. Sometimes guests report seeing him, too, sometimes not."

"You're certainly calm about it."

"Now I am. It's…he's rather obstinate at times. You know there was a time I couldn't see him at all. But Scott was persistent while I was resistant. I guess that sort of sums up our entire relationship when he was alive. Even when we were married we didn't always communicate very well. That's how I ended up here. Don't misunderstand me. I loved Scott with all my heart. But what was a problem for both of us back then were big dreams and not enough conversation about making them a reality. I just wasn't as savvy about picking up on how much Scott really needed to come back to his hometown to raise his family here. Maybe there was some premonition on his part that he didn't have very long to live. But now, he's here for good."

"Why? Why do you suppose he's still hanging around? Shouldn't he want—to get to the other side—or something?"

Jordan narrowed her eyes. "He loves this place, Keegan, the town, the people. He cares for them in a way I never could have predicted. In my opinion, with Scott it's the 'or something.' I don't want him to leave, Keegan. This is his home. Why don't you ask Hayden how he got to her last fall right after she got here?"

"Hayden's seen him, too?" That was a revelation she hadn't seen coming.

"Oh, yeah. According to her, Scott got her through a really rough time last year. They forged a bond."

As Keegan chewed on that the rest of the afternoon, she thought the whole thing with Scott just kept getting weirder by the day.

But the scientist in her, plus a heavy dose of old-fashioned curiosity needed some detailed answers.

Robby Mack Stevens woke late in the afternoon in a seedy motel room in Reno, Nevada, with the hangover from hell and Candy, a hooker leftover from the night before.

He'd somehow gotten sidetracked on his very first visit to Reno. He thought he'd been so clever sidestepping Las Vegas for the smaller arena that claimed to be "The Biggest Little City in the World."

Robby had tested John Gold's luck and gotten pulled

into gaming, which he discovered he wasn't very good at because blackjack had pretty much kicked his ass.

He hadn't had any better luck at craps or for that matter poker or the slot machines.

On the other hand, he'd found cocaine and meth readily available to anyone with the bucks to pay the going rate on the street.

No wonder he'd gone through Terri Lynn's saving accounts in less than three weeks. Because of that, today was the day to exit Dodge. Or in this case get the hell out of Reno, put the city and his experience in his rearview mirror for good. It was past time for him to find this backwater town called Pelican Pointe and take care of Cord Bennett.

But first he had to get rid of Candy. He kicked at her butt a couple of times before she groaned in annoyance.

"What? What time is it?

"Time to get your ass out of my room, that's what. Now!" he hollered when she continued to lie there.

He'd managed to buy an old Saturday night special, a .25 caliber Bryco off Candy's pimp for fifty bucks.

As luck would have it, Robby was armed, motivated and ready for a long, overdue showdown.

Chapter Twenty

March went out like a lamb and gave way to the roar of April showers. Spring storms already assured that the month got a jump on rainfall. As a result the landscape around town came to life, making everything pop with an array of colors. Wildflowers bloomed in major doses of Indian paintbrush, poppies, and purple thistle.

Even the sand dunes seemed to come alive with fresh crops of thriving beach grass. There was still no sign of Robby Mack Stevens.

Cord began to think the guy had headed south, down to Mexico and avoided California altogether.

He stayed busy as he watered down the troughs, dumped grain into the feeders, cleaned the stalls. It was good, sweaty work that kept his mind from worry.

After finishing in the barn, he went to wash up and noticed his cell phone dinged with a new text message and voicemail.

One glance at the digital readout told him it was from Gabe Bennett. The guy had kept his promise to keep in touch. In fact, hearing from him had become a weekly occurrence. It was tough enough getting used to the idea of having a father, let alone one who insisted on keeping him in the loop.

Cord couldn't say he minded though. Hell, on some level it gave him a kick. Here he was in his mid-thirties and he could admit a thrill every time his phone rang and it was Gabe.

What a difference thirty days could make in a man's life.

He had a woman he cared deeply about in his life. For

the first time he had a father, a connection to family, someone who seemed like he genuinely cared for him despite the wasted years of not knowing each other. But with every phone call, every text message from Gabe, father and son seemed to grow just a little closer, a little easier with each other. They'd go over their day, or exchange a work-related incident, even a joke or two.

For the first time in two years, Cord had a steady job, a place to live, a woman in his life, and a future. He had to admit he was happy.

What more could any man want?

At lunch time, Keegan decided it was time to talk to Hayden Cody about Scott. She had several ruses she could use to stop by the shop. For one, Keegan hadn't thanked Hayden for all the children's book donations she had provided that they had given away as door prizes during the open house.

Two, there were any number of books on plants she could pick up under the guise of trying to become a better gardener.

And three, she could pretend to check out all the little knickknacks Hayden had stocked since her last visit.

Even though her budget was tight, it didn't mean she couldn't indulge in an herb-scented candle or two, the ones Hayden had taken to making and selling herself. The woman even had an online store.

Keegan went over all those ploys as she walked along Ocean Street with the smells of the sea at her back, courtesy of the spring breeze drifting in off the water.

When she reached a golden-colored, Spanish-style stucco house with a red-tiled roof, she read the brand-new, hand-painted shingle outside the brightly painted, red front door that read, "Hidden Moon Bay Books."

Lilly's work, Keegan decided. It was nice to see the

people in Pelican Pointe taking care of their own for a change. She knew it hadn't always been that way.

She entered the store to the jingle-jangle of a bell and looked around. The place had undergone a dramatic renovation. No longer the empty shell of a house belonging to Ethan's grandmother, Autumn Lassiter, it was now so much more than the town's first and only bookstore.

In addition to books, the chic little boutique offered homegrown herbs, gift baskets stuffed with homemade soaps, an array of scented candles, and a line of creams and lotions.

The minute Hayden appeared from the back, Keegan exclaimed, "Wow! You've done amazing things with this place in such a short amount of time. This isn't just a bookstore."

"I know," Hayden said with pride. "Once I opened the doors, I couldn't stop ordering things to stock and set around. And I really lucked into finding this wonderful lady in San Sebastian who helped me discover just the right process for making the soaps and candles."

"Ah, I thought you were using Autumn Lassiter's recipes for that."

"I was, but after a couple of months playing with the formula, I wasn't getting the quality I wanted or felt comfortable selling. Shelly and I were able to play around with the ingredients enough to finally come up with a product we could both be proud of and market."

"Is Ethan still writing? Is he still trying to find a publisher?"

Hayden got a moony look on her face. "He is. And one day he'll be a famous mystery writer with a wife who owns her own bookstore."

"What happened to the idea of self-publishing? For awhile it was all around town Ethan planned on going that route."

"Self-publishing isn't easy no matter how many people say it is. It takes commitment and hard work. Right now,

Ethan's been a little too busy with his official duties to dedicate time to promoting and marketing his books. But he'll get there. You wait and see."

"I've no doubt he will."

"I have something for you." Hayden reached under the counter and took out a blue envelope with Keegan's name scrawled on it. "Lilly and I are planning a baby shower for Jordan. This is your invitation, my house in two weeks."

Keegan opened the flap and oohed at the card. "How sweet-looking. If my grandmother were alive, I've no doubt she would've knitted her a baby blanket in powder blue."

"I wish I knew how to knit." Hayden glanced around her own store. "I've got a book here on the subject—in the how-to section. Wonder how long it would take me to learn. Of course it's too late to start now for Jordan, but—"

Keegan got the hint. "Wait. Are you pregnant, Hayden?"

She beamed. "Just barely. Don't tell anyone. You're the first one I've told outside of Ethan, of course. I thought it would be a nice little surprise to spring on the guests at Jordan's shower."

"Oh, it will. Ethan must be walking on air. And Lindeen Cody must be about to burst at finally getting a grandbaby."

"Lindeen doesn't know yet. We plan to tell his folks on Sunday at dinner."

Keegan scanned all the books on the shelves, waiting for just the right time to bring up the subject of Scott.

But Hayden zoned in on something that seemed to be troubling Keegan. "Were you looking for a particular book?"

"You have a lot more selection than you did the last time I was here."

"I get new titles in every week. I sell more books than I do all this other stuff combined. It seems the town really was in need of a place to buy affordable reading material. They even buy Scott's old college textbooks because it seems they're still in use at UC Santa Cruz. The students here even buy his programming manuals. It seems when it came to books, Scott Phillips never threw one away."

Hayden sighed. "I hated parting with them until one day he finally told me I had to let them go."

Keegan's mouth dropped open. Here was her opening. "You had a conversation with Scott Phillips about his textbooks?"

Hayden didn't hesitate. She looked Keegan straight in the eyes and replied, "Not had. I do have. I talk to him all the time. He comes and goes in here just like he does the rest of the town." She tilted her head to study Keegan. "Let me guess, you've seen him and think you're going crazy or something?"

"I've seen him and I'm not sure what to think. Why do you think he hasn't moved on from this realm to the next? Why is he still earthbound like he is?"

"You've been talking to Wade, haven't you? Well, let's put it this way, I have no idea. Frankly, I don't care why he's here, only glad that he is."

"Jordan mentioned you and Scott forged a bond last fall. Is that true?"

"Absolutely. If not for Scott, I don't think I'd have found my purpose here."

"But you and Ethan fell in love. Wasn't that your purpose, why you stayed here? You fell in love with Ethan. End of story."

"Of course, I fell head over heels in love with Ethan. But that certainly isn't the simple end to a very complicated relationship with the man. We're very different, Keegan. Without Scott's words of wisdom in that regard, my future would've been murky at best with Ethan."

Hayden shook her head. "You really don't get it do you?"

Perplexed, Keegan admitted, "I guess I don't."

"Okay. Let me see if I can simplify things. Do you honestly think I ever considered living in Pelican Pointe, let alone married to a deputy sheriff? When I got to town I was on the run, truly messed up, Keegan, really confused about my past, lacking confidence in my own abilities about my future. I'd been taken in by a very clever con man and was on the run from said bad guy. I was hoarding a secret, one I couldn't tell anyone for fear that they might arrest me, or judge me. Either way, my self-worth was pretty much zero."

"So a ghost helped you with all that? Scott's been bugging the hell out of Cord. And—"

But Hayden didn't let her finish. "Maybe Cord needs bugging. Did you consider that? Cord arrived in town after being in a dark place for a really long time, Keegan. He has major issues. Maybe Scott is trying to help him the same way he helped me."

"You really believe that?"

"I do."

"But why?"

"Never did I ever think I could be this happy after the mess I'd made of my life in Chicago. Life has unexpected roads with unexpected twists and turns and outcomes, Keegan. Come to think of it, I'm pretty sure I've driven down every one of those unexpected roads. In fact, Ethan was one of those endings I didn't see coming."

Hayden held her hands out wide and looked around the store. "And all the while those roads led me right here where I ended up married to the most wonderful guy in the world, and in eight more months I'll have Ethan's baby." Her hand automatically rested on her flat stomach. "I'm running my own business in a place I never, ever would've sought out in a million years. And just look at all I have now."

"But he's a ghost, Hayden. Scott doesn't belong here, walking among the living, scaring people."

"Says who? Of course he belongs here. If not here, where? This is his hometown, Keegan, the place where he's most comfortable, the place where he grew up after his parents died. From my standpoint, I'd say Scott

Phillips knows exactly what he's about. He's seen heartache up close and personal. He knows the town and the people in it better than anyone. Personally, I don't want him going anywhere else."

All of sudden, Hayden moved closer, got very serious. "Keegan, you might be a smart person, a scientist, someone who has always gotten your answers out of books. But unless you've gotten to know Scott firsthand, you really have no idea why he's hanging around the town he loves."

After Keegan left, she couldn't get past Hayden's words. She decided to walk back to the center and get her truck. It seemed the only way she could hope to widen possibilities was to find her own solutions. The only way to discover the answers might be to enter the belly of the beast.

But first she had a stop to make.

Keegan moved through Eternal Gardens as if laden down with a heavy burden instead of three bouquets of flowers. The last time she'd walked these grounds, she had laid her grandmother to rest. Two funerals in a short span of fifteen months was really too much for anyone to bear.

The sadness she felt had her wondering if Cord would ever get past his beloved Cassie enough to take a serious chance on anything long-term with her.

When she reached the Fanning plot, she knelt down to place two identical sets of red roses on the graves of first Porter, and then Mary Fanning. She paused, remembering the first prayer Mary had ever taught her as a meek, five-year-old child. *Now I lay me down to sleep. I pray the Lord my soul to keep. If I should die before I wake. I pray the Lord, my soul to take.*

Tears welled up before she changed direction to search for the plot marked Phillips.

She wandered around a bit until she came across four headstones lined up in a row. The first two belonged to Scott's parents. The last pair, that of his grandparents. The fifth headstone was Scott's.

David Scott Phillips
Beloved Husband and Father
Died In Service to His Country

The urn in front of the marker held a dozen long-stemmed, pink tulips. She stood there a minute before deciding to add the white roses she'd brought to the number. She slid in the stems, one by one, stepping back to examine her work.

"Thanks for coming. Those are nice. You really didn't have to do that though."

Recognizing the voice, Keegan sucked in a breath, made a slow, deliberate turn to see Scott standing three feet from his own grave. She fought the urge to take a step back in retreat.

"No need to be scared," Scott cautioned. "I rarely have any reason for violence these days."

"Easy for you to say," Keegan stammered. "You're…everywhere."

"I try to be."

"Why?"

"Why not?

"You're a puzzle to me."

"I see that. It's not so difficult to understand. I love this place." He lifted his head to the sky, threw his arms out wide. "I'm home, exactly where I want to be. For me, this is my heaven." He looked over at her. "Your grandparents were extraordinary people. They want you happy, Keegan."

She heaved out nervous frustration. "I saw you in town. It freaked me out. And you've been bugging Cord. And you're coming and going the other night scared the crap out of both of us—" She ran out of steam and finally blurted out, "You saved Cord from killing himself New Year's Day, didn't you? The gun jammed because of something you did. That's the only explanation."

"Not much different than you saving him from drowning. Is it?"

"But that's...how did you do something like that? Ghosts aren't corporeal. Contrary to popular belief or urban legend, ghosts can't maneuver things around."

"Ah, so now you want me to spill all my ghostly secrets on the first visit? Why? Aren't you grateful Cord got a second chance, Keegan? Of course, it didn't last long before he tried again. But lucky for him, you were there that night."

Keegan couldn't argue with that, so she sat down cross-legged on the grass, pulled up a long blade of tender shoot to run through her fingers. "He's trying to get his act together now. I try to help but—"

"It's up to him, Keegan. You can support him, be there for him, but the rest is up to him. Don't you think?"

"I'm in love with him."

"I know."

"He'll never be over Cassie."

"Don't count on that."

"What? Why?"

"Don't sell yourself short, Keegan. True love when it happens levels the playing field—considerably."

"But right now it's one-sided." She studied Scott's face. "Isn't it?"

"You're asking the wrong person."

"A woman doesn't ask a man if he loves her. He's supposed to—"

Scott shook his head. "Women. They have all these rules of what is supposed to happen, what men are supposed to know how to do. You didn't believe Cord when he told you he saw me, talked to me, and yet here you are, standing in the cemetery having a conversation like I'm real. Throw away the rules, Keegan. For once, let your heart guide you."

"It's too soon anyway. I shouldn't have told you."

Scott laughed so hard he held his hand at his sides. When he recovered, he said, "You think I'm going to run through town shouting Keegan's secret? Who am I going to tell?"

"You talk to Cord all the time. And besides, he couldn't believe you held back the info about his father."

"Some things are meant to be learned over the natural course of time. Such was the case with Gabe Bennett. Those things that are dangerous, however, now those are another matter entirely."

That night Robby Mack didn't get any farther than Lake Tahoe. A throbbing headache forced him to pull over for the night and sleep in the car. The meth he'd consumed before leaving Reno made him nervous and edgy.

He counted the bills in his wallet.

Whether it was the drugs or the fact he had less than twenty-five dollars, he decided the convenience store he'd passed ten miles back would have to do. It was remote and didn't have that much security around it. He knew because he'd already checked.

He pulled out a stocking cap from his bag, reached to make sure he hadn't left the gun behind, and shot a quick U-turn.

He stretched the knitted fabric over his head and prepared to do what he had to do.

To make his way to Cord Bennett he needed money for gas.

And he'd do anything to get it.

Keegan dragged Cord to Santa Cruz under the guise of shopping for Jordan's baby shower gift. She really wanted to get him out for an evening, hopefully get him to relax for longer than a couple of hours.

The guy had been a walking bundle of nerves since he'd found out Robby Mack was on the loose. He needed a breather and Keegan was determined to make the outing fun.

Even though guys usually avoided shopping like the plague, unless it was for a bigger flat-screen TV, their first stop was a baby boutique downtown that specialized in providing everything for mothers-to-be.

Keegan browsed knowing exactly what she wanted, a knitted blanket for a baby boy that looked handmade. It wouldn't of course be done by Mary Fanning, but if she found what she was looking for, she thought it might be an addition to any nursery that could be handed down from one generation to the next.

When a fiftyish woman noticed the couple perusing layette sets, she stepped from behind the counter and wanted to know, "When are you due, dear?"

"Me?" Keegan gaped a few seconds before looking down at her belly.

At the question, Cord instinctively ogled Keegan's stomach, as well. His brow creased. He needed clarification. "We are here for Jordan, right? Is there something you want to tell me?"

But Keegan finally got her mouth fully operational. "It's not for me. I'm shopping for a shower gift for a friend."

"Ah. Did you have anything in mind?"

With that straightened out, Keegan went into detail about what she hoped to buy.

"I've got just the thing. Follow me." The sales clerk led them to a cherrywood crib set up in the corner decorated with an ensemble that included the fitted sheet, knitted blanket, bumper guard, and dust ruffle. "I know it's for a boy, but the mint green really pops."

"Wow, it does," Keegan agreed as she ran her hands over the incredibly soft fabric. "What do you think, Cord."

She turned and noticed he had turned a rather interesting shade of green himself.

"This is for Jordan, isn't it?" Cord wanted to know.

"Oh. Cord, of course it is." Her eyes twinkled with hilarity, delighted that he felt so uncomfortable about standing in a baby store. That is, until she realized something else was going on. Turning to the woman, Keegan went on, "If you gift wrap, I'll take all four pieces."

Beaming, the sales lady asked, "Cash or charge?"

"Charge," Keegan answered as she dug out her Visa. But when the woman walked back to the cash register, Keegan shifted to Cord and asked in a huff, "Okay, what is it? Did I cross some invisible line here that has you freaking out for some unknown reason?"

Without answering her, Cord bolted outside, leaving her standing there rather embarrassed by his abrupt change in behavior.

Once out on the sidewalk, Cord ran his hands through his hair. How the hell did he intend to explain this to Keegan? He paced up and down on the cement, stressing all the while about that particular memory. When exactly had it buried itself deep inside his psyche? And why did it have to pop up now and ruin his evening out with Keegan? He desperately wanted a whiskey. Sweat beaded down his face.

By the time Keegan exited the shop carrying her gift for Jordan, she saw a troubled man, a different man entirely than the one who had accompanied her to Santa Cruz. The joy of the trip gone, she wheeled on Cord. "What the hell was that all about in there? What's wrong with you anyway? For crying out loud, I'm not pregnant! And if this is how you act when you think I am—"

Both hands flew to his face, scrubbed downward. "I was back in another place, another time, with someone else."

"Don't be coy. Why don't you just say it? You mean Cassie? You were back in time with Cassie?"

"Yes, Cassie."

"What does shopping for a baby gift have to do with—? Wait. Cassie got pregnant? That's a little tidbit you forgot to mention."

"It's complicated."

"No, no, it really isn't, Cord. I think I deserve the truth."

"Of course you do. Let's cross the street to the café over there, sit down where we can talk, get something cold to drink."

"All right," she said thoughtfully. She really didn't like the sound of this.

But after he grabbed her arm and led her to the little coffee shop, they took a booth in the back.

She placed an order for iced tea she didn't want—waited for him to get his thoughts together—and maybe his act. Because God, he acted like he really needed the time.

"There are a few things that have come out in therapy."

"Okay."

"Things I didn't want to remember about Cassie. Things I guess I blocked. It seemed better somehow if I could set aside her faults and forget about her shortcomings and concentrate on all the good. It turns out there wasn't that much good."

That was the last thing she thought he'd say. Her brow tensed up. "What do you mean?"

"I'm getting to it." He took a deep gulp of iced tea that seemed to help him buy more time before going on, "I came back after my second tour in Iraq to California, landed at Los Alamitos."

"Because you were in the Guard here."

"Right. Cassie had flown from Virginia to here, met me at the airport along with all the other family members welcoming the unit home. Keep in mind my tour had lasted twelve months that time. Cassie and I hug, we kiss, we go through all the bells and whistles of small talk and then head out to check into a hotel. Here I think we're going to have a helluva reunion and then we get to our room."

He took another long slug of tea. "She tells me she's four months pregnant."

Keegan's mouth wanted to drop open but she fought the urge to let it. Instead she merely reached out, laid her hand on his.

Cord noted her eyes couldn't hide the surprise or the sorrow.

"Yeah, that's about the reaction I had. Okay, maybe a little more. Obviously the baby isn't mine. But she tells me she loves me and wants to try and make a go of it. I storm out of the room, go downstairs, hit the bar. I get drunk.

"Next day, she begs me for another chance, wants me to forgive her, blah blah blah. A couple of days go by, I reconsider and we agree to try to make a go of things. I know it sounds crazy, Keegan, but I loved her, or at least I thought what I was feeling at the time was love. Anyway, we get an apartment. I go back to my job in construction. We go shopping for baby stuff on a weekly basis."

"Like we just did."

"I guess so. Anyway, two months go by, she miscarries at six months. Things are strained between us. Then to top it off, I get called up for a third tour. She leaves California, goes back to Leesburg to be with her family. I head back to Iraq, wondering, worrying the entire time that I've got a girlfriend stateside who I know for a fact is not faithful to me." He let out a huge sigh. "I'm sorry I freaked out back there."

"You said things were coming to light in therapy. What things? Was that it?"

"No. If I list all the ways Cassie could be manipulative it just makes me sound petty."

"It doesn't."

"In a way it does. She's not here to defend herself. But when I'm sitting there talking to Dr. Pontadera, it's therapeutic. I feel like I'm finally purging myself of all those years I wasted with Cassie."

"Did she ever own up to who was the baby's father?"

He shook his head and looked away.

"But you have your suspicions, don't you?"

He met her eyes. "After the fact, yes."

This time her mouth did drop open. "Oh, my God. Robby Mack?"

He nodded.

"Anything else you'd like to tell me?"

"These revelations are fairly humiliating, Keegan."

"Cord, we all have things in our past that we're embarrassed about. You want to know what I think?"

"Sure."

"I think you wanted family, someone in your life to love so badly, you settled for the one person you thought might make that a reality. You wanted the illusion of a life with Cassie and thought she was the one who could make you happy."

"That's the same thing Dr. Pontadera said."

"See. Piece of cake. One psych class and I'm an authority," Keegan said with a smile.

"I wouldn't say that."

She grinned. "I'm not sure I'm sorry this happened or glad. I had no idea Cassie was so—controlling."

"Could we talk about something else?"

"Sure." She signaled the waitress. "I want a huge slice of that chocolate cake and don't be stingy. And could you load it down with chocolate ice cream? What about you, Cord? What do you say we have our dessert course first?"

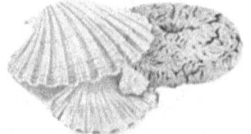

Chapter Twenty-One

"Absolutely not," Nick barked for the third time in a span of fifteen minutes.

Patrick Murphy stood in the kitchen at Promise Cove and did his best to talk Nick Harris into throwing his hat in the ring for Sissy Carr's old seat on the town council. Since the matter of Sissy's resignation had been settled, the special election to replace the woman had been scheduled for June. Murphy was running out of time to talk Nick into getting on the ballot.

"It wouldn't take all that much," Murphy claimed. "It would really be more like an honorary position anyway."

Nick sent him a disbelieving look. "Come on, Murphy. I didn't ride into town yesterday. I know damn well you guys find a reason to meet every time the wind changes direction. I've got a baby due in under two months, which I might point out is the busiest time of the year for the B & B, too. I don't have time to campaign around town."

"You'd be a shoo-in, no campaigning required."

"No."

About that time, the bell chimed they had installed at the front door to indicate a guest. The bell didn't actually ring, it buzzed so it wouldn't wake a napping two-year-old.

When Jordan started to move to answer the door, Nick waved her off. "No, I'll get it. You've been on your feet too long as it is today."

As soon as Nick was out of the room, Jordan leaned over to Murphy. "I'll talk to him. He'd make an excellent candidate for the city council."

"Not only that, but the board of directors has finally

forced old man Carr out at the bank. All those bad loans finally took their toll on his rep."

"Not to mention his daughter's sneaking off to be with Kent. People might not have been surprised at her actions but they were upset she stole money. Now that Ethan has positively ID'd her remains and knows she didn't drown, it's looking more and more like Kent might've killed her."

Murphy nodded. "Ethan thinks the two of them might've gotten into an argument shortly after they boarded Easy Money. Kent maybe snapped and hit her on the head with something, dumped her body into the ocean."

"I know what Ethan thinks happened. But it took a long time for the body to wash up on shore."

Murphy made a face. "According to Ethan, it was in terrible shape what with the elements taking their toll for so many months."

Jordan picked up her tea, sipped. "Just what the town needs—a murder mystery."

"Well, wherever Kent is, I hope they catch him and he pays for the attempted arson out here and for—whatever else he's done."

"We've always known Kent was a sleaze."

Murphy changed the subject back to the topic foremost on his mind. "I'm thinking Nick would make a fantastic replacement as president of the bank. He has the experience and since he's been here in town more than a year now, a sense of what Pelican Pointe's citizens need from its lending institution."

Jordan frowned. She wasn't sure she liked the idea of Nick going back to wearing his banker hat. But then, he should have the opportunity to decide that for himself. "Okay. I'll talk to him about that, too."

In the entrance hall, the moment Nick opened the

front door his first impression of the "guest" standing on the porch was that of the joker. Instead of garish, over-the-top makeup though, the man's smile was too wide and didn't reflect the coldness Nick saw in his green eyes.

The man had done a poor-ass job of bleaching his hair.

"Did you need something?" Nick asked a little wary of the stranger.

"I know. I know. I don't have a reservation. But the guy in town sent me here, said there were no motel rooms to be had within fifty miles. Your place is it."

Nick noted the man's nervous ticks and recognized a drug addict when he saw one. He weighed the pros and cons of letting this guy into their home. Finally, practicality wore out. Who was he to judge what a lodger looked like?

But there were more ways than one to get rid of the unsavory type. "This is our peak season. The rates are two-ninety-five a night."

The guy whistled through his teeth. "You're kidding? That's a little pricey for my tastes." Even though he had the credit card he'd stolen from some guy named Jerry Mason, it was only a matter of time before the issuer caught on and cancelled the card. Now that he was this close to Cord Bennett, Robby didn't dare take the risk.

Nick eyed the man's nervous demeanor. He decided there was no way he would come off the room rate for this guy.

"But you have a vacancy, right?"

"I have one room left and it's booked through the weekend. That means it would be available for one night only, which is tonight."

"I'd sure like to take a hot shower but two-ninety-five is highway robbery. What do you guys have in there, gold plates or something?"

This guy's credibility dropped to a negative. Nick wanted to get rid of him now even more than he had when he'd first opened the door. "The price is pretty much in line with all the other B & Bs up and down the coast with a view of the ocean. This is a tourist town, which means tourists are our bread and butter. What did you say your name was?"

"Gold. John. I guess I'll drive on down the road then until I find me a Motel 6."

Nick nodded, never bothering to mention he'd be driving for another two hours on the interstate before he found a motel of any kind.

Instead Nick merely said, "You do that." And shut the front door in the man's face.

After leaving Promise Cove, Robby followed the route he'd already mapped out. Thanks to the info Terri Lynn had discovered some weeks back over the Internet, he knew Cord Bennett worked as manager for Taggert Organic Farms.

Lucky for him, when Robby drove past the fruit stand, there stood Cord Bennett behind the counter arranging baskets of vegetables. Robby itched to take him out, once and for all. The idea of Bennett writing letters to every judge, every prosecutor, every shrink, involved in his case, didn't set well with Robby. Now that he had him in his sights, Robby lifted his foot off the gas, slowed his progress.

Just as he was about to reach under the seat to grab the .25 he'd hidden there, a truck pulled up near the gate to the farm. Robby watched as two men got out and started unloading large containers of produce.

What a bumpkin? Robby thought as he floored the accelerator and took off down the coastal road heading back into Pelican Pointe, making sure to keep his speed under the radar.

As soon as Robby got to town, looking for a place to spend the night became his top priority. After making several trips up and down Main Street, he tried the side streets. Circling the residential neighborhood like a vulture, all he needed was to locate one abandoned house. But when he couldn't find what he wanted, he headed toward the ocean. If he had to sleep in the car, he wanted a beautiful spot where he could hear the sound of the surf.

On this side of town though, he got lucky. There were several rundown storefronts along the docks. If he could get into one of those he'd have himself a place to stay, maybe even for a couple of days until he figured out the best way to get to Bennett.

He turned the car into the first narrow opening at the end of the block that led to the back lot of a derelict building. Looking around, it was obvious the only action the brick structure had seen in decades was an active tagger bent on leaving a string of graffiti that didn't make a bit of sense. There were broken windows on all three floors but someone had stopped at the first after deciding it was a waste of plywood.

Uneasy, Robby looked around for the best spot to hide the car. When he decided parking it behind a Dumpster was his best bet, he edged the vehicle farther down the dead end, as close to the garbage container as he could get without putting scratches on the paint.

The pavement was ragged with bumps and broken asphalt, so much so he had trouble maneuvering the Mustang into position.

Still pissed off about not being able to spend the night at the comfy B & B, he exited the car with a considerable chip on his shoulder. He decided to lock his bag in the trunk until he discovered what the place offered in the way of lodging.

He stepped around the potholes, walked down the alleyway and realized he'd have to pilfer a flashlight for later when it got dark.

Right now though, he made good use of the light he had. When he pushed open a door in the back he wondered what kind of people didn't even have the good sense to lock up a building. But glancing around what looked like a former newspaper office, the emptiness answered his question.

There was nothing of value anywhere. Checking out each room, all he found were bare walls, an abundance of trash littering the concrete floors, peeling paint, and rotting wood.

A back staircase offered the only way up, but he had to make his way around discarded condoms, Styrofoam food containers, and other disgusting debris to get there.

Finally when he reached the top, he picked out a corner where the windows faced west with a perfect view of the ocean.

When hunger got the better of him, he went looking for a place to eat and discovered there were no fast-food joints. What kind of stupid-ass town didn't have a golden arches? he wondered before spotting The Hilltop Diner. If he ordered the cheapest thing on the menu, he could stretch the three-hundred dollars he had in his wallet until he could steal what he needed.

The Diner looked like a malt shop right out of the sitcom *Happy Days*. In fact, the entire town looked like it hadn't seen a new idea since Nixon held office.

Robby took a seat at the counter and noticed a few stares from the other patrons. It seemed he had overestimated his "California" look. It didn't exactly make him blend in with these stuffed shirts.

It wasn't until he picked up a menu that he spotted his mug shot hanging behind the counter taped to the mirror. Automatically, he dropped his head. Out of the corner of his eye though, he studied his reflection and then the photo they'd taken the night they'd booked him into the Leesburg jail.

The two images of the same man looked totally different.

He relaxed and ordered the dinner special, two fish tacos with rice and beans. His ears pricked up when he noticed the table to his left, a circle of old men, seemed content to discuss the town's hottest couple, Cord and someone they called Keegan.

What were the chances another Cord lived in a town this size? Had Bennett found himself a honey?

All he needed to learn now was where he could find this Keegan.

After he chowed down on the food, it didn't take him long to coax people on the street into telling him little tidbits about Keegan Fanning.

How lucky could he get? Not only did he learn she ran a marine rescue center, but it sat right across the street from his new digs.

As he walked back to his "accommodations" for the night, he wondered why anyone in their right mind would want to save a bunch of smelly animals.

Whatever the reason, he began to formulate a plan.

That night Robby set up house in his empty shell of a building across the street from FMRC. Having the penthouse suite on the third floor was a side benefit where he could keep an eye on the man he wanted dead. Because at the moment, Cord Bennett was across the street making out with the very hot, Keegan Fanning.

Robby dug out the pair of binoculars he'd lifted earlier using his five-finger discount at Ferguson's Hardware. Even in the darkness, he scanned the vast compound of noisy, dirty animals. He wasn't sure which was worse, the ugly-ass, big, brown birds or the slimy-looking things with flappers that slithered along the ground.

To him, every one of the ugly creatures deserved a bullet to the brain.

But the woman they called Keegan seemed to dote on them. And Cord was no better. He followed her around like an underling as she fed the little bastards a fishy concoction that almost made him lose the supper he'd just eaten.

He barely recognized Bennett. He'd forgotten how tall the asshole was. And his hair was so long he looked like a damned hippie.

Robby watched as the couple made their way across the property wrapped up in each other. For the first time in two days, he missed having the hooker next to him.

When the pair disappeared inside a house, Robby got busy stacking several dirty but flat cardboard boxes for his bed.

Despite the broken panes of glass from the various busted windows that let in the chilly night air right off the ocean, his "bedroom" for the next couple of days, wasn't all that cold. Of course, that could have been due to the whiskey he'd stolen courtesy of the only grocery store in town and consumed over the last hour.

Draining the bottle of its last swig, Robby settled down to sleep.

After a long day at the farm, Cord couldn't think of a better way to spend his evening than curled up with Keegan. Because the chilly spring evening demanded a roaring fire, he set the wood he'd stacked to flame.

When he turned and saw her sitting at her little desk working on another grant application, his heart seemed to stutter in his chest. He took in her long, lean body in the flickering glow. Yearning slammed into him.

After dimming the lights, he crossed over to the docking station, slid his iPod into the slot, hit the Play button. The tenor voice of Teddy Thompson filled the room singing *In My Arms*.

He knew he had her attention when her head popped up. "Who is that? Oh, his voice is incredible. I love this song. *That* isn't on *my* playlist."

He grinned. "No it isn't. I downloaded a couple of new songs I thought might be good for times like this."

She tilted her head. "Times like this?"

"When I ask you to dance." He held out a hand. "Come on. Teddy Thompson used to tour with Rosanne Cash's band. I got hooked on his music when I worked security detail at one of his concerts." He tugged her up and into his arms. "Dance with me."

She rose and went into his arms. Nothing in her life had ever felt more right than him holding her like this.

They swayed, comfortable in each other's embrace as the shadows around them mirrored their movements on the wall.

He kissed her hair. His mouth nibbled an ear, an easy skim of lips along soft flesh. An intake of breath, a whisper of warm words, he glided his hands along her back. A lick of her neck, a faint bite to sensitive shoulder, he brought her up against his hardness.

They were hip to hip.

It didn't take much seduction or ambiance on his part for her blood to heat. But then it never did. She touched his cheek, brought his mouth down to cover hers.

She ran her hands through his mass of hair, enjoyed the thrill of knowing he wanted her.

They eased down to the rug.

Hands unbuttoned and tore at clothing. They groped, touched, stroked. Gentle became fierce. Need lapped and took over reason.

Bodies slicked to rhythm and song until the concerto exploded into a brilliant flash fire of dreamy soft blues.

When he picked her up and carried her to bed, when he pulled her against him in the dark, she knew the tides had brought them all the way home.

The next day Robby Mack managed to evade the curious townspeople by escaping to the country. He decided to go back and check out Taggert Farms for himself. He didn't, however, count on a fully staffed operation. There were workers everywhere, in the fields picking produce, in the orchards picking apples, guys loading trucks. They manned the vegetable stand, which meant he had to forego the front gate.

He parked a half mile down the road pulling off into a scenic overhang, a spectacular spot to sit and take in the ocean and the horizon. Grabbing his gun from the glove box, he got out of his car, went over to the cliffs just for the hell of it and took in the rocky beach below.

It had to be a thirty-foot drop to the seascape. It didn't take long for him to get bored though and for him to lose interest in the scenery.

He had to remember the reason he'd made the trip here in the first place.

Jogging back to where the white fence marked the end of the property, he vaulted over the railing and took off through a clearing until he got to the cover of woods.

Robby walked the surrounding area, spying on the workers, hiding behind trees or stumps or whatever he could. Only when he made his way closer to the barn, did he catch sight of his target.

Bennett was shirtless. The scars on his chest visible, the scars he'd put there. A feeling of satisfaction moved through him knowing he'd tried to take the man down once before. He might've failed at it, but at least he'd tried. That had to count for something. He wouldn't make the same mistakes he'd made that day in the church when he'd waited too late to turn the gun on Bennett.

He might not be able to get inside the rescue center without a big production, but he would lure Bennett out into his trap with something he seemed to care about now. The redhead told him what he'd already figured out about Cord's loyalty to his beloved Cassie. The man obviously didn't have a clue two years ago and still didn't today.

Good thing he intended to fix that little nugget as well.

On the walk back to the Mustang, Robby heard one of those nasty beasts that crawled along the ground on flippers causing a ruckus on the beach below. He was sure of it. He followed the din, craned his neck over the side of the railing to see what was so noisy. Sure enough the thing sat on the rocks, barking for all it was worth. Even from this height, he could smell the stench.

He took out the .25 from his coat pocket, leaned over a bit farther, took aim and fired.

Amid the kale and the rows of lettuce, Sammy's head lifted at the sound of two shots. "Was that gunfire?" he shouted to Silas who stood at the opposite end of the vegetable patch.

"Sounded like that to me," Silas returned.

"We should go get Cord."

But Cord had already heard and came out of the milking station on the run. "Did you hear that?"

"Yeah, it sounded like it came from out on the road," Silas noted.

All three men hustled toward Cord's truck. Cord took off down the driveway sending gravel flying every which way.

When they reached the end of the lane, Cord looked left then right. "This is nuts. We don't even know where the shots originated."

"Take a right," Silas directed. "We should at least check out the immediate area."

"Good call," Cord agreed as he turned the pickup southward. One pass, then two, slowly along the highway and they found nothing. But then Cord snapped his fingers.

"We need to check out the scenic overlook. I've seen tourists stop there to take photos from the panoramic view."

"And what? Today they bring a gun?" Sammy remarked.

"Maybe they were hunting something," Silas pointed

out.

"Nothing down on that section of rocks except the occasional seal," Sammy revealed.

"What did you say?" Cord asked.

"Seals get stranded there after bad storms sometimes, like the kind we've been having."

"Jesus. Why didn't I think to check the cliffs first?" With that, Cord braked, shot a U, and headed for the overhang.

They pulled into the deserted lot and jumped out of the vehicle at the same time. But it was Cord who made his way to the railing first and leaned over to scan the rocks. "Shit," he uttered. "Some son of a bitch shot a seal. Look, there. It's a mess. I need to let Ethan know."

"Yeah. And you should call Keegan. She's helped out a time or two when other people have killed marine life around here," Sammy suggested.

"Damn." Cord dug out his cell phone, first to dial 911, and then punched in Keegan's number at the center.

His instincts wanted to protect and shelter. But he knew Keegan would have none of that at least not until later when he could get her alone. He gutted it out as he relayed what they'd discovered on a pristine stretch of shoreline meant for beauty not carnage.

Somewhere out there a cowardly shooter was willing to take out a weapon in broad daylight and kill a seal for no good reason without batting an eye.

Twenty minutes later he spotted Keegan pull up behind his truck he'd left parked on the side of the road. It didn't really surprise him that she'd manage to beat both Ethan and Steve Childs, the park ranger, to the scene.

Once out of her vehicle though, she raced to where Cord stood along the guardrail. "Are you sure he's dead? Maybe I can—"

"He's dead, Keegan. There's too much blood and he hasn't moved the entire time we've been standing here. I'm sorry, honey. I'll go with you."

They made their way down the same steep hillside,

chucked full of scrub brush, eucalyptus, and scraggly wild sage they'd taken the night she'd climbed the rocks to get to Sam, the harbor seal pup.

This time though there would be no rescue.

When they finally reached the stretch of gravelly beach and the remains, Keegan stared at what she estimated was a two-hundred-pound gray seal, probably no more than a year old.

Blood matted the fur. The surrounding rocks dripped red.

"Oh, my God. What would make anyone do something like this?"

"I don't know, baby. Some people are just plain mean."

Tears filled her eyes as she reached out, ran her fingers through the seal's soft, short coat. Keegan knew her job was to document, take photos of the grisly scene. That's why she was here.

So she did her best to close off her emotions to the miserable sight and get to work. It was tough to take. Unfortunately this wasn't her first animal shooting, but it always got to her just the same.

How anyone could become used to this, she didn't know. She didn't understand the kind of human nature that could mete out this kind of senseless cruelty on purpose to a defenseless animal.

Obviously the harbor seal had been used for target practice.

"He was just sitting on the rocks, minding his own business when someone took him down from that observation area up there," Keegan reasoned, pointing to the two entry wounds, one in the head, one in the neck. "And the size of the holes tells me it wasn't that big of a gun. But it got the job done whatever caliber it was."

"That took some skill. He had to be a helluva shot."

"Exactly."

Squawky birds were circling overhead, waiting their turn at the carcass. The blow flies had already arrived.

Keegan looked skyward, sighed. "We need to get him

out of here before the scavengers swoop down and that means I need to get started. The sooner I finish, the sooner we get to bag him."

Cord watched her professional demeanor slip into place. But he could tell it cost her in sorrow and anguish because she'd gone pale at the gore of it all.

She unzipped her camera case, took out a professional Nikon, and started snapping photos in rapid succession.

Cord had never been one to understand the shooting of animals. Yes, he'd been to war. Yes, he'd killed in combat. Yes, he had been trained to kill by the military. But this—killing something just because you could, because it was there took—

Suddenly Cord got a sick feeling in his gut. Could Robby Mack Stevens be responsible for this? To what purpose?

But with Robby Mack, he knew damn well, the man did not need a reason to kill. And since Robby already had a taste at killing humans, killing an animal would be sport, a walk in the park.

Just because they hadn't seen a sign of the bastard, didn't mean they needed to drop their guard and get sloppy now. Not for the first time, Cord wished he had never been stupid. He wished he still had that little .22 for security reasons.

He rubbed his chin and sighed. It couldn't be helped. Stupidity had to be dealt with and paid for and then moved beyond to get to the other side.

He just hoped like hell, it didn't cost him Keegan.

Cord heard voices coming from the ridge up above and knew Ethan Cody and Steve Childs had arrived.

As soon as she turned and spotted Ethan and Steve, Keegan squeaked out, "Right now I have all the pictures I need of the scene. But I'd like to get the seal to the center as soon as possible and be there when Bran does the necropsy, digs out the slugs."

"Get them to me, Keegan, and I'll enter them into the system just in case," Ethan offered.

"Thanks. Then I guess let's get this guy bagged and transported. Steve, are you ready?"

Steve nodded. "It sickens me every time I see something like this."

"Yeah. It never ceases to amaze me how low man can go."

Chapter Twenty-Two

That night, Keegan stood alongside Bran Sullivan as he performed the necropsy on the seal inside one of the exam rooms they routinely used to heal.

But there would be no making better tonight.

From five feet away, Cord observed the process with his hands stuffed inside his jeans pockets.

He watched Keegan use her tape measure to gauge the size and length and then jot down information in the file before shifting focus to assist Bran.

She began by handing off instruments, one by one, when needed.

But it was Bran who dug out the first bullet to the head, used the forceps to drop it into a stainless steel bowl.

"Well, I'm no marine or animal expert, but I do know a .25-caliber slug when I see it," Cord revealed, leaning closer for the first time since entering the room.

Bran worked on getting the second one out of the neck. This one seemed to take longer to reach. But when he bounced the metal into the cup, he told Cord, "See if it matches the other."

Cord examined, concluded, "Both are .25-caliber slugs."

"You want me to open him up all the way, Keegan, finish up the exam?"

"It's up to you, Bran. I could use the data, I guess, but at this point, we know how the poor thing died."

"Yep, that's a certainty. I could take blood and tissue samples, check for disease, might be able to use the info to enhance your study of the pollutants in the area. See why he was on those rocks to begin with."

"Then let's do it. You okay over there, Cord?"

"I'm holding my own."

"This one thinks he's tough, huh Keegan? One surgery under his belt, now his first necropsy and he's ready to roll." But Bran assessed the man, who up to this point had possessed a helluva lot more grit than any of the other knuckleheads Keegan had brought around. "Ever thought of pursuing this line of work, Cord?"

"You mean work around animals? You know I already do."

"Tough all right, but a little slow on the uptake," Bran retorted and winked.

Keegan eyed Cord and smiled before bobbing her head in his direction. "He's resistant to that way of thinking, Bran. He's hung up on age. It's too late for him to think of changing careers."

Cord snorted. "What are you guys talking about? The vet thing is a pipe dream, something Keegan mentioned in passing."

Bran harrumphed and declared, "When someone has a knack and they disregard it why are people always surprised when that chance up and goes away?"

After that, Bran let the topic drop as he finished his dissection.

Keegan did the same as she began to concentrate on taking then bagging the slew of specimens she needed.

But an hour later, Bran was the first to shed his goggles and mask. He threw his scrubs in the discard pile and went to the sink to clean up. When he began to pack up, he admitted to Cord, "Well, whoever did this, it was a deliberate act. But you both knew that already. I'll drop off the slugs to Ethan on my way home for all the good it will do."

"You've seen this before, I take it? People shooting the marine life in the area?" Cord asked, wanting desperately to believe this had nothing to do with Robby Mack. But what were the chances?

"Sure, it happens. I've seen people take a gun to their

own dog and not because it was ailing or sick but just because they got pissed off about something. It takes a mean son of a bitch in my book to shoot an animal just because they can."

"We agree on that," Cord muttered.

"You aren't thinking it's this same guy Ethan put the flyers up all over town, are you?"

"I don't know. I do know the man's capable of something like this and much worse."

"Then I guess we all better be looking out for you and Keegan." With that, Bran slapped Cord on the back, said his goodnights and was gone.

After jotting down all the data, after labeling the specimens, Keegan rechecked her notes, shut off the recorder and finally called it a night. She stretched her back, tossed her gloves in the trash, and walked to the sink to wash up.

"I could use one of your infamous massages right about now, Cord Bennett. What do you say to heading home and making the most of our evening? I could use a tension reliever."

He went over and kneaded her shoulders, kissed her neck. "That's my job. I take it very seriously. Know something else?"

"What?"

"After watching that necropsy, I'm fairly certain I may never be able to eat meat ever again."

She chuckled. "Yeah. Right. You, give up pepperoni pizza? And bacon? I'll believe that miracle when I see it."

He tugged her out of the exam room and into the crisp, night air. They walked through the compound under a starry sky.

"I'm serious. The entire time I stood there, I'm thinking I know why you don't eat meat of any kind, why your grandparents didn't eat it either. It's not a bad plan when you work around animals all the time."

"Cord, you don't have to become a vegetarian—for me."

"Haven't you heard? The nutcase is making all these changes in his life. What's one more when it comes to diet?"

"But you love bacon."

"Ah." A glazed look formed in his eyes. "The perfect food that can be eaten anytime of the day or night, for breakfast, lunch, or dinner, a main dish or in a sandwich. Yeah, I concede bacon might be a major obstacle, but I'm willing to give it a try."

"Hmm, that means I'll have to give up something for you."

"Why?"

"It seems only fair. Something I love. It can't be chocolate though. Or ice cream."

"Chocolate's a food group, it's definitely off the table. And ice cream is a necessary part of life."

"How about bread?"

"Bread's unrealistic. Look, Keegan, you haven't touched a drop of alcohol since you met me."

"But that's just so you won't be tempted. I'm not that big a drinker. I don't even like beer all that much," she lied.

"Uh huh, right. I'm giving up bacon, you're giving up alcohol. This relationship is one for the books."

"Give and take, that's what Porter and Mary Fanning believed. Compromise ruled the day."

"Compromise, huh? How about I negotiate you into bed?"

"I thought you'd never take the hint."

On his third day in Pelican Pointe, Robby woke to the sound of another barking seal.

His back hurt. Something inside his head hammered trying to get out. If the thing didn't shut up...he grabbed for his pistol only to realize the racket echoed from clear across the street.

How did anyone put up with that fucking noise all the time?

He rolled on his cardboard bed and decided to hell with this, no more sleeping on the floor, no more filthy living conditions. He was ready to get out of this stinking town, which only meant one thing.

Today had to be the day.

As thunder boomed overhead, signaling another spring storm forming offshore, Keegan spent her morning squirrelled away at home, in her grandfather's office, which doubled as a third spare bedroom. Guinness sprawled at her feet. She noticed the dog shudder at the sound. The canine did not like thunder.

"It'll be okay," she reassured him as she reached over, scratched his head and turned on the radio hoping to catch the weather forecast for the immediate area.

She shifted her focus back to her task and the email she had to write. Before long the reminder to donors took shape and she hoped it would be enough to keep FMRC at the forefront if they happen to get the urge to open their checkbooks.

Sometimes it sucked trying to solicit donations. But it wouldn't hurt to keep in touch on a regular basis with the center's core benefactors.

She silently wondered if her grandfather ever tired of the chore and tried to think whether or not she remembered him grumbling about it.

She decided it couldn't be helped though. Contributions were vital.

The open house had been a huge success, more so than she'd ever dreamed. They'd raised enough to keep the center open through August. In fact, the whole street-fair experience had sold her on making the event an every year occurrence.

When thunder rumbled again in the distance, she glanced out the window to see a mean-looking marine layer forming on the horizon.

When her cell phone chimed, she pivoted to check out the display. And grinned when she saw it was Cord. She fought the funny feeling in her stomach and wondered if she'd ever get tired of that little extra thud of the heart. "Hi."

"Hello gorgeous. How about I take you out to a late brunch, some place exotic, like the Diner, they serve breakfast all day. We'll both order a stack of pancakes six inches high. How's that sound?"

"Only if you order blueberry and I get pecan. That way—"

"We eat off each other's plates. Got it."

"You read my mind."

"Yeah? I do that a lot. See you in about an hour."

"It's a date."

She clicked off the call and sighed at getting to hear his voice. Wow! Hayden had been right. When was the exact moment she'd gone moony over Cord Bennett?

Weeks ago, she decided.

She went back to finishing up the correspondence. Once that was done, she closed out of one window and opened another. This time, she went to the center's website to update current photos of the pelicans. While there she decided to upload new videos Pete had taken of the rest of her brood, especially Minnie and Bumper. The pictures showed the progress of both mother and son. Never underestimate the appeal of cute sea otters playing together in the water when you were begging for money, Keegan resolved, as her downloads completed.

She was about to tackle a stack of bills when her two-way radio crackled to life. "Abby to Keegan. Over."

Keegan picked up the handheld device. "Go ahead, Abby. Over."

"Where are you? Over."

Keegan sighed. Abby was a go-getter but sometimes she could be irritating. "I'm locked away at home trying to get some work done. Over."

"Because when you're in the office there are too many distractions? Over."

"Exactly. What's up, Abby? Talk to me. Over."

"Got a call about an angry harbor seal making a fuss near the Wilder Ranch State Park watershed. Over."

"Copy that. The weather's getting nasty. I'll have to push it to beat the storm though. Heading out now. If I get to the boat in the next fifteen minutes ETA will be half an hour after that. Over."

"Roger that. Be careful taking the *Moonlight Mile* out in this storm. Over."

Keegan chuckled. Okay, maybe Abby was more like a mother hen than an irritation. "Can't be helped. You get any more details, radio me. Over."

"Copy that. Will try and get more info to you. Over."

"Roger."

Keegan grabbed her cell phone, dialed Cord's number. When she reached his voicemail, she clicked over to the message icon instead and typed in the text: *Pancakes will have to wait. Off to rescue harbor seal at Wilder Ranch. BBL.* ♥ *K*

She dropped the phone down into the pocket of her mackinaw, threw on her rubber boots, and stuck her Raiders cap on her head. When Guinness stood up all ready to beat her out the door, she shook her head and commanded, "No way. You're staying home this time, out of the weather."

She dashed downstairs, opened the front door and stepped out into a California gale, whipping in off the water.

The *Moonlight Mile* stayed moored in Smuggler's Bay steps from the center for just this reason. Getting underway usually took no more than fifteen minutes. But today with the wind building into gusts, it took her longer to work the lines from bow to stern. By the time she finally headed out of the bay into open water, the blackening clouds on the horizon looked downright ominous. She couldn't help it—a chill crawled up her spine.

She made the turn south, all the while keeping one eye on the menacing sky.

By the time she reached Wilder Ranch State Park, the swells from the approaching storm battered the boat. The wind punched like a boxer fighting for his life in the fifteenth round. Because she hadn't been able to locate the seal from the *Moonlight Mile*, she lowered the dinghy. She'd use it to motor over to the shallower inlet where she could disembark easier in the high tide.

Once she got closer to the rocks, she cut the motor and dropped the knobby anchor, gathered up her gear and waded onto shore,

Choppy waves as high as ten feet slammed into the surrounding cliffs. Keegan glanced around for firmer footing. As she made her way up the rocks, one slippery step at a time, it occurred to her, she didn't hear the barking of an angry seal.

In fact, all she heard was the roar of the sea.

Fat drops of rain began to tap on the brim of the Raiders cap. Keegan hugged the craggy rocks like a lover, trying to hold on against the chilly wind, all the while scanning the jutting boulders for any sign of wildlife.

Maybe it was too sick or injured to bark now, she thought. After all, it had taken her over an hour to get to this spot.

But still, a feeling of unease pricked along her common sense. She'd been at this for years, and she'd never had a seal stay this quiet for this long unless...

She searched along the crags and crevices of the watershed. So far all she saw was the slick, mossy surface that threatened her footing.

Maneuvering farther into the small cove, she caught movement out of the corner of her eye about the same time her walkie-talkie crackled to life.

Just as she hit the button to speak into the radio to tell

Abby she couldn't find the seal, a man's voice startled her.

"Drop the radio. Throw it into the water. You won't be needing it."

Even from five feet away, the guy stank from the smell of sweat and liquor. His clothes were filthy. Not only did he look disheveled, but his eyes were cold and glazed over, like he might not be all there. But Keegan knew immediately she was in trouble. "Robby Stevens, right?" she surmised looking past the bleached hair and hazel-green eyes that didn't look real. The image of his mug shot filtered through the disguise.

"That's right. And we're going to stay in this spot until fuck-buddy Bennett gets here."

"There was never any seal?"

"Of course not. After Bennett joins us he's going to watch you and me, while we get to know each other in the biblical sense."

At FMRC, Abby eavesdropped on the entire exchange. Somehow Keegan had managed to keep the receiver open long enough for her to determine the boss was in trouble.

With her hands shaking, Abby picked up the wall phone in the exam room and dialed Ethan Cody direct.

"You're delusional."

"Just drop the radio and I'll show you how delusional I am."

Keegan let the handheld device slowly slip through her fingers. It landed at her feet. She could only hope the receiver still worked to transmit her location. She knew she'd kept her finger pressed to the switch long enough for Abby to discern that she needed help.

But that idea crashed and burned when Robby kicked the device onto the rocks below.

"What do you want?"

"I want you to call Bennett, tell him you need help with the animal you've been looking for."

"No."

When he started to backhand her, she saw the arm start to come down and dodged the blow, which infuriated the man all the more.

But then he simply pointed the gun at her head and cocked the hammer. "The last woman who defied me, I put in the ground. Would you like to make it two for two? I don't have to keep you alive. I can get Bennett here without you. But I've seen you two together. Since he cares for you, you're the bait."

"I can't call. I left my cell phone back on the boat." Which was a lie, but he didn't need to know that. She slipped her hand inside the mackinaw and groped for several buttons, hoping like hell she remembered the location of each icon on her display. She recalled how spotty cell service was here even under the best of circumstances. But maybe she might get lucky and someone would pick up a weak signal.

But she would not lure Cord to his death. That much she had already decided. She stalled for time but Robby immediately caught on.

"Look, don't mess with me. I've had a rough couple of days. I've been living right across the street from that fucking zoo you call a home."

"Across the street? Well for...for how long?"

"Three miserable days."

Pelican Pointe didn't have the greatest cell phone

service. Because of that, Cord didn't get Keegan's text message until he reached the city limits sign north of town. Since he'd come this far, he decided he might as well help her with the seal.

He pulled over to the shoulder of the road so he could text back. *Need help? On my way now.*

He punched in the coordinates for Wilder Ranch State Park into his GPS and veered back onto the highway. He had just driven past the Hilltop Diner on Main when he spotted Ethan's police cruiser, making a right hand turn off Beach Street, lights flashing.

Ethan spotted Cord about the same time and motioned for him to pull over.

The minute Cord got out and walked up to Ethan's patrol car, the look on the deputy's face told him something bad had happened.

Ethan blurted out, "Looks like Robby Mack has Keegan."

"Shit. Son of a bitch used her with a bogus call."

"Abby overheard the entire exchange. Stevens wants you."

"Then what are we waiting for?" Cord snapped as he dropped into the passenger seat.

"I don't have time to argue. But this is an official police matter, Cord. Remember that when we get there. Promise me you won't do anything stupid."

"Who me? Sure, Ethan, whatever you say." Cord would have agreed to anything at that point because all he wanted to do was make sure Keegan was okay. "Either way, I'd just follow you."

"Yeah, that's what I thought you'd say."

The rain poured down as Robby shoved Keegan into the watershed. They sloshed through the pounding surf as it continued to crash up against the rocks.

"Where are we going?" Keegan shouted. "This is crazy. We stay here, we'll drown. The tide's coming in and the rain's picking up. Don't you see that?"

"Shut up. You're a mouthy bitch." He shook his head. "Why is it you women can't keep your mouths shut for five damn minutes to let a man think?"

About that time he heard the unmistakable sound of a cell phone ding coming from her jacket pocket.

"Hand over the cell phone. Now!"

Even though he had a madness in his eyes that gave her the willies, she reached in, dug out the phone. Without winding up, she threw it as far into the water as she could.

"You bitch!" he screamed.

This time she took his fist straight on. It knocked her back a step and for a minute she saw stars. She tried to shake it off because she needed to keep her wits and hold it together. She had to remember this man had already taken the lives of six people, seven if he was telling her the truth about the last woman.

Robby Mack scrubbed a hand down his unshaven face. "That's the way you want it fine. We'll use the dinghy to cross the swell and get over to the boat, use the radio there to tell Bennett what I want him to do. Let's go!"

She started moving with the gun in her back. Keegan calculated the situation, timed her statements so that she could get him talking. "Why do you hate Cord so much?"

"That's easy. He took Cassie away from me. We were doing fine until that bastard entered the picture. Stupid idiot never realized I'd woo her back again and again every single time."

Keegan narrowed her eyes at that as she climbed into the motorboat, started to pull up the anchor. "She cheated on Cord?"

She already knew of course, but since she deemed she needed to keep Robby talking and distracted, it might as well be about Cassie.

"Every time he left for Iraq," Robby bragged. "Stupid bitch didn't have a faithful bone in her body. She cheated right under his nose. And Bennett was too desperate to ever catch on or let her go."

All at once, Keegan brought up the anchor to the level of the skiff. She swung the heavy weight with everything she had into the side of Robby's head. She heard bone crack and the thud of him hitting something solid on his way down.

The gun went flying out of his fist and landed somewhere on the rocks. Keegan didn't bother to check where. She rolled the unconscious man to the side of the raft and pushed him with her foot into the angry sea.

She pivoted around to pull the starter cord on the motor. When it kicked in, she throttled back, sped full out toward the Moonlight Mile as it bobbed in the deep surf.

Because of the high tide, it took her ten long minutes to reach the trawler. She climbed aboard, scrambled to the radio. "Mayday! Mayday! Mayday! This is the *Moonlight Mile*. I need help at Wilder Ranch State Park. Over!" she screamed breathless into the mic before going into further detail about what had happened with Robby Mack.

She kept it short, talked in clipped tones, trying to remain calm. Just then, she caught sight of Robby struggling with the current to get out of the tide and climb up to the rocky shore. She noted the gaping wound to his head, still bleeding as red liquid dripped down onto his neck. But the sight didn't faze her.

She relayed this latest fact to the Coast Guard dispatcher. "He's up. He's wounded but he's up. Keep Cord Bennett away from this place. Stevens wants him dead."

But Cord at the moment, watched as the deputy sheriff barreled down the narrow road leading into the park.

Cord did his best to keep his anger from simmering over and losing control of his emotions. "Do you have any idea what he'll do to her, Ethan? Robby is one mean son of a bitch. I told them that after I got out of the hospital. He may want me dead. But he'll kill Keegan just to get back at me."

About that time Cord spotted a lone, blue Mustang sitting in visitor parking, and pointed out, "I've seen that car around town and a couple of times out on the Coast Highway."

Ethan pulled up behind the car blocking it in so there was no chance of Stevens using the vehicle for escape. Automatically, he ran the plates.

While Ethan was busy with police procedure, Cord jumped out. With his heart thudding in his chest, he started running for the shoreline along the cliffs.

He knew if Keegan had been sent to look for an endangered seal, there was no better place than the bluffs and the rocks to search.

"Cord, get back here," Ethan yelled as he waited for dispatch to come back with the registration information.

But Cord had already disappeared around the bend.

With her field glasses, Keegan scanned the coastline from the deck of the *Moonlight Mile* as Stevens stopped to catch his breath on the rocks. He slumped down at one point to one knee.

And then there was Cord in her line of vision racing along the edge heading straight for Robby Mack.

She cried out in warning, but she was too far away for anyone to hear her shouts.

On the bluff, the two men eyed each other before Cord went over and dragged Robby Mack up by his shirt. "You fucking bastard."

Cord threw a fist into his face, and then pummeled him again and again. Robby finally went down with a bloody nose and two bashed eyes.

But when the man rolled over near the edge of the boulder, he came up pointing the little Saturday night special at Cord's chest with a shaky hand. "I wanted another chance at you, and lo and behold, here you are.

You think that fucking bitch was so saintly, don't you? That baby was mine."

"Yeah, I know."

"You made her miscarry with my kid, didn't you?"

"Unlike you, Stevens, I don't hit women."

A cunning glint moved into Robby's eyes. "Every time you deployed to Iraq, Cassie came back to my bed, cozied up to me just like always. I tried to talk her out of marrying you, but the bitch just would not listen."

"I figured that out, too, after the fact. I don't give a shit anymore."

Robby threw back his head and hooted with a homicidal laugh. "I decided she needed to pay for defying me—in a big way—the bonus round was I'd make you pay, too. But you lived."

A certain part of Cord's past died right then and there. He'd known it, but hearing Robby corroborate details, the humiliation of it all drained away, finally putting a cap on that chapter of his life once and for all.

"Where's Keegan?"

"That fucking bitch, I took care of her the same way I took care of Cassie."

Blistering hate filled Cord's eyes. "You've always been a mean son of a bitch, Stevens. You think you're so tough as long as you stick to beating up women. I checked on you, Robby boy. As far back as seventeen you've been hitting little girls. You even have a rape conviction in your past. Why don't you throw down that peashooter and fight me like a man? Oh, that's right, you don't you have the guts. Come on, Robby. Come on, take me on. You know you want to."

Stevens cocked the hammer back…

From behind Cord, Ethan took aim and fired. The bullet from his .45 hit Robby Mack square in the forehead knocking him back, one step, then two.

Stevens lost his footing and fell onto the rocks below with a thud all the while the choppy surf pounded up against the cliffs in an angry rhythm.

Cord stood over the edge looking out in the direction of the *Moonlight Mile*. The moment he spotted Keegan in the little dinghy alive and well, he dropped to one knee. Her arms waved wildly in his direction as she bobbed up and down in the high tide trying to make her way back over to shore—and to him.

He finally took the breath he didn't know he'd been holding.

When Ethan came up behind him and peered down at Robby's body spread out on the jagged boulders below, he laid one hand on Cord's shoulder. "He could have killed you."

"I thought he'd killed Keegan." Cord did his best to squeeze the tears out of his eyes.

"The Chumash have a legend about men like you. I think you must be a warrior who refuses to die. How many lives do you have, anyway?" Ethan asked jovially.

"Just the one. And I'm getting pretty damned sick and tired of having a gun shoved in my face."

Later, after they'd dealt with crime scene investigators and spent hours giving their separate statements in an official capacity, Keegan and Cord sat on the sofa at her place in front of a roaring fire.

She had her legs stretched out and her feet in his lap. Cord used his long, lean fingers to massage her instep, her toes.

Guinness snored softly on the floor next to the couch.

"I can only imagine what it must've been like for you to confront that asshole. After what he put you through, it isn't fair. The man was deranged."

"Mean," Cord corrected. "Unbalanced, sure, but he needed to be in prison not taking up a bed in a mental health facility. Hey, I told you I'd already figured it all out anyway. It doesn't matter, not anymore. For the first time in a long time I truly feel that part of my life is done. I've got a brand-new start in a new town, even have a relationship with my father I never thought I'd ever have. The only way I could get any luckier is knowing I have you in my life. I want you in my life, Keegan."

"I'm right here, Cord."

"That isn't good enough. I love you, Keegan. I want to make my life with you. Can you see spending your life with a recovering alcoholic? I'll never be able to take a drink."

She abruptly sat up, leaned into him. She ran her hand down his cheek and said, "We're all recovering from something in one form or another. And besides, I love you, I have for weeks now. If you don't believe me, just ask Scott."

His brow furrowed. "What does that mean? What does Scott have to do with us?"

She stroked another line down his jaw. "Ask him sometime."

Epilogue

Four months later
First day of fall classes

"There's nothing to be nervous about," Keegan assured him when she saw Cord fidget with his backpack.

"Easy for you to say, Miss Three Degrees," Cord replied in mock disdain. "Why do I feel like I'm six again and this is my first day of school?"

"I don't know, maybe because you have on brand-new sneakers. Or that you insisted you needed to buy new jeans and shirts. Or it might be the fact your backpack has all new school supplies in it. Yeah, it's probably that."

"Smart ass."

"Now see, your snappy comebacks will do you proud in class. Just don't make a habit of it, or fall asleep no matter how dull the professor is, or in some cases, the TA."

"Too bad TA doesn't stand for tits and ass." When he saw the look on her face, he grinned. "Okay, I don't feel six anymore. But the first time around I was really into college t and a."

She bumped his shoulder. "I bet you were. Teaching assistants are usually hot. So you be sure to stay away from any t and a, or I'll be forced to show you my nasty side."

"I'm pretty sure I've already seen your nasty side. Come to think of it, I really prefer your dirty side." To prove it, he leaned in, gave her a quick tug on the lips until he got a nice little moan out of her. "I haven't been in a classroom in almost ten years."

"It'll come back to you. Now shut up, buck up, and get to class."

"How about you be my personal TA?"

"I'll show you t and a—later. Quit stalling."

"You've got lab first thing this morning, right?"

"Yep, on my way to Anatomic Pathology now. We'll meet up in the student union for lunch, okay with you?"

"That's the plan."

"Cord, you'll do fine. Think about the two of us practicing veterinary medicine together in the not so distant future. Both of us taking over Bran's practice and making it coincide with our work at the center. College is mostly a ton of reading anyway and you like to read, so—"

"You really think I can do this?"

"Baby, I know you can. All your courses transferred without a hitch. And the advance placement cut a good nine months off your curriculum." She kissed his cheek and slapped him on the butt. "Now, get going. You don't want to be a straggler on your first day. I'll see you at lunch."

"Maybe I should've gotten a haircut."

"Are you kidding? I love it long. It looks great, you look great. Now go."

Cord trudged off, his long legs eating up the ground. He'd be pushing forty by the time he completed his internship. But he could do that at FMRC. He shook his head. He'd done crazier things he supposed than setting out to become a veterinarian at this late stage of his life.

When he got to the Life Sciences Building, he pulled open the door and stepped into the hallway, scanned the nameplates beside each door.

After finding his first class, Molecular and Cellular Biology, he settled into his preferred seating, a desk in the very back of the room.

There were some things that stayed the same and never changed, he thought.

And some things did. Even though he didn't need the financial help, his father, Gabe, had agreed to foot the entire bill for his stint in college and vet school. In fact, Gabe had donated a very generous sum to make sure FMRC stayed afloat for the rest of the year.

Cord had to admit that in a matter of six short months, Gabe Bennett had become a permanent, steady fixture in his life, something Cord had never thought possible. Only three hours away, the man made a point of visiting him often and when that wasn't feasible, he still would text or phone Cord almost every day.

Cord couldn't believe his good fortune in the father department.

Or his good luck. Keegan had agreed to marry him over Christmas break.

While he waited for class to start, Cord nervously drummed his fingers on the wood and decided to open his textbook. He had to look twice at the signature line on the inside front cover that listed all the students who had owned the book over the years. There scrawled on the second line was the name Scott Phillips.

For some reason, Cord felt compelled to thumb through the book.

There it was, practically in the middle, sandwiched between pages 260 and 261, a piece of paper, folded in two, and used like a bookmark at the beginning of Chapter Ten, Biomembrane Structure.

Cord slipped it out, unfolded the note.

I told you it wasn't your time to go, that you still had a lifetime of things to do. And that's the fun part. Make sure you never take life for granted again.

Grow old, Cord, live life every day like a precious gift because you never know from one day to the next what the dancing tides will bring to shore.

Dear Reader:

If you enjoyed *Dancing Tides*, please take the time to leave a review. A review shows others how you feel about my work. By recommending it to your friends and family it helps spread the word. If you have the time, please Tweet/Share that you've finished Dancing Tides.

If you do write a review, by all means let me know via Facebook or my website.
I'd love to hear from you!

For a complete list of the author's other books visit her website.
www.vickiemckeehan.com

Want to connect with the author to leave a comment?
Go to her Facebook or blog
www.facebook.com/VickieMcKeehan
www.vickiemckeehan.wordpress.com/ blog

Go to the next page for a preview of
Lighthouse Reef

Lighthouse Reef

Prologue

Twenty-five years earlier
Pelican Pointe, California

The waves crashed up against the rocks. The wind whipped in gusts while a slice of moonlight trailed along the sand, glistening like silver. On the deserted stretch of beach, three young men huddled in front of a campfire they'd built up trying to stay warm in the chilly, damp night air. Two were brothers—the other an older tag-along already of legal age they'd talked into buying beer and cigarettes in the neighboring town of San Sebastian— where you could purchase liquor if you were twenty-one.

But San Sebastian was farther inland and it didn't offer the Coast Highway to tour up and down cruising for chicks, especially in the summertime, or during spring break when babes wearing string bikinis were as common as surfboards. Oddly, that was usually the best time of year to pick up hitchhikers, too.

Not four hours earlier, the trio had set off an alarm on Main Street when they'd broken a window to get inside Ferguson's Hardware store. Their plan had been to rob old man Ferguson, take whatever cash they could find. Who knew Ferguson had gone and installed an alarm system? Probably something the son had come up with to impress his old man, a step toward progress, signaling a change in ownership one day in the not too distant future. Something to show the town he deserved the cushy job he'd fallen into as daddy's right-hand man.

After all, nepotism ran strong in this shit water of a town, didn't it? Fathers turned the reins over to their sons to inherit the business, whatever the business happened to be. It was a practical matter, a legacy that had held its own ritual for years and would continue to do so for future generations.

Future generations? What a joke that was. Like anyone with a brain would stay in Pelican Pointe their whole life and hope to have a future here.

Flames rose higher on the fire as they took turns tossing more driftwood onto the pyre hoping to make it more like a bonfire.

"Why do you want to do that?" the younger one asked. "We're just attracting attention to ourselves."

"Shut up," the older brother barked. "Didn't we just gather up all this wood? It's freezing out here in the mist. Besides, I call the shots. Don't forget that," he warned as he chucked another log into the blaze, making the tips of the flames shoot up higher, as if trying to reach all the way to the top of the bluffs where the lighthouse sat high atop its craggy perch.

Up to now, the discarded beer cans that littered their feet were the only true indication the three had been drinking. But as they got drunker—they also got more surly—and louder. Nasty tempers began to clash as they always did between these same companions and flare like rockets on the Fourth of July.

The youngest, barely sixteen, spared a glance in the direction of the young teen girl they'd tied up earlier and placed close to the fire. Her eyes told him she looked scared to death. Not an hour earlier, his brother had stuck a gag in her mouth to shut her up and keep her from screaming. "What should we do about her?"

The older brother didn't take long to think about it. "Let's take the bitch up to the lighthouse. Whaddya say we go up there and have ourselves some fun. We'll put it to her good and hard. No one will hear a thing."

"He's right. The longer we stay down here on the beach, the more we risk somebody could come along and spot us," the tag-along agreed without much hesitation. "But shit. How do we get the bitch up there? You feel like toting her all that way?"

"Hell no. We'll stick her in the back of my pickup while we make our way through town. That way it just looks like it's the three of us same as it usually does."

"Then let's do it."

"I'm in. How do we choose which one of us goes first though? Should be the oldest that gets first dibs, dontcha think? Since that's me—"

"No. No different than the way we always do things. I go first, then my little brother. You last."

"Why does it always have to be your way?"

"Because it's my damn truck that's why. Now shut the fuck up and help me get this bitch loaded up. Anymore crap from you—?"

"Okay. Okay. No need to get your panties in a wad. How much do you think she weighs?"

"How the hell should I know! The three of us should be able to handle her though." With that the oldest brother went over and pulled the terrified girl to her feet. He brought out the knife he carried and stuck it to her throat. He looked into the blonde's brilliant-blue eyes and wondered what it would be like to watch the life go out of them. He'd been thinking about it a lot lately, reading about it, too. Tonight he had his chance to see what it was like for himself. He just had to bring the others around to his way of thinking.

"Grab her feet," he ordered the tag-along. To his brother, he yelled over the sound of the wind and surf, "Open up the tailgate."

"What about the fire?"

"We'll come back. For what I have in mind, this won't take that long at all."

Don't miss these other exciting titles by bestselling author

Vickie McKeehan

The Pelican Pointe Series
PROMISE COVE
HIDDEN MOON BAY
DANCING TIDES
LIGHTHOUSE REEF
STARLIGHT DUNES
LAST CHANCE HARBOR
SEA GLASS COTTAGE
LAVENDER BEACH
SANDCASTLES UNDER THE CHRISTMAS MOON
BENEATH WINTER SAND
KEEPING CAPE SUMMER (2018)

The Evil Secrets Trilogy
JUST EVIL Book One
DEEPER EVIL Book Two
ENDING EVIL Book Three
EVIL SECRETS TRILOGY BOXED SET

The Skye Cree Novels
THE BONES OF OTHERS
THE BONES WILL TELL
THE BOX OF BONES
HIS GARDEN OF BONES
TRUTH IN THE BONES
SEA OF BONES (2018)

The Indigo Brothers Trilogy
INDIGO FIRE
INDIGO HEAT
INDIGO JUSTICE
INDIGO BROTHERS TRILOGY BOXED SET
Coyote Wells Mysteries
MYSTIC FALLS
SHADOW CANYON
SPIRIT LAKE (2018)

ABOUT THE AUTHOR

Vickie McKeehan's novels have consistently appeared on Amazon's Top 100 lists in Contemporary Romance, Romantic Suspense and Mystery / Thriller. She writes what she loves to read—heartwarming romance laced with suspense, heart-pounding thrillers, and riveting mysteries. Vickie loves to write about compelling and down-to-earth characters in settings that stay with her readers long after they've finished her books. She makes her home in Southern California.

Find Vickie online at
https://www.facebook.com/VickieMcKeehan
http://www.vickiemckeehan.com/
https://vickiemckeehan.wordpress.com